Deadly Harvest

Laura Amour Thriller, Volume 2

David Wickenden

Published by David Wickenden, 2019.

DEADLY HARVEST

First edition. November 17, 2019.

ISBN: 978-1999279127

Written by David Wickenden.

Also by David Wickenden

Laura Amour Thriller
Deadly Harvest
Deadly Harvest

Standalone
In Defense of Innocence
Homegrown

Watch for more at davewickenden.wixsite.com/dave-wickenden.

Dedication

This goes to my family, who help me, inspire me and support me. Nothing without you guys.

Acknowledgments

The writing of a novel is a long process. We're talking usually about 70,000 - 80,000 words. If you're nailing a 1000 words a day, that is still around three months of steady work. Most of this in self-imposed, solitary confinement. Writers do occasionally come out of their caves to intermingle with the real world, but a part of us is still immersed in the fantasy world that we've created within ourselves. We've been known to talk to characters that are not really there, as we struggle with a plot point or the frustration of having to kill one of our favorite characters to create more tension. Please do not hold it against us. This is just creativity at its core.

It's during these times that we get to meet and talk to some very helpful people. I would like to thank one of these people who dropped everything to share his time, expertise and support for this project. Although a tour of a crematorium might sound morbid, Allan Morley of Parklawn Cemetery and Crematorium walked me through the entire process and made it sound so fascinating.

I would also like to thank all my beta readers who kept me honest and helped me make this story the best it could be. Some of these are tremendous writers in their own right and the fact that they took the time to help me show that we are not competitors but rather collaborators. I would like to thank K.M. Pohlkamp, author of the award-winning *Apricots and Wolfsbane*, Melissa Adams, reader-extraordinaire, Rick Eles and my fellow first responders, Jennifer Amyotte and Joan Desabraisare.

Finally, I would like to thank Carol Tietsworth for catching all my goof-ups. The manuscript shone after her incredible care.

Any shortcomings are mine alone.

Chapter One

Laura Amour's blade drew across the sentry's throat, cutting through muscle, tissue and cartilage. It spoke to the knife's keen edge. The man staggered in surprise as wind drew the arterial stream of blood into the night sky. She shuddered at how easy it was to take the man's life, regardless of his sins. That he would not have hesitated to take her out with the Russian 12.7mm "Vychlop" or Exhaust-silenced sniper rifle didn't sooth her. Grabbing the bulky barrel before it fell, she guided the body to the flat rooftop as it collapsed rather than allow it to fall three stories to the street.

How this man held a Russian, spoke of influence and money or the Russian Mob. What the man was doing guarding a brothel with such a weapon was a question Laura couldn't even begin to fathom.

In her typical methodical approach to her goal, she had started two blocks out, searching for any sign of a trap. She left nothing to chance because there was no coming back from dead. From a street back, she had made out the silhouette of the sentry propped up against a brick chimney as he faced the street.

Before advancing on the man's position, she spent over an hour searching for any other hidden guards. It had taken her another twenty minutes, crab-walking across the roof to reach the man unobserved and unheard. Crouched beside the dead body, she drew in a ragged breath as the stress bled out of her. She shook her arms to release the tension of being coiled for so long.

Once her breathing settled, she leaned over the edge of the three-story tenement building, gazing upon the St. Denis district of Paris. A sudden slamming of a door and the quick scurry of feet across the paving stones made her pull back into the chimney's shadow. Across the street, the stout figure of a man was making a fast retreat. Angry Parisian French followed the retreating figure, proving her right. The poets called it the language of love, but what she could make out, it was anything but, unless the pair was into masochistic sex. Laura cringed at what the woman claimed she would do to the man if he ever returned.

And it would hurt.

Ignoring the couple below, she turned her attention towards tonight's target. The building may have been a copy of all the others in the neighborhood but if her information was accurate, what was happening inside would shock even the rougher patrons of this side of Paris. From the exterior, there was little to raise an eye towards. The shaded windows leaked light around the edges.

Six months ago, she had been living a quiet life in a Caribbean paradise, far from the ugly realities of today's world. She was also licking her wounds from her last crusade that saw her lose her country and her best friend.

It only took a message from the head of Canada's spy agency, CI-SIS, to have her jumping back into the fight. Children were at risk. There was no way she could sit by while that happened. What surprised her was that Darren Forbes sent her an intelligence package that identified a highly-placed politician in the French government suspected of running a huge human trafficking ring. One that dealt with children.

Tonight would be her first attack against this organization. But it was more a fact-finding missions rather than a tactical strike.

"LAURA," A VOICE CALLED over the afternoon traffic. "Laura, par ici!"

She looked across the busy street to see Aline waving her hat in the air to catch her eye. She smiled and raised a hand to show she saw her new friend. Careful of the aggressive drivers hurrying to go nowhere, Laura danced across the distance, her two shoulder bags bouncing as she threw herself into outstretched tattooed arms of the excitable teen.

The girl, one of thousands of prostitutes that serviced the Paris night-life, kissed her with zest on both cheeks before guiding her to the table that had been their meeting place for the past couple months.

"I was so surprised to get your message," Laura said as she dropped in her regular chair pushed deep in the umbrella's shade.

"But that's just it. Something's changed," said Aline, flicking a line of ash from her cigarette. "They told me not to come by. That they were trying some new acts and that they would call me when they needed me."

"Any ideas?" Laura asked, sipping on her coffee, watching the woman over the rim of the cup.

"No, but the bastard became hostile when I complained. He threatened me. That's a first with this place. They normally treat us good."

"What happens to the children? Are they sheltered off-site?"

"No.... Well, now that you mention that, I don't know. I think the kids stay inside the building. A soft cage, but still a cage. Now though, I don't know what will happen to them. It'll depend on what kind of new act they're talking about, I guess."

Laura made a point of pulling a notebook and pencil out of one of her bags and opening it to the last entry. The cover she had used to approach the young street worker was that of an investigative reporter searching for clues to a growing number of missing children. One of the major documents that the intelligent report she had received was an Interpol report revealing thousands of refugee children had disappeared after arriving in Europe from war-torn or impoverished locations across the globe. Many had arrived from countries that included Thailand and Cambodia, traveling alone with no parents or guardian and no one claiming them. Either before or after being documented by social services in the different European cities, these children disappeared. The authorities had investigated, but had concluded they were run-a-ways.

Bullshit! Not *that* many.

Hundreds if not thousands of Syrian refugees, fleeing the fighting between Syrian dictator, President Bashar al-Assad and the rebels had reported losing track of their children in the race across the Mediterranean through Greece, Macedonia, Germany and Italy. Efforts by the International Red Cross and other agencies had found and reunited many children with their families, but nowhere near the vast amount missing.

"Tell me about the cages."

"I've seen them in the display room, down from my own," said Aline.

"Display rooms?" Laura asked, blue eyes narrowing as she tried to visualize what Aline was telling her.

"Oui, they have these rooms, where they display the merchandise to the customers. Normally, it's a bedroom scene, but for some younger ones, it might be a playground setting, with a swing or a rocking pony."

"That's sick."

"You won't see me argue about that, but honey, men and women pay me to whip their asses so they can get off, so I'm not Mother Teresa either."

"Yeah, but at least you have a choice in the matter."

"Oh, you think so? Fuck Laura, you are naive," Aline said, holding up her skirt, to show several needle marks walking across her inner thigh. "Not much choice."

Laura argued, but Aline stopped her cold with a look. "You've never lived on the streets. I saw that the first time I met you so don't talk about shit you know nothing about."

"But that stuff can kill you," she said, grabbing the other woman's hand.

"On the streets, there are worse things than death," the young prostitute said, her dark brown, doe-like eyes going still. "Ask the little ones. They'll tell you."

The woman looked out over the street, not taking in the view, but watching something from the past, like a sad episode from a canceled television show. With a shudder, she pulled out and lit a cigarette, as if the act would dissipate a hurtful memory.

"Anyway, you can't see the customer. He's behind a one-way mirror deciding what fetish to satisfy," Aline said, as if it was normal. She pulled an unruly lock of her dyed vividly red hair back into place under her cap.

Laura closed her eyes needing a moment to disassociate from the tragedy before her. If someone could live such a life and think it was normal; that they treated people that way, then society had failed people like Aline. Prostitution may be the world's oldest profession, but it seemed to be worse today than at any other time in history — at least more visible — she knew technology and the Internet had helped it grow exponentially in her lifetime.

Aline turned to look Laura in the eyes, "You don't think they'd hurt the kids, do ya?"

"Now who is being naïve?" Not waiting for an answer, she moved her coffee cup over and leaned forward. "How many children does that place have?"

"Two to three. They move them around a lot. For security."

"What can you tell me about the building, Aline? Ways in or out?" Laura asked.

Aline stopped and looked at her. She reached a hand out, running her fingers across Laura's short blond stubble down to her cheek. There was so much intimacy in the gesture that Laura shivered at her touch.

"You had better be careful amant. These people will kill you in a second even if you are a reporter."

The guilt at this ongoing lie ate away at Laura. She had come to know the woman well over the past few months and liked her company. Laura regretted their friendship would end soon and the danger she brought upon the girl if her employers were to link the two of them together was more caustic than she might have imagined when they first met.

LOOKING ACROSS THE rooftops, Laura saw the one entrance of the brothel that Aline had said was left open.

The rooftop patio was occupied.

At a table that was setup in the roof corner, overlooking the street, two men sat smoking. She heard the murmur of their conversation but the distance and the city noise swallowed any distinct words. One man, dressed in a dark pullover sweater and slacks sat with his feet crossed on the table, while the other stood with his arms folded like he didn't want to wrinkle his suit.

Picking up the "Vychlop", she sighted the rifle across the distance, pulling the scene right into her face. For a brief second, she was tempted to use the Russian rifle to eliminate the two guards. With such a tool, it would be so easy. But from this angle, she could not be sure there weren't any video cameras focused on the area. She couldn't risk losing the element of surprise for the sake of ease.

The guards finished their cigarettes and left the deck.

Through the scope, she noticed they allowed the door to swing shut on its own, not bothering to lock it.

Laura rose to a crouch and made her way to the rear of the building she had been watching from. She checked the lane-way that separated the next row of buildings for people. Seeing none, she pulled on the straps of her backpack to ensure they were tight, ducked under the wires and reached out to the bars on the utility pole. She lowered herself to the ground using the bars and slinked into the shadows.

She skirted any light from doors and windows that might back-light her as she moved. A small break between buildings allowed her access to the street. The heavy overhead trees cast a tunnel of shadows across the street and like a wrath, she moved to the other side. She found another break in this row of buildings that allowed her to the lane behind her target building. She scrambled up another hydro pole, raised her face over the roof's edge, her eyes sweeping both sides for any sign of a sentry. She crept to keep any noise to a minimum, crossed three buildings before stepping onto the suspected brothel.

Laura yanked off her backpack. She pulled out a holster and strapped it across her right hip. Three extra fifteen shell clips in pouches lined the holster's belt and there were more in her pack. She hoped that she would not need them. Aline advised her there were seldom over three or four men guarding the building and the human property. They were there to protect the money, the manager, and the merchandise — in that order. They locked the manager out of sight behind a camera and speaker system. The client saw only the escort they paid for. Entry to the back rooms opened with a credit card for the client or a proximity card for the guards.

Above her, the wind picked up, and she felt and heard the first of the heavy raindrops hit around her. It would provide perfect cover for her once she finished here tonight.

Pulling on a lightweight balaclava that covered her light hair and face, Laura pulled out the silenced 9mm Browning BDM. She pulled back the slide and ensured a shell filled the chamber. Laura took a deep breath and dropped onto the rooftop deck with the pistol aimed at the glass window of the door leading into the building.

Seeing nothing, Laura crossed to the entrance and dragged the door open, allowing her pistol to lead the way. She listened as she descended for any sign of someone on the stairs ahead of her but the building remained silent. Descending the flight of stairs, she peeked around the corner and spied the first camera Aline had warned her about on the second-floor landing. It was a rotary mount. She gritted her teeth at the near fatal mistake. Should have used a small mirror to check the position of the camera before moving into the hallway. Something else to think about. I can't afford any more mistakes.

From her pack, she pulled out the collapsible wand with a small mirror attached and eased it around the corner. She watched as the camera made its arch towards her position and then tracked its way to cover the lower landing. When the lens disappeared, she moved down the staircase to stand beneath the camera. The only noise in the heavy silence was the small motor that rotated the camera. That might change in the next couple seconds, depending how attentive the security was. From the side pocket in her backpack, she pulled a small metal tube that looked like an asthmatic puffer. She held it below the camera lens, shook the can, making sure that the nozzle faced the glass lens. The motor reached the end of its arch and paused for a split second. It was what she was waiting for. Tilting the tube so it faced the lens, she depressed the trigger and a fine spray covered the optics lens rendering it blind.

She stepped up the stairs, putting the tube away and with the pistol at the ready, waited to see if the blind camera would cause a response. After a ten-minute spell, she eased herself around the corner and headed for the next landing. She repeated the same technique of blinding the surveillance camera and raced back up beyond the second-floor landing and waited for someone to come and check the equipment.

One camera not working was one thing, but a second? The main floor door opened with a thump and the scrape of a shoe. Seconds later, the unmistakable snap of a pistol being armed came to her. Crouched low against the inside wall of the third-floor landing, Laura held her pistol aimed forward, waiting for a target. Stealthy movements approached and the guard's firearm angled up the stairs towards her position. When his face became visible, she squeezed off a round that took the man in the forehead, the silencer loud in the enclosed stairwell. The man's pistol clattered on the wooden stairs. Unsure if he had a partner, Laura dove across the landing, her firearm searching for a target, but the area was clear. She jumped to her feet, slid to the next corner and with a snap of her wrist, she extended the telescopic mirror and checked the stairs below her.

Nothing.

She returned to the dead guard and recognized him as the guard from the roof with the suit. She rifled through his pockets and found the access key card Aline had described. The plain white plastic card was unremarkable but it would open most of the doors for her. She felt no guilt about killing the man. He'd chosen human trafficking for a living and all it entailed. He should be fortunate that she didn't make him suffer as so many others had.

She tucked the man's gun into her backpack along with the two extra clips from his suit coat pocket. She moved back to the corner and used her mirror again to ensure the way was clear. At each corner, she repeated the drill. Better to be overcautious rather than dead. They had drilled this into her during the building clearing exercises she'd taken part in back in her old life as a PTSD counselor for first responders. They'd taught her too well.

On the first-floor landing, she halted and from her pants pocket, pulled out a snake inspection tool and her smart phone. She had already synced the two together so only needed to turn on the power of the endoscope and the picture from the camera showed up on her phone. Ensuring the LED lights were off, she slid the tiny camera under the door that led onto the main floor. The view under the door opened across the phone's screen and she had only enough time to pull back before the door slammed open, just missing her head. The second guard stepped into the stairwell and his eyes widened as he almost tripped over her.

Laura scooped up the pistol from the floor and grabbed the man's sweater with her other hand. She pulled him towards her, ramming the bull-nosed silencer into his chest, firing two rounds. He stiffened in the split second it took for his brain to signal his body that he was dead. She allowed him to roll off her as he collapsed.

As she regained her feet, Laura noticed the door had closed behind the man. She pushed the camera back under. Smooth glass covered the walls of the hallway, but none of the display rooms were lit up. The hallway beyond was dark. There was no one else waiting for her, and she saw no camera in the dim light. The manager might know there was an intruder. Until the guard told him otherwise, and that wasn't about to happen soon, he'd be on guard. Would he call for help? How long before reinforcements showed up?

She swiveled the camera and saw that the hallway disappeared around a far corner. In her mind's eye she pictured the building and knew the staircase burrowed through the center of the structure. According to Aline, the command center was at the back of the building with the display rooms near the front.

Clients made their choice and then it allowed them access to a second or third story where their purchases awaited their pleasures.

Either way would take her to the command center. She retracted the inspection cable, put her equipment away, taking seconds to grab the man's weapon and ammunition. She reloaded her own weapon before opening the door and crept into the hallway. Laura sat still for a few minutes pushing her other senses outward while her vision adjusted to the low light. No sound emanated within the building, like it was empty of life.

With her gun pointed in front of her, she moved to her left and followed the wall to the corner. The mirror showed nothing, so she continued on, lifting and placing her feet with care so she made no noise. There should only be the manager according to the information she pulled from Aline, but situations changed and she wanted to be ready for anything.

The wall she crept beside was all glass. Try as she might, Laura could not determine what was on the other side of the glass because of the low light. There was no way to know if there was a victim or another guard watching her move through the Stygian darkness and her nerves were screaming at the possible threat.

A muffled shot followed by a burning sensation along the side of her neck, felt like someone laid a branding iron against her skin. She rolled towards the sound and squeezed off three fast shots into the bank of windows across the hall. With a crash, one of the large panes of glass fell to the floor, shards sliding in all directions. Although her shots did not hit her assailant, it and the explosion of glass threw off his next round. The report was loud in the hallway, but the flash showed Laura where the hidden guard stood. She unleashed multiple rounds at the flash so fast that her gun's silencer seemed to purr like a contented cat. A dark shadow crumpled and fell out of the display room with a sigh. Keeping her gun trained at the dark mound on the floor, she crawled forward. The man was dead.

She touched her neck feeling the burn and her glove came away wet and shiny with blood. A half an inch more... Sticky wetness spread through her sweater. From her pack, she pulled a self-adhesive four by four bandage and covered the wound by feel. The only issue she now had was this white target near her head, but there was no sense leaving her DNA all over the building.

The gun report would have signaled anyone else in the building. She stood up and ran to the next corner and chanced a quick look towards where the command center was. Through the glass, she saw that the room was lit and lay empty. Had the manager fled or was he the dead man behind her? She crossed the hall and slid towards the door to the command center. Locked from the inside and there was no place for her to use the access card.

Peering into the room, she saw a desk with several video feeds. Off to one side of the console, a red light was flashing. There was no way to know what the light indicated. There might be an army of re-inforcements on the way. A back door in the room lay open.

Laura turned and hurried back to the display room where the guard had shot from. Stepping through the opening, she moved through a darkened child's bedroom. At the rear of the room she found a door leading to a hallway. The walkway ran along the outside wall of the building. This was how they transported the girls and children to and from their display cages. She followed the interior wall with her hand as there was zero visibility in the dark.

At the corner, she listened for any movement or breathing before she extended her mirror. Farther down the hall, light from the open door of the command center pushed back the blackness. Gun extended, she eased herself towards the room, ready for anything.

A quick glance showed that room was still empty. She flicked off the light before entering the room, the low light from the video monitors the only illumination. No sense making an easy target of herself.

Her eyes skipped across the bank of video screens and centered on the only one with movement. She watched as a full-grown man waved a gun at a bunch of children, herding them away from the camera. If she went by their size, the children seemed to be different ages. Two of the larger children each held a toddler in their arms.

There was no volume from the feed but she could tell that the children were close to hysterics.

Over each monitor, there was black labeling tape with white lettering. Over the monitor with the children, in French was the word "sous-sol". Basement.

The staircase she had descended when she entered the building ended on the main floor so there had to be separate entrance to the basement. If the man in the screen came from this command center, then there must be another way.

She had to find the entrance, and fast. The red light on the console continued to flash.

Chapter Two

Laura left the command room and followed the hall into the darkness. Trying not to make any noise, she slowed herself and placed each foot carefully. She didn't need to warn the man with the gun of her location. It also gave her eyes a chance to regain some of the night vision she had lost due to the office lights.

With one hand sliding along the inside wall trying to feel for any doorway or opening, she moved forward. Muffled crying came from somewhere ahead of her. *I'm coming.* Biting her lip, she had to force herself from running blindly towards the fearful cries. Getting herself shot was not going to help those children.

She came to another left turn and after checking for any threat, eased around in a low crouch. The children's voices became much more distinct once she cleared the corner.

A louder man's voice tried to hush the children with a vicious hiss. *"Tais-toi, sinon je vais vous faire du mal."*

So, you're going to hurt them? Not if I can help it.

Laura's hand ran painfully into an obstruction. With the 9mm in her other hand, she reached forward to trace out a door frame in the pitch black hallway. Pressing herself to the outside wall of the unlit walkway, she transferred her pistol to her other hand. She reached out with her free hand and rattled the doorknob.

Splinters of wood exploded past her head as the man on the other side of the door fired a three-round burst from a submachine gun through the barrier. The loud report from the gunfire was cut off by a chorus of terrified screams that sounded like a choir from hell.

Laura allowed herself to fall noisily to the floor, banging her pistol on the floor. The man on the other side of the door pounded up a set of wooden stairs and yanked the door open to finish her off. When the door swung open, he was outlined by the light below. Giving him no time to aim the evil looking M56 at her prone figure, she fired a double tap from her silenced pistol. The rounds tore into his chest, knocking him backwards down the staircase. A barrage of rounds struck the ceiling as the man's trigger finger tightened in a death grip. The gun clicked empty before he hit the bottom of the steps. Laura jumped up and followed, her gun aimed at the body where it came to rest in a disheveled heap at the foot of the stairs. Almost as if on a switch, the small voices that echoed their terror off the concrete walls of the basement were silenced in surprise.

Laura moved down the stairs carefully, her eyes and gun sweeping the dimly-lit basement for other threats. Huddled together up against an ancient furnace, were a group of children of different ages.

"Anyone else?" she whispered in French.

"Oui," said a black girl who was about fifteen. "There are two or three more men upstairs."

Laura noticed how the eyes of the children followed her pistol as she moved. She holstered it and gave them a friendly smile. Eyes dropped to the floor rather than meet her's. With a sigh, she shook her head. "Not anymore." She stepped over the man's body and crouched down in front of the group of children who stared at her with open fear.

"Police?" asked the girl, one arm around a smaller girl of about five or six years.

Laura shook her head, "No, but I'm here to help. Are there any others?" indicating the children.

The girl shook her head causing her beaded braids to whip back and forth. "Non. They just arrived this afternoon," she said indicating the six other children. Her head dropped to the ground. "I've been here for almost a year."

Laura's heart went out to this brave young woman but she felt her blood begin to boil. The horrors this kid must have gone through...She reached over and placed a hand on the other's shoulder in a gesture of compassion but removed it as she felt the girl flinch at her touch.

"What's your name?"

"Gabrielle," she said, her chin rising. Laura could see the girl's dark brown eyes seemed to harden with an inner strength that surprised her. Most victims of sexual abuse lacked self-esteem and confidence. But she sensed iron in this young woman.

"Other than the front entrance, is there another way out of here?" Laura asked her. She walked to the dead body at the bottom of the stairs. Reaching down, she picked up the submachine gun and released the clip. Empty. The man did have a handgun which Laura retrieved and released the clip.

"Only the tunnels," Gabrielle said behind her.

Laura looked up from where she was searching the man for another clip and asked, "What tunnels?"

"The drainage tunnels for the rain," she said pointing over her shoulder with her thumb. "Although there is one area that comes close to the Paris Catacombs."

Laura thought about using that as an escape route, especially as she knew that there might be reinforcements bearing down on the building at that very moment. But the idea of getting lost underground with a group of children held so many other risks. The best plans are the simple ones. She thought about the roof access and discarded that as well. Gabrielle and one or two of the older kids might manage, but the rest would not be able to navigate the roof system in the dark, let alone climb down the utility pole.

She looked over the other children. Scared, red eyes watched her with barely suppressed terror. It was obvious that all of them were pre-teen. Two were no older than five years. "Can you understand my words?" she asked in French. And then again in English. There was no recognition in any of their expressions.

"They do not speak English or French. I'm not sure what language they do speak, but it might be Arabic." Gabrielle said. "One of the guards mentioned that they were Muslims."

"I'm going to go and make sure it's safe to move out of here. Can I give you a job to do?"

Gabrielle nodded without hesitation.

Pulling her back pack off, she pulled out the other ammunition clips that she had taken off the other guards. Fortunately they were all 9mm therefore interchangeable. She quickly showed the girl how to unload the pistol clips and load the longer submachine magazine. Once she saw that the girl knew what she was doing, she put her finger to her lips and made sure all the other children understood her. Shouldering her backpack, she took the stairs two at a time, using the flashlight to move faster in the blackened hallway. At the command post door, shielding the light, she peeked in to ensure there was no threat. Seeing none, she slid into the chair facing the video monitors.

She saw that the one displaying the basement showed the children huddled around Gabrielle while she diligently worked at the task Laura had given her. She smiled at the girl's spunk. Checking the other monitors, she quickly found one that showed the entrance to the building. In the low light given off by the streetlights, she could see sheets of rain water marching across the pavement. The rain would help cover their departure. It might mean exposing the children to the cold late winter weather, but anything would be better than staying in this building. With a quick flip of the switch under the monitor, she saw the street in the opposite direction. It also showed a car and a cargo van sliding to a stop in front of the building, rainwater splashing across the sidewalk. All four doors of the car swung open and five men dressed in dark clothing launched themselves into the night, weapons at the ready. Another four fanned out of the van and spread out across the street to offer an over-watch.

So much for leaving by the front door.

Without waiting, Laura reached back to her backpack and withdrew a fragmentation grenade. Pulling the pin, she wedged a chair up against the hallway door, the grenade held snug by one of the chair legs. Carefully, she removed her hand, ensuring the explosive would stay in place. She turned, picked up her pistol and followed the hallway back to the basement.

As she descended the stairs, she heard a fearful gasp and a sea of upturned faces met her. Gabrielle stood and handed her the magazine while indicating a small pile of bullets on the floor.

"Grab them, quick." The abruptness in her voice made the younger girl look up.

"Change of plans. How do we access the tunnels?" Laura said.

"Behind the old furnace," Gabrielle said lifting her chin in that direction. "It's how they transport us into the building."

"Show me," Laura said, waving the other children to be silent and to follow.

Gabrielle moved forward confidently around the ancient coal furnace with its multiple water pipes leading away from the boiler. To Laura's amusement, the children followed on the older girl's heels like a bunch of chicks following the mother hen. This might just work out. The group stopped in front of a floor to ceiling set of wooden shelves. Gabrielle was leaning into the end of the shelf, her shoulder braced against the old wood, pushing with all her might. Without questioning the young girl, Laura squeezed around the gaggle of children and lent her weight to the shelf. The entire structure began to slide smoothly along some kind of hidden rail, exposing a darkened tunnel that led away from the room.

She handed her flashlight to Gabrielle. "You lead and I'll bring up the rear," she said lifting the smallest child, a girl, up into her arms. From her pant leg, she pulled out a second flashlight and after turning it on, gave it to the child to hold. She guided the kids through the mouth of the tunnel before pushing the sliding shelves closed. For a split second, she thought about leaving another grenade but she only had one more and might need it later on.

Almost because she was thinking about it, there was a muffled explosion over their heads, causing dust to cascade over the group.

"Let's move," Laura whispered.

She grabbed the small hand of another child, a boy with dark curly hair and watched Gabrielle lead the way through the pitch black tunnel, their steps echoing off the walls.

Laura coaxed the children to a slow run with Gabrielle leading with the flashlight. The light the child held bounced haphazardly across the walls and ceiling. The light and shadows danced across the slime-covered walls of the tunnel. It reminded her of a macabre laser show that would have been at home in an episode of the Walking Dead.

How many other fugitives had braved this same gauntlet to escape those who would do them harm? She knew that the French Resistance had used many of the same tunnels to move through the occupied city to avoid Nazi patrols during the last war.

She held the boy's hand to ensure that they were not separated and to help give the small child some comfort.

We're only as fast as the slowest.

Laura had to shove the automatic rifle back over her shoulder as it bounced around awkwardly from her running motion. The spare pistol, which was shoved down the back of her pants, scraped her butt with its front sight. The moisture she felt proved that it had broken the skin.

What'd I do for a combat harness? With all its clips, compartments and built in holster, her hands would be free, but this was supposed to be a reconnaissance outing.

Her foot hit what should have been a shallow puddle. It turned out that a layer of stone was missing and she stumbled, almost pulling the little boy down with her. Somehow she didn't drop the child in her arms, but the flashlight flew from the little hands, hit the wall and rolled down its sloping side, startling the group ahead of her.

"It's okay," she said in a tight whisper, as she regained her balance. She scooped up the light and gave it back to the child. She needed both hands free to carry the two youngest. All she could do was to keep herding them forward.

The light revealed an increase in the water that followed the curved walls to the pathway. Laura suspected that the storm had increased its assault on the world above.

The boy began to whimper, even as he continued to run. Laura wondered if the little one had recognized the danger as well.

Just as she noticed the water on the tunnel floor was flowing in the same direction that they were running, she heard Gabrielle call out a warning.

"Careful. Stop!"

She slowed down and moved around the collection of bodies to where Gabrielle stood. The tunnel floor which was made up of ancient cinder blocks dropped into a deep chasm. She could hear the water splashing somewhere below where they stood, but glow of the flashlight did not reach the bottom.

Gabrielle's light swept across the tunnel and crossed over a railed causeway before returning back to reveal an avenue around the sinkhole. The structure was a metal bridge that hugged the round-sided wall. Iron handrails stood on either side but the base was spotted with two large rusty holes. Gabrielle skipped across the bridge with little care to the danger below and pointed the light back so that the walkway was illuminated.

"It's solid, just watch the holes," the young girl said.

Laura tried to lower the child from her arms, but her arms clung tight in a death grip around Laura's neck with her legs twisted around her chest. With no time to argue, Laura let go of the child so that she hung from her neck like a human necklace with a whimper. She stepped over the first hole and picked up the boy in one sweeping movement, not giving him time to protest and passed him over to Gabrielle who dumped him unceremoniously onto the wet stones.

She urged the next child in line and helped them over the larger hole to the teen who guided them over the second hole. It took only seconds to ferry all the children past the chasm. When she passed the last over, she wrapped her arm around the little girl and stepped across.

As she cleared the bridge, Gabrielle shut off her light and whispered urgently, "Behind you."

Laura twisted around and in the distant could see three lights bobbing in the darkness. The pursuers either knew of the tunnel or had found the entrance. She reached up and pulled the light from the child's hands which caused the little girl to begin to fight her for the flashlight. When Laura flicked off the switch, the girl gave off a terrified keening that echoed off the tunnel.

"Keep the light moving forward so we can see where we're going, but try to shield it with your body."

Without comment, Gabrielle turned and they continued on. Laura pressed the little bodies to follow in a slow run. The men behind them would catch up to them in minutes at this rate. She had to do something to slow them down. When the group rounded a turn in the tunnel, she ran around the group of children so that she was in line with Gabrielle.

"I need you to take these two so I can deal with the ones behind us. Can you handle both?"

"Of course!"

Not giving the child any warning, she pulled the girl off her and into Gabrielle's arms. The stones magnified her terrified scream and the whole group faltered. The cry ended abruptly as she found another neck to cling to. Laura pushed the young boy into the older girl's embrace and the group began to move forward at her urging. Making sure the group hadn't lost anyone, she turned back towards the approaching threat.

They would be most exposed and vulnerable while crossing the metal bridge. Using the wall as a guide in the dark, she stumbled blindly until the tunnel arched back towards the chasm. She cleared the turn, the noise from the falling water magnified and she slowed and crouched low to the cobbled floor.

Ahead of her, she could see the bobbing lights that looked like fireflies dancing across a dark meadow. Making sure her hood covered her hair; she bent her neck so her face was partially pointed to the floor so that the approaching lights had little to reflect back. She was able to see flashes of legs and arms in the bouncing glow.

They didn't slow down as they approached the massive drain, but angled towards the bridge telling Laura they were familiar with the subterranean escape route. She waited, ready in a shooting stance with both hands wrapped around her Browning; the safety in the fire position.

The first man crossed the bridge, his light pointed at the ground to avoid the missing steel. He stepped back onto the tunnel floor, he pivoted and shone the light back for the next man. This helpful gesture lit up both of the other men. Laura took advantage of the situation and fired twice at the last man in line. Both shots hit him square in the chest, folding him into himself, dead before he hit the ground. The flashlight flew from his hand, sending light beams across the tunnel's ceiling before landing with a clatter facing away from the chasm and its bridge.

As the second shot left the gun's muzzle, Laura took two side steps closer to the two remaining men before sending a double tap towards the closer man's back. He was already turning and only one of the 9mm chunks of lead caught him in the back. The other took him in the side, under the armpit, spinning him forward so that he fell across the bridge, his light lost to the waters below.

The last man caught on the bridge, was sharp enough to flick the switch of his light off after the first two spits of Laura's silenced attack, plunging the entire tunnel into darkness. For long seconds, neither Laura nor her opponent moved. She knew that her adversary was listening for any movement that might indicate where she stood. She was doing the same. He might be exposed on the bridge, but the darkness sheltered him as it did her. You couldn't rely on luck to hit a target you couldn't see.

It was a waiting game. Whomever made the first mistake would die.

Chapter Three

The seconds stretched like a tightened spring. The darkness of the tunnel seemed to close in on Laura, who waited with growing nervousness, barely breathing. The urge to take in a deep breath seemed to grow with each passing minute as she waited for some sign to indicate where the third man was located.

The real issue was the children were getting farther away as she waited. Only three of the guards had come through the tunnel. Depending how many were neutralized by her grenade trap, there were still more on the loose. If they knew about the tunnels, the others maybe racing to cut them off. She had to move to protect the group of kids she had so recently freed.

Slowly, she reached into her pocket and eased the flashlight out. The scrape of fabric on the rubber casing seemed loud to her and she braced herself for a bullet, but nothing happened. Readying her pistol in her right hand, she lifted herself from the crouch to her full height. She flicked on the flashlight's switch and lobbed it sideways towards the wall in a flat trajectory that made it look like she was running.

The man took the bait and unleashed three or four shots at the moving target. Sighting on the muzzle flashes, Laura fired inches higher and was rewarded by a grunt and clang of a metal on metal. In her mind's eye, she saw the same trick she had played earlier in the basement, and was wary of being caught.

In the darkness, she heard the man's wet cough that became a death rattle. Placing each step down carefully to avoid making any noise, Laura moved towards the thrown flashlight. She circled so she came from the darkened side and didn't reveal herself. Keeping her gun arm extended, ready to shoot at any movement, she reached for the lamp. She kept the flashlight away from her body so that if the man shot at the moving light, it stood a chance of missing her.

She angled the light towards the chasm and saw that she needn't have worried. The man lay with one leg through the rusted bridge, the other extended over the chasm. Bright crimson bubbles protruded from his lips and she knew that he was hit hard in the lungs. He was slowly drowning in his own blood.

Quickly, but cautiously, she checked each of the other men. The other two were dead and she stripped them of any ammunition she found. Just as she straightened up from the last corpse, she caught sight of something on one of the men's hands. Peering closer, she saw that it was a tattoo in the web of the man's right hand, between the thumb and forefinger. It looked like a *fleur de lis,* but with a ring at the bottom. Within the ring, there were two lightning bolts crossed together. She aimed the flashlight at the closest body near her and saw that he was marked with the same symbol. She didn't know what it meant but knew that she had to get moving. Sliding her smart phone from her interior chest pocket, she snapped a photo of the body art before setting off down the tunnel.

Gabrielle and the children had made good time. It seemed to take forever for Laura to catch up to them. She was impressed by how well the older girl had kept them together and coached them along through the dark underground waterway. Most kids her age would be busy texting about boys and experimenting with makeup, but Gabrielle handled herself like a twenty-something. Of course, the life experiences couldn't be compared. These men had stolen her childhood.

Little heads turned in fear at her approach but Laura saw the tense shoulders relax as they recognized her. They didn't know her at all, but they knew she was helping them escape.

"How much farther?" she asked Gabrielle in a tight whisper.

"This tunnel joins the main sewer system in a couple of minutes. There is an access point to the street around the first corner."

"Are you sure?"

"Yes. Sometimes, they take me to the client so there is no chance of him being seen."

"Okay," Laura said touching the other girl's shoulder in sympathy. "Let me lead, just in case there's someone waiting ahead."

Even in the limited light, fierce determination lit Gabrielle's face and Laura gave her a quick hug before moving forward. Using her light, she sprinted ahead so that she had time to explore before the group got too close to the tunnel's entrance. The tunnel floor became covered with chunks of broken limestone and she had to slow down to avoid tripping. She moved forward, clambering up a mound of dirt and stone that led to a rough hole, high up on the dead-end wall. It looked like this tunnel had been walled off in the past and the people of the building had reopened the access to move the children to and from the house unseen.

Laura had known that there was an incredible tunnel system under the ancient city. Stories from the Second World War were told of the Resistance using them to counter and outflank their Nazi occupiers. In other sections of the subterranean world, millions of people had been buried in an attempt to empty the overflowing cemeteries within the city. Had she known that she'd be navigating the sewer system, she might have taken one of the multiple tourist excursions, both legal and illegal, as part of her operational planning.

Pulling herself up the incline, she shielded the light so it would not give her away if anyone was waiting on the other side of the wall. Just before she crested the broken section of limestone, she clicked off the light and traded it for her pistol. She eased her head over the lip of the opening and did a quick check for threats. She had taken care of three in the tunnels and at least one with the grenade trap, but there were still a bunch unaccounted for. They could be waiting just out of her sight. Pulling the collapsible mirror out of her pant pocket, she checked the tunnel but saw nothing that alarmed her.

Sitting on the ledge of the opening, she twisted her legs and dropped down to the cement below, gun at the ready. The tunnel was larger with water separating two walkways. Farther up the tunnel she could see a platform that crossed the stream of water that moved with alarming volume and speed. She guessed that the water was heading towards one of the outlets that fed the Seine River that meandered through the city. Looking downstream, the tunnel disappeared into the darkness.

Laura was so tensed in anticipation of confronting armed enemies that she jumped when Gabrielle's head poked out of the entrance. She waved the girl forward to hide the fact that her heart was in her throat. With one more look up and down stream, she holstered the pistol and reached up to grab the first child that slid out of the entrance. The child's legs were kicking up and down as she searched for something solid to step on, but calmed when Laura grabbed her by the waist and helped her down. One by one, the children dropped to the cement walkway where they looked around with excited eyes. Their faces and clothes were covered in mud and dust, but they didn't complain as they waited against the tunnel wall.

Gabrielle passed her flashlight to Laura then jumped down and landed in a crouch. She brushed her hands on her pants as she took in the tunnel, pointing upstream to the makeshift bridge. "Across that platform and up the path to the first alcove, you'll find an access ladder that comes out in a back alley."

Laura nodded and indicated the fast flowing water. "Keep tight to the wall until we have to cross over. If one of us falls in there's no way we'll be able to outrace the current."

There was a steel handrail running along the side of the tunnel and Laura had all the children grab hold of the support before shuffling towards the crossover. At the platform, Laura had the ensemble stay in place as she quickly crossed over and gun in hand moved towards the hidden alcove. Sure enough, there was a metal ladder bolted into the cement wall that reached up to a manhole cover in the surface above. She retraced her path to the bridge and as with the other bridge in the first tunnel, she stood over the racing water and helped the kids cross, one by one. Gabrielle smiled at her as she followed her across. They made a great team, considering they were strangers to each other.

As they moved forward, a loud metallic grinding followed by a bang, echoed through the sewer. Laura motioned the children to be quiet as she pulled out her pistol and followed the wall to the edge of the tunnel where it turned into the alcove. She arched her neck so she could see into the room without exposing herself and saw shadows moving above the ladder. Someone was descending from above. It could have been a maintenance person, but she didn't think so.

Pulling back behind the corner, she pulled the backpack off and groped inside until she found what she was looking for. Readying the object in one hand and the pistol in the other, she turned the corner as a man's legs came in view. Whether she made a noise or he sensed her, his head snapped towards her and eyes glared. He stopped his descent and reached into his jacket, even as Laura brought her own weapon to bear. He let out a yell and dropped six feet to the tunnel floor, turning in midair. While he dropped, his jacket swept up and Laura saw the man clawing at a revolver in his chest holster. He never cleared it.

Laura fired twice into the man's chest and he crumpled where he fell. Above him, she heard the frantic curse of at least two more men and then felt cement slice her pants as gunfire slapped the ground at her feet. She stepped back a step and holstered her pistol. With her hand free, she pulled the pin from her last grenade and counted, "One one thousand, Two one thousand," before stepping forward and lobbing the deadly ball straight up the ladder shaft.

Even with the explosion being above ground, the blast nearly deafened her as the sound drove through the hatch and reverberated through the tunnel. She looked back where Gabrielle and the children all were holding their hands over their ears, the whites of their eyes dancing in the darkness.

She motioned Gabrielle forward but didn't wait for the girl. Laura turned and threw herself up the ladder. Just before she left the relative safety of the sewer, she pulled her pistol. With the bulbous silencer leading the way, she poked her head through the manhole and checked the area. Two bodies lay torn to shreds. She pulled herself from the hole in time to hear a vehicle door open and caught sight of a pair of feet under a cargo van. The man came around the back end of the van, weapon in hand, she squeezed off two more shots. It was like the dog who runs full tilt until it reaches the end of its rope. The man's chest stopped moving but his legs flew out from beneath him so that he crumpled in a heap.

The first of the children was ascending the ladder with the help of Gabrielle. Laura pulled the child up and out of the hole and motioned for her to stand beside the van. The girl stood in shock over the remains of one of their attackers and Laura had to hiss at her to look away. The child may not have known the language, but turned her gaze away from the bloody corpse. *At least it wasn't you, sweetheart.* When the last of the smaller children were pulled from the sewer entrance, Laura left Gabrielle to finish the exodus while she checked the vehicle. The explosion would bring the police and she had to be clear of the area before they showed up. With the terrorist attacks over the last couple years, the police were extremely equipped and trained to respond in force to anything that might be an attack on the country or its people.

She found the keys in the ignition and hit the button to unlock the doors. Running around the front of the van, she slid the side door open and lifted the smallest child, the girl, into the darkened vehicle. She began to cry at the quick, rough handling but Laura shushed her even while she grabbed the boy and slid him beside her on the bench. The others were able to load themselves and as Gabrielle pulled herself from the manhole, Laura ran back around the front vehicle and started the engine.

She waited impatiently as Gabrielle helped the last of the children into the rear compartment and closed the sliding door behind her.

"Try to get them belted, just in case this gets rough."

Chapter Four

Not waiting for an answer, Laura engaged the transmission and stomped on the gas. The Mercedes Sprinter jumped forward, and she heard, rather than saw Gabrielle fall back onto some kids. There was a surprised holler followed by at least one child crying.

"Sorry," she called back and slowed the vehicle to a normal speed. Speeding through the night would definitely draw attention to them, so she took a deep breath to help push down the adrenalin. At the end of the alley, she pulled the Mercedes onto the rain-covered street. There was little traffic in the area and Laura felt exposed. Unsure where the tunnel system had left them, she arched her neck, looking for landmarks that would help her get her bearings. She knew she was north of the Eiffel Tower, but the tall buildings that marched down the street gave no sign in which direction it lay.

At the next cross street, she slowed and leaned over the steering wheel to check in both directions. Over to her right, she could see the lit peak of the Tower which gave her an idea of where she was and where she needed to aim for. She turned the wheel hard to the right. A wall of white punched her in the face. The Sprinter's contained compartment magnified the crunching of metal and breaking glass. The airbag deflated almost immediately as the van pitched forward in the path of the turned wheels.

Something dark slammed into the dash beside her with a groan. It disappeared under the panicked cries of the children. She had to concentrate on focusing on the limp form of Gabrielle to recognize that the girl was an unconscious casualty of the crash. She reached down and her hand came up sticky with blood. Please don't be dead.

Hold on. She wiped her hand on her pants and gripped the wheel. They had to find somewhere safe so she could inspect the girl.

In the side mirror she saw the crumpled front end of a dark sedan, steam hissing out from under the hood. While she watched, someone threw the driver's door open and a man in a suit stepped out, gun in hand. Grabbing the transmission, she put the vehicle in reverse and slammed her foot onto the gas pedal. The van reacted immediately, and she had little time to brace herself before it slammed into the sedan. The impact knocked the other vehicle backwards, the driver's door catching the gunman in the chest, flinging him into the night as if he was weightless. More screams resounded through the van.

Laura dropped the transmission into 'drive' and once again stomped on the gas. This time, the inertia slammed her back into her seat like a carnival ride gone off the rails. Feeling a trickle coming from her nose, she swiped at it and her eyesight blurred in pain as the realization of a broken nose became clear. She blinked multiple times to clear her vision as the tenement buildings flashed past her. It was all she could do to stay in the road's middle.

She threw a glance back at the mirror and saw that sedan was limping forward but a second car had joined the chase and was closing the gap between them. At the next cross street, she put the van in a rubber squealing slide, bouncing off the parked cars on the side road. This road opened to a full four lanes and she let the vehicle have its head, the engine roaring its approval. But it was no match for the car that grew in the mirror beside her. The rear interior of the cargo van lit up from the approaching headlights and she swiveled the rear mirror so it didn't blind her. It had rendered the cries behind her to a nonstop whimpering bleat. She activated the switch on both the driver's and the passenger's window so they lowered into the doors. This way there would be no chance of flying glass in the event that she had to shoot through them.

She recognized the large Red Cross Hospital as she screamed past it and knew she was still a distance away from the Paace de Clinchy where the National Police would set up their first parameter if they were responding to the explosion and gunfire. They would close on the origin of the explosion once they ensured no one had slipped through their net. She was taking a big risk of being arrested but there was no way she would lose her pursuers unless she had help. There was also no way she would allow these kids to fall back into the hands of these sick bastards.

The frustrating thing was saving a handful of children wouldn't change much. The criminal network would just move and set up shop elsewhere. She had been hoping to find answers that would have let her move up the food chain to the next layer of the criminal hierarchy. Only by cutting off the head, would she make a difference.

The car behind them was speeding up and trying to get around them.

"Hold on," she yelled over her shoulder, not knowing if the kids understood. She swung the wheel and jabbed at the brakes, causing the sedan to crunch into the back fender and scrape against the parked cars along the street. The chase car fell back for a moment, but then tried the same maneuver again on the other side. Laura pulled the van in the other direction and realized immediately she had fallen for the bluff. The other driver quickly returned to her side of the roadway and with a roar of the engine, slid in beside the van. She yanked the steering wheel again, slamming the side of the van into the heavier car to no real effect. The lightweight utility van only bounced off the vehicle. He could force her into the row of parked cars on the right side of the road or push her into a light standard. It was only a matter of time before he pulled ahead of her and then it was game over.

Snapping a look forward ensuring there was nothing in front, she risked a look at the car beside her. The front tire was even with her door. For a second she thought about shooting out the tire until she glimpsed movement in the side mirror. The rear window was down and a mean looking uzi poked out. Obviously they had the same idea. She reached for her pistol as she tugged on the wheel. The van slammed into the sedan forcing the man to pull back his gun. Locking her hand on the steering wheel to keep the vehicle straight, she reached over and walked several shots across the front windshield. She must have hit something as the car lurched hard to the left and ground into several parked vehicles before righting itself. It had fallen back and Laura once again slammed the gas pedal down.

The rear window exploded in a hail of bullets, showering the children with safety glass. This sent another chorus of screams.

"Dammit," she said through clenched teeth.

The van drifted through the bend in the road and in the distance she could see the flashing lights of the police roadblocks. Ideally this is where she had hoped that the criminals behind her would break off the chase, but they had other thoughts. The second car moved forward and took the lead, a bloom of steam obscuring the front windshield. Why? The trafficking of children was widespread so a few kids lost shouldn't be something to die over. The number of pursuers and the efforts to recapture them said otherwise.

It must be something about these particular children.

Putting the mystery behind her for the moment, she pushed the van to its limits; pedestrians, tourists and show-goers flashing past in a blur. She knew if a person or car cut across the street, she wouldn't be able to avoid a collision.

She grabbed her backpack and tossed it onto the roadway at the same time as she swerved so the car behind her could not come aside. She tried to drop it and turned into the driver's side so those ahead would not see her doing it. Yanking the release on her belt, she shed her holster and pistol, followed by her gloves and balaclava. When she left the vehicle, she wanted to look like an injured, terrified woman, not a one person army. It wouldn't fool anyone for long, but she hoped it would allow for a temporary illusion.

She could see the GIPN and RAID logos on the shield and vehicles up ahead and knew she faced some of the best urban anti-terrorists in the business. Any mistake on her part would get her killed.

Fortunately, those following behind were helping her case by the almost constant barrage of gunfire directed at the van. She drove hunched over the wheel, bracing for the impact of one of those incoming rounds.

As she barreled towards the barricades, the line of riot shields, deadly MR-73 assault rifles propped over them, split to either side as smoothly as an RCMP Musical Ride, leaving a gap for her to slip through. Behind the wall of ballistic hardened shields stood two heavy-duty personnel carriers which would trap her once she entered the safety of the uniformed ring.

Those shells that missed the van could be seen crackling into the shield wall or ricocheting off the equipment. A few of the outlying police officers returned fire so they could shoot at the vehicles behind the Mercedes van. But she knew instinctively that several other rifles had a bead on her.

Two hundred yards out, she took her foot off the gas, the needle on the speedometer buried beyond the 120 km/hr indicator and switched to the brakes. The van's brakes locked, and the van slid in an almost straight line towards the gap in the blockade. A sudden flash behind her distracted her, and she attempted to look behind but both side mirrors were gone; by being crushed against the parked cars or shot away, she would never know.

The van slid between the gauntlet of riot shields and heavily armored police officers and rocked to a stop. Laura kept both hands on the wheel, her head bent forward as a group of gun- wielding officers surrounded the front of the vehicle, rifles pointed at her, looking for a reason to riddle her with holes.

One soldier, a woman, reached beyond the shield she held ready and opened the driver's door. In a crisp voice she commanded "Slowly, keeping your hands where I can see them, get out of the vehicle."

Laura, her lower face covered in blood from the broken nose, cried in what she hoped was a terrified voice, "The children. They tried to kill the children."

The effect on the officer was a softening and widening around the eyes. No other features were visible under the armor. Laura spied a nameplate on the outside vest that spelled, RACHELLE, with the three stripes showing she was a Capitaine.

"What children?"

"In the van. Please check on them. They might be hurt. Gabrielle is not moving," She didn't have to pretend for the last. Her terror for the spunky kid was real. It must have been convincing, because with a nod from the female officer, one of her comrades leaned into the vehicle and seeing Gabrielle lying in between the front seats and the smaller ones behind, yelled for a medic.

She felt hands slide expertly across her body searching for weapons. Beyond the barricades, Laura could see both cars that had pursued her were smoking ruins, covered with bullet holes. One was on its side, with a dead man pressed up against the inside window. Finding no weapons, the woman said, "What the hell happened tonight?"

"I'm a teacher at the International School," Laura said, trying to look terrified, "and we were coming from a play when these men tried to kidnap the children. They even threw some kind of grenade at the van to make me stop, but I wouldn't — ." She wrapped her arms around herself and looked off into the night, blinking to hold off a deluge of tears.

"It'll be all right. One officer will take you to the police station so you can give us a statement."

"Can I see the children?" she said biting her lip. "Just to make sure they are okay."

"Yes, of course."

The woman and two other soldiers escorted her to an ambulance. There was no mistaking that she was still under suspicion. The police were allowing her a little leeway because of her injuries and the children, but until they confirmed her story, they were not taking any chances.

A group of armed officers, their faces covered with balaclavas surrounded the children for security reasons, but Laura could see it did nothing to calm the young ones down. The two youngest cried out when they saw her and ran to wrap their arms around her legs. She bent down and picked them both up and walked over to a stretcher. She hugged both to her chest until the worst of their crying came under control. Over their heads, she smiled at the other children who sat quietly on the back step of the ambulance. She didn't have to turn to know the children's reactions were being watched and gauged by the officers.

In the back of the ambulance, they lay Gabrielle out on a stretcher as a medic wrapped white gauze around her head to hold a bandage to the back of her head. She looked so small on that white sheet and it pulled at Laura's heart.

She looked at the officer and indicated Gabrielle. Once the woman nodded her permission, she stepped into the rig and crouched down beside the medic. She looked at him and asked, "Is she going to be all right?"

The man nodded. "She has a nasty lump on the back of the head. We'll check her for concussion, but she should be fine."

"Oh, thank God!" she said putting her hand over her mouth.

Behind her, a shout when out and she heard several weapons being cocked. Looking over her shoulder, her hand instinctively reaching for the holster that was no longer there, she saw a number of anti-terrorist soldiers holding their weapons at the ready. The Capitaine, crouched with her Smith & Wesson 686 revolver out and pointed at something out of Laura's sight. Even as Laura watched, the woman lowered her firearm and cursed under her breath.

"Andre," said the Capitaine, to the taller of the two officers. "Watch the woman and children." She holstered the revolver and stomped off towards whatever had spooked her and the other troops.

"No problem," replied the man to her back.

Laura continued to play the worried educator, moving among the children, giving hugs. The kids played their parts to perfection without even knowing it, but it was only a matter of time before someone realized none of them spoke French. Her guard gave her space to reassure her wards, but his rifle was always at the ready and she knew instinctively there would be no catching him off guard.

From their position at the rear of the ambulance, she could view more of the scene. What particularly caught her attention was the heated exchange between the Capitaine and a tall, distinguished man. He had bureaucrat written all over him. He was in his mid- to late-fifties with charming dark hair, gelled back, with just enough gray at the temple to give the impression he was experienced. He wore a tan overcoat that boasted a suit beneath. What really stood out were the two heavily muscled 'suits' that stood to either side of him, both with the regulated earpieces descending under their collars.

He was using his size to intimidate the Capitaine by leaning over her, but Laura saw that neither the young officer, nor her fellow assault team members were backing down. In fact, it shocked Laura to see that the other soldiers held their weapons at the ready as if prepared to hold off the bureaucrat with force if needed. Even from fifty feet away, Laura could feel the electric tension sizzling in the night air. He looked over towards Laura and the children, his glare was malevolent.

The man's mouth tightened in a hard line and he pivoted on his heel and pounded away, the two bodyguards having to break out into a run to catch up. The man's rigid form screamed repressed rage.

The Capitaine looked away from the man's receding back and spoke into her radio mic.

"Right away, Capitaine," said Andre, their stern looking guard. He walked over to Laura and said in a low voice, "Please have the children move into the rear of the ambulance."

"What?" Laura asked with genuine surprise. "What's happening?"

"The Capitaine will explain later. But I need to get you and the children into the vehicle." At a command, the medic left Gabrielle's side and Laura helped the little ones onto the side bench, opposite the stretcher. With a new place to explore, the children sat open mouthed and wide-eyed as they took in their new surroundings.

Laura knew something out of the ordinary was taking place and was helpless to do anything about it. She had to keep playing the victim until the opportunity to escape cleanly presented itself. To make matters worse, one of the ambulance attendants was replaced by the heavily armored anti-terrorist, Andre, in the front compartment.

The rear door opened, and the Capitaine climbed into the vehicle and sat beside her. Leaning her rifle between the corner compartments of the vehicle she pulled off her helmet and balaclava. She shook out her short brunette hair, scratching feeling back into her scalp.

"So," she said with a smile that was as much a smirk to Laura, "what have you gotten yourself involved in this time, Laura Amour?"

Chapter Five

"How long have you've known?" Laura asked, eying the beautiful, yet deadly anti-terrorist who made room for herself in the van's back.

"I've followed both your careers; the academic and the more recent nefarious one. It took a few minutes, but I knew I recognized you from the beginning." Her eyes roamed across the row of children, pausing on Gabrielle before returning to Laura. "My name is Rachelle Deschamps. From your present company, I'm guessing that you're in my country for the same reason you fled your own."

Laura stared at the woman, knowing her bluff was finished. Her fight was over, because there was no way she would attack a cop, even if it meant going to jail. The police were not the enemy and as crazy as the media and her own government had portrayed her; she knew the difference.

She nodded. "My information spoke of a vast number of children, mostly Syrian, but other nationalities as well disappearing across Europe. Except for the older girl," she said indicating Gabrielle, "these arrived through the underground tunnels this afternoon. We're running from the ones who run the brothel."

"But that makes little sense. There has to be more to it than that. Who are these kids?"

"I don't know. Even if they spoke English or French, which they do not, I've only been with them for an hour." She met the intense scrutiny of the police officer. "All I can tell you is that there were extensive resources sent to retrieve or silence them."

"More than you know," the Capitaine muttered. "You saw the man back there at the blockade? Did you recognize him?"

Laura shook her head, her mind going back to the distinguished looking bureaucrat.

"Why would the Minister of Foreign Affairs of France be interested in a human trafficking case? Specifically, why would he risk his reputation and position for these children?

"That was the Minister? Coutu?" Laura said unable to keep the surprise from her face.

The Capitaine nodded her head, "Oui. Michel Coutu. He demanded that I hand the children over to his people. That he even knew they were in your vehicle told me that something was off. Do you know something about him I don't?"

"Is that why you had us leave so fast?" Laura said sidestepping the question.

"Yes. Coutu is powerful and has the ear of the President. I told him to get me written orders but until that time, they were material witnesses into a possible terrorist attack." She closed her eyes and pinched the bridge of her nose as if to ward off a headache. "I may have destroyed my career, but I wasn't going to just hand them and you over to him without a good reason."

"For their sake, thank you."

"But there's always the question about you Laura. Are you going to fight me?"

"I only fight those who exploit or abuse children, Capitaine. If you've been following my story, you know that."

"I do, but I will still have to get you to put these on," she said pulling a set of handcuffs out of a compartment on her belt.

"Well, you might want to reconsider for the time being," Laura said indicating behind the police officer with her chin.

Unsure if it was a trap, Rachelle seemed uncertain on how to react. Finally, she turned her head to the side and reminded Laura of a chameleon who was trying to see in both directions. If the situation wasn't serious, she would have laughed.

"Unless you have an escort, that car has been following us for some time," Laura said.

Rachelle looked back at her and then keyed her mic. "Andre, we may have a tail. Be-"

At that moment, as the young man in the front passenger seat leaned forward to better view the vehicle behind in the side mirror, his head exploded in a spray of blood and brains which coated the inside surface of the windshield. In a panic, the driver slammed his foot onto the brake pedal and it threw everyone forward. The safety hand loops built into the unit's ceiling saved both women swayed with the motion but the children slid forward and across Gabrielle's unconscious body. Laura grabbed the closest one by the back of her shirt and this helped slow her down so she was unhurt. The two who sat forward took the bulk of the shifted weight but it was only momentary as the driver swung the wheel towards the road's center and sped up. A sudden glancing blow to the vehicle's left side suggested that he avoided something solid alongside of the road.

Through the narrow windows in the rear doors, Laura spied the vehicle slide back into the lane behind them, its lights harsh and penetrating causing her to pull back out of its glare.

"They're behind us again," Laura yelled over the cries of the little ones.

The Capitaine leaned forward and reached for her rifle, but it had fallen and slid under the stretcher.

Laura pulled the smallest girl to her and passed her back to the officer. "I should be able to reach it from here." She dropped to the floor on one knee and could grab hold of the rifle's strap. Because of the stretcher being folded onto itself, there was not enough room to pull the weapon through. Sliding the strap along the floor, the weapon followed to the top of the stretcher's frame where she could grab it by its stock and pull it through. When she turned, she stared down the barrel of the lethal Smith and Wesson.

Over the revolver's sights, the Capitaine's glare was intense. "Hand it over, slowly. You're still a fugitive."

Laura complied. "You will need my help. There are at least two, maybe more."

The woman stared at Laura in uncertainty. She looked over her shoulder at the pursuing car and back at the window between the cab and the rear of the ambulance, its surface dripping with her partner's life. She turned back to Laura and handed her the revolver. "I want it back after," she said, her eyes drilling into Laura's.

Laura nodded. She accepted two speed loads which she dropped into her jacket pocket.

"They haven't shot the ambulance so they need the children alive. How can we exploit that?" Laura asked.

"They've isolated you and the children by killing Andre," Rachelle said. "If I had the resources, I would have someone ahead to force the ambulance to stop. If we're going to do something, I think sooner is better."

Laura looked back toward the cab and on the wall over Gabrielle she saw a circle of holes beside a knob. A radio speaker. She turned the knob and said, "Hello, hello."

The reaction to her call was the heavy jerking on the ambulance. It had startled the driver and he almost lost control of the speeding vehicle. The rig swayed dangerously as the driver fought the inertia of the top-heavy ambulance. Laura waited until he was running straight before she tried again. She shook her head at the amused grins of the older kids as if they were on an amusement ride. She only hoped it didn't jump the rails.

The second attempt was more successful as the driver answered back in a shocked and trembling voice. Laura had to repeat herself a couple times before the driver understood what they expected of him. He had to look back to see she was armed before he agreed to stop the rig. He didn't like the idea of more killers waiting up the road for them, either.

While Laura and Rachelle waited for the next straight piece of open roadway, her French partner shut off the overhead light to the back compartment.

"No sense giving them an easy target."

They saw the red glow off the ambulance's brake lights reflecting off the following vehicle's windshield, just before they felt their weight shift forward. The other car slowed with them and as they rocked to a stop, they each kicked open a rear door of the ambulance, weapons leading the way.

The passenger door opened and the barrel of a shotgun protruded from the opening and angled towards the two women. It was all the threat they needed. Laura squeezed off a shot at the shotgun-bearing man through the corner of the windshield that took the man in the side and sent spider web cracks across the front glass. He staggered from the heavy caliber pistol round but continued to push the long barrel between the door and the front post of the window. Laura took one step forward as she repositioned her aim to take the man in the neck. The shot flung him backwards and he lay still on the ground while his weapon clattered to the pavement.

Rachelle didn't hesitate either. The assault rifle pulled tight into her shoulder, stitched a line of holes across the window, just above the steering wheel. Not waiting to see if her shots had hit home, she sidestepped the front of the car; her rifle ready.

Laura followed suit on her side of the vehicle. She rounded the passenger's door and could see the driver was dead, missing half of his face. With her revolver extended, she leaned in quickly to see movement in the rear seat.

"One moving. Back seat," she announced.

The interior light showed a splash of crimson paint across the back seat and window. It became obvious that the heavy rifle rounds had gone through the driver and hit the man in back. Snapping her head for another look assured her that there was little threat. The man was gasping for air, trying to fill lungs that were rapidly filling with his own blood. At his feet, she could see a machine gun with a long silencer. Probably the weapon that had killed Rachelle's partner, Andre.

"He's no threat."

Rachelle opened the door and viewed her handiwork. She pulled the automatic gun from the floor and threw the gun over her shoulder by its strap. Two clips lay on the seat beside the man which she collected as well.

Laura was stepping away from the car when she caught sight of the man with the shotgun she had shot. She recognized his profile and leaned down and rolled him over.

"Capitaine, you'll want to see this," she said, tilting her head to the ground.

The police officer rounded the car and stood looking at the corpse.

"I'm sure this was one of your Minister's bodyguards," Laura said. "I recognize him from the blockade."

"Fuck!" Rachelle slammed her hand on the car's hood in anger.

While the officer dealt with her anger at her superior's deceit, Laura following a hunch, reached down and grabbed the man's hand. She had to work the black, leather glove off his hand, but found nothing. Checking the other hand showed her what she suspected.

"Do you recognize this?" she asked the cop.

Rachelle, her temper under control, at least visually, bent to examine the man's hand. Unable to see in the low light, she lifted the hand towards the car's interior until it became more visible.

"Part of it is a symbol of the Legion. I'm not familiar with the crisscrossing lightning bolts, though."

"The Legion? As in the French Foreign Legion?"

"Of course," Rachelle said in an off-mannered way as if it could be no other. Laura could see the woman considering what this could mean, but it wasn't long, as she dropped the hand like it was burning her.

"The men that pursued us in the tunnels each had the same stamp on their hands. I've taken a picture."

"Good. I'll get one of my people to look into it, but we have to get off the streets. And hide this," Rachelle said, indicating the ambulance.

"Can't we go to your headquarters?" Laura asked as she moved towards the rear of the rig where several anxious faces looked out at the carnage that seemed to follow them. The clinical side of Laura knew these children would need some major counseling after this was over or they would suffer from the violence and terror of their situation. If they were refugees from the Syrian conflict, they may already have seen too much.

"Not now, with the Minister involved. I'm not sure who I can trust from inside the government. Now that this involve members of the Legion, I'm worried about my people because many have military backgrounds, including *from* the Legion."

The police officer cut off and peered into the back of the rig and then sidestepped the rear bumper of the vehicle. "Damn, we lost our driver. He must have taken off running as soon as the shooting started."

"Can't blame him. Unless he was a military medic, being shot at isn't something they would have trained him for."

The officer looked at Laura thoughtfully and then said, "I'm guessing you have a place to go to ground. Is it somewhere that we can hide us and seven children until we figure our next move?"

Laura nodded. "I have just the place, but we need a change in vehicles. They'll be looking for this one, more so once the driver gets a hold of his people, if he hasn't already."

"Let's get it off the street first and then worry about finding another." She pulled out her cell phone and pulled the battery and the SIM card.

When the officer looked over at her, Laura said, "Not to worry, mine's a burner."

The woman just nodded.

Laura jumped in with the children while Rachelle took over driving. They were still within the city that the officer knew well and even though Laura got lost with all the twists and turns; it didn't take long before they stopped outside a set of tall metal gates. The officer left the vehicle and used the headlights to illuminate a padlock that kept the gates closed. Using a pick lock gun, which helped jump the tumbler pins within the padlock, the chain fell away allowing the gate to be opened. In seconds, they pulled the ambulance through the wrought-iron fence and moved deeper into what turned out to be a massive cemetery. Minutes later, parked between two large mausoleums, the ambulance shut down, leaving the area in dark shadows.

With little discussion, Rachelle left the group to find another vehicle. Laura sat with a child in each arm, humming an old lullaby and rocking them gently into a restless sleep. She covered the others with one of the wool blankets she had found in a wall cabinet. In the darkness, even she dozed off until a groan from Gabrielle brought her back to full awareness.

She moved one of the little ones onto the lower part of the stretcher, ensuring the blanket covered her. With her now free hand, she reached over and squeezed the older girl's arm. She felt Gabrielle stiffen at her touch, but shushed her and whispered, "It's okay, you're safe."

The girl relaxed and asked, "What happened? Where are we?"

"Long story. Quick version is you hit your head and have been out for a while. We're waiting for a police officer to get another vehicle so we can take you somewhere safe."

"And the kids?" she asked weakly, running her tongue across her dry lips.

"All good, thanks to you. Now rest."

It was all the coaching she needed, and the girl drifted off. Laura leaned back, the little boy stretched across her chest, his breathing a steady purr.

Without meaning to, Laura took her own advice and fell in a light sleep. Startled awake, she jumped when the rear door of the ambulance opened to reveal Rachelle's shadow.

"Laura?" the woman asked to the darkness.

"Here." She wrapped the child up in the blanket that covered him and carried him out into the night. "Any luck?"

"Yes. It's a cargo van with no seats, but it should do the job."

They transferred the children from one vehicle to another. There were a few grunts, groans, and whimpers, but none completely awoke. Even Gabrielle, whom she walked over to the van and laid her on the metal floor with a blanket for a pillow, was barely aware. Sliding the side door closed as easily as she could, she made sure her revolver was secure in her jacket pocket, before climbing in through the passenger door.

As they passed through the cemetery's gates, Rachelle ran back and re-locked the gate. They should not find the ambulance until at least the morning.

Chapter Six

Laura actually had several safe houses scattered around Paris in the event she needed to disappear. It was always better to plan ahead even if she'd never needed it. There was no reason to tell this police officer about the other locations. She might still need them. She guided Rachelle out of the city and into the Parisian countryside, northeast of the sprawling capitol. Just outside of the small village of Amblainville, she pointed out a narrow lane that led to an old farmstead which had been rented out for the season.

It took a few minutes to unlock the door and turn on a few lights. The house was cool, and she turned up the heat before heading back out to gather the children. Twenty minutes later, all the children were spread throughout a number of bedrooms and the two women were sitting quietly in a spacious living room with their own thoughts.

Having been closed up, the building was damp and cool, so Laura busied herself starting a fire in a large stone fireplace. There was plenty of wood stacked, enough for a few days, but if they were planning on using the farmstead any longer than that, more would have to be split and piled. She hoped the children didn't mind canned soup, because until she had time to shop, it limited their eatables. She didn't even have milk.

What she had was wine, and she opened a bottle. She returned to the living room and handed a very full coffee mug to Rachelle and sat opposite to her.

The police officer smiled her thanks. "I guess we're not too different," she said raising her glass in salute.

"Well, if I knew I was coming home with guests, I would have prepared something stronger."

"Now, we could be sisters."

"So tell me about this Minster of yours, sis," Laura said over her mug.

"As I told you, very powerful. He has attempted to interfere in local matters in the past, so there is no love lost between him and my agency. He is supposed to be in charge of foreign affairs so it is curious that he was would be involved in what you have told me should be a criminal element."

"Except for the Legion members."

Rachelle's eyes narrowed. "If it hadn't been one of his bodyguards, there would be nothing to tie him with this, except for his continued intrusion at different incidents involving GIGN. I have to inform my superiors,"

"Can you trust them?"

"I don't know," she said with a vacant look in her eyes as she stared into the fireplace.

"There must be someone in your team who is beyond reproach?"

"There are a few, but I'm trying to figure which one would be the best to approach. My running off with no authorization, and no notification will cause all kinds of trouble.

The two sat quietly and Laura realized the woman needed time to get her head around the problem. Only the snap of the fire interrupted their thoughts. Sitting quietly with a stranger would normally have been uncomfortable, but Laura didn't feel that way at all. She suspected that it was because they had fought and faced danger together. It was the same brother-in-arms bond that many soldiers felt after a battle. They might be on different sides of the law, but the two women were both warriors.

Finally draining her glass, Rachelle said, "Okay, I can think of one person that might help. I'll keep it short, in case others are watching for me."

Laura nodded. "It's getting light out. I will move the van into the storage building, in case it's been reported missing. I have a spare vehicle, but it's much too small for the bunch of us."

Laura switched the vehicle around and returned to the house to find Rachelle asleep on the couch. Her phone rested beside her in pieces, like she had stripped down a weapon for cleaning. Resigning herself to take the first watch, she covered the anti-terrorist with a blanket and watched through the window as the yard become brighter with the coming day.

LAURA WOKE TO SMALL little hands framing her face. When her eyes fluttered open, she found herself staring into a pair of small, dark eyes that resembled black opals. The dazzling smile was the only thing to eclipsed them. The child said something in a bird-like voice and her smile grew even larger.

"Good morning to you, Miss Sunshine," Laura replied with a smile. The little one let out a happy squeal and took off running down the hallway that led to the bedrooms. Laura could hear other voices back that way but could not understand the strange language. She sat up to find Rachelle entering from the kitchen with two steaming cups of coffee.

"It's not wine, but I figure it help kick start your day," she said handing over one mug. "I drink it black, there is sugar in the kitchen, but no milk."

"It's perfect. Thank you." She tucked her feet under her knees and warmed her hands around the cup. "Any news?"

"No. I've been waiting for you to wake up before turning on the television."

Pulling the blanket that had covered her bare legs, she sipped the steaming coffee and twisted her neck muscles to release the stiffness. Fresh pain made her flinch and her fingers explored the bullet crease from the previous night. She had forgotten about it. The wound had scabbed over, but was still tender. She would have to clean it to ensure it didn't become infected.

"You got lucky," Rachelle said.

Laura nodded. "The guy shot from hiding, through two panes of glass. Must have screwed with his aim. He had me cold."

Rachelle stared at her for a moment and Laura figured she would say something further, but the woman kept quiet. Instead, she switched on the television and surfed a few channels until she came to a news channel. It didn't take long before the anchor was talking about the events of the previous night. Laura didn't need to know the French language to understand that the police knew of her involvement. They posted a full facial of Laura on the screen and there was an expose' of her past.

The story flowed into the scene of the shootout with the men in the sedan and the ambulance. The camera shot, taken from far back showed the dark sedan and one body by the passenger's door, covered by a sheet. The interview with the driver of the ambulance proved that the press arrived before the police. The poor man was a train wreck as he tearfully described Andre's murder and how both the Capitaine and the woman with the children killed their pursuers. Questions were being raised by the Press about whether the police Capitaine was working with Laura. The official response from the GIPN was that the entire situation was under investigation.

Rachelle shut the television off in disgust, dropping the remote onto the couch. She stalked out of the room and Laura heard the door leading to the courtyard open and close.

There was nothing Laura could say that would make the situation better. She had to allow the young police officer the room she needed to deal with the information. They were allies of necessity but when everything settled, Laura knew that the Capitaine would do her best to bring Laura in to face justice. She wasn't the enemy, but she had a job to do and from what Laura had seen, the young counter-terrorist was superb.

Pulling on her slacks, she got up and walked towards the giggling coming from down the hallway. She poked her head into the doorway of one bedroom and saw her young escapees were gathered around a ball of fur that was chasing a length of string across the hardwood floor. She marveled how these children reverted to the high energy, playful and happy kids so quickly after their horrifying night. There were sure to be nightmares over time, but children seemed to bounce back after traumatic events better than adults. Maybe because they didn't take themselves so seriously.

One by one though as they recognized her presence, the laughter died out. She could see fear creeping back in their faces and stiffness in their shoulders. The kitten used the moment to attack the string. She smiled at the group to calm and reassure them. Crouching down on her knees, she reached out and tugged on the string so the tiny claws pounced at each lurch. With a flick, she snatched the line from the kitten and twirled it into a spin over its head. The little head followed the moving target and crouched low, its tiny muscles quivering in anticipation. A sudden lunge and the feline lost the string only to fall in the lap of one child in the circle. This brought forth a course of delightful squeals and the game was back on.

After a while, Laura extracted herself from the circle and backed out of the room. Crossing the hall, she checked in on Gabrielle and found that she was just waking up.

"How are you feeling?" she asked, sitting on the side of the bed.

The young girl gave her a tired smile and nodded. "I could get used to waking up to giggling," she said, her voice dry and in need of water.

Laura patted her on the arm and left the room. She returned minutes later with a glass of water and helped prop the girl up so she could drink.

"Thanks. That was great," she said as she allowed herself to sink back onto the pillow.

"I'm afraid it's all we have," Laura said, brushing the braids away from Gabrielle's face. With flawless skin of youth and her dark haunted eyes, the girl was incredibly beautiful. "I will have to do some shopping. I'm sure once they fully exhaust the kitten, I will have some hungry mouths to feed.

"Where are we?"

"We're about an hour outside of Paris. In the country." She could see the girl mull the information over but, she said nothing. "You're safe here, Gabrielle," Laura reassured her, and the girl closed her eyes as if to fall back to sleep.

Laura stood up and left the room, and although she didn't look back, she would have sworn the girl's eyes watch her go. She walked back to the front of the house and spied Rachelle out in the yard pacing back and forth. Regardless of the woman's strategy planning, Laura needed to feed the children. She strode outside and waited for the woman to acknowledge her presence.

It took a minute before the police officer looked up and the startled expression told Laura how deeply she had been concentrating.

"What is it?"

"I have a houseful of hungry children with no groceries. How do you want to handle this?" It was immediately apparent that this was an issue that the Capitaine hadn't even considered.

"Unless you plan on loading us all back into the van which might be a target now, you're either going to trust me to stay with the children or go get groceries," Laura said spelling out the problem in plain language.

"I'll go," Rachelle said without hesitation. "With your face plastered all over the media, someone will be sure to report you. What do you need?"

"Everything to feed two adults and a bunch of kids for a few days. I could use a hair coloring kit and if you can find coloring books and markers, it would give them something to do. A soccer ball, too, if you see one."

"Are you planning on setting up a home?"

"We both know that there has to be a reason, that they used so many resources last night. These specific kids have a high value to someone and until we can figure out the why and to whom, there's no way we can just hand them over to the authorities."

"Yeah, but —"

"Something big is going down, and it's not just happening here in France. The Interpol report I mentioned spoke of thousands of children going missing right across Europe. A lot of them are from among the refugees, but some are being flown in from outside countries with no guardians and they disappear before they ever reach Children Services."

The woman didn't back away, and she impressed Laura with her courage.

"Coutu is dirty, Rachelle," she said in a mater-of-fact tone. "When you get back, I'll share what I have with you."

Laura handed her a set of keys for the car and a credit card, "It's clean. Pass-code is 1298."

Rachelle wordlessly took the items and headed for the car.

Chapter Seven

Michel Coutu surrendered himself to the rich leather chair, his eye on, but not seeing the crackling fire in the massive stone hearth. The earthy aroma and the slow burn of the cognac helped ease the stress of the situation so he could contemplate his position with an uncluttered mind. Tongues of firelights danced across daunting portraits of the Coutu heritage, stern expressions that spoke of unbending authority and ruthless defense of all that they called their own. The Coutu family had been a force to reckon with since the Revolution when they helped topple the monarchy. It was a family jest that even a sewer rat could pull itself from the gutter and rise to a position of power within the government. All you need was a little luck, a wise choice in alliances and a willingness to crush any who stood in your way.

The Industrial Revolution both helped and hindered his family's fortunes. Quick fortunes were made by those quick and smart enough to grasp the technological changes sweeping the world. The rise of the middle class destroyed the feudal agricultural lands as the poor flocked to the cities for employment.

Both World Wars created as much opportunity as risk for the Coutu family. By the time the First World War ended, they had taken control of the black market, controlling the flow of alcohol and prostitutes for which soldiers from either side were happy to exchange for the script they were paid. Shipments of rations and war supplies were often lost and resold to neighboring allies and occasionally to the other side.

With the infrastructure firmly in place, new opportunities presented themselves during the Great Depression and set the stage for the main event, the Second World War. Working both sides was always profitable. Huge payouts were especially sought for British and Canadian fliers who had been shot down over occupied France. His father, Guy, was equally comfortable running raids against the Nazi storage depots as he was whispering names and places of hidden French Resistances fighters. These usually were those who interfered or suspected his true alliance.

It was after the war that his father took on a more presentable facade. Through another questionable business arrangement, he acquired one of the country's largest newspapers. Although the paper brought enormous profits to the family, it also produced one of the most lucrative surpluses.

Information.

Dark secrets, troubled businesses, insider information. It all ran through the paper and therefore through the opportunist hands of Guy Coutu. Using the gems of information to turn a quick profit or influence a corrupt politician's vote was child's play for the master of manipulation. Keeping multiple layers between him and those who did the actual wet work kept the illusion of respectability while increasing his power and influence in the highest circles.

From the moment of his birth, Michel Coutu's position in France's society was set. The best schools, the finest tutelage. Under the firm guidance of his father, they groomed him for some of the highest offices in the country's leadership, all the while having him learn the family's true business holdings and workings.

The step-up from publisher to politician was easy enough especially when your strongest opponent bows out of the race due allegations of sexual misconduct. Those allegations, with photos and signed statements had already been in the man's dossier even before he put his name forward. The contest was so one-sided and Michel had won by such a majority that any questions as to where the information had come from were quickly lost in the celebrations.

He heard the muted ring of a phone from a distant room and sipped his drink as he waited for Clara to bring him the phone. Since the death of his wife, Selena five years ago, the phone would be for no one else. Had he been involved in his current enterprise when the cancer had struck her down, he may have had the means of saving her. That thought alone kept nagging him in the dark hours of the night. For all his money and influence, he had held her as she breathed her last breath against his tear stained cheek, powerless to help her.

The door cracked to the study allowing light to creep across the floor. The soft whisper of footsteps scratched the heavy stone floor, until Clara stood beside his chair, the encrypted phone in her hand.

"Monsieur? It is Antoine."

He nodded and took the phone from her. He waited until he heard the door close behind her, extinguishing the harsh light.

"Report."

He listened to the man on the other end of the line read off what facts had been pulled from the scene where his team had attempted to stop the ambulance and retrieve the children. There was little information not already known.

"And this woman? Who is she? Who is she working for?"

His lips thinned in exasperation to Antoine's reply. "And Capitaine Deschamps has not reported in yet?"

He put his glass down on the table, knowing it would soon snap in his hand if his temper continued to grow. He took a long slow breath in an effort to calm himself, before he said, "Keep on top of this. The minute the good Capitaine calls in, I want a team ready to take her into custody for aiding an international terrorist. Same with the children. Once they are in the social system, our inside people can collect them once things settle down. This shipment has already been bought and paid for and for obvious reasons, we must deliver. You know how exacting the selection process was. There are no immediate substitutes. As for this Canadian, I want the biggest manhunt put together since the Terror." He was referring to the hunt for Royalists following the Revolution and the mass executions.

This time there would be only one death.

Not waiting for a reply, he ended the connection and stared at the offending device. With an effort, he carefully placed the phone on the side table. It would not do to lose control at this stage of the game. Now was the time for clear thinking and a show of decisive command. There was too much at stake. The Eastern Europeans would pounce on his organization the minute they sensed a weakness. That was a war that could jeopardize the entire empire.

If he could salvage and complete this sale, it would be the start of a new era for his organization and put him in a position to never have to worry about any competition again.

Staring into the flames, he recalled all he had read about this Amour and her crusade against child abusers in her home country. He also went over the insider information that had come from the Canadian Foreign Minister at the last NATO conference on global terrorism. The woman had an impressive record. She helped spark a grassroots protest that not only forced the government's hand into producing harsher penalties for crimes against children, but the unintended result was the toppling of the government in the following election.

He had no way of knowing how his operation had attracted the attention of this woman, but she would find that he neither had the moral nor legal restraints that had constrained her last opponents.

Picking up his cognac, he emptied half the glass, closing his eyes as it began its burning descent. He smiled to himself as a plan evolved. He turned the strategy around in his mind to view it from multiple angles but could see no fault. It would draw this Amour to him like they drew a tiger to a bleating lamb tied to a stake. Once committed, there would be no escape.

And then it would be business as usual.

Chapter Eight

A roar of triumph and laughter came through the open window of the farmhouse. Laura and Rachelle were discussing the latest news, but the soccer match in the courtyard kept interrupting their conversation. Gabrielle had felt well enough to make the walk outside and sat in a lawn chair as the unofficial score keeper and referee.

"So, you're saying we're both wanted by every police force that France can muster?" Laura summarized.

"Yes," the police officer nodded. "Except, I'm wanted for questioning for aiding and abetting a known International terrorist while they basically want you dead or alive."

"Don't sound so jealous," Laura said with a smile.

"You don't seem so worried," Rachelle said with a look on her face that was a mixture of confusion and disbelief.

"I've played this role before. I don't underestimate the surrounding forces. I plan to avoid them."

"Like last night?" Rachelle said, the sarcasm dripping off her tongue.

"It was a calculated risk. The protection of the children was more important than my getting caught. With the group chasing us and all the gunfire, I knew where your group would create a blockade."

Rachelle sat up, the surprise clear in her expression. "How?"

Laura stood up and walked to the window overlooking the courtyard. "Other than my previous training," she said over her shoulder, "I've spent six months reviewing all your tactics, weaponry and response procedures."

"But-"

Laura pulled out her smart phone and signed into an encrypted cloud service. She brought up the different counter attack Operating Procedures for RAID and passed the phone to the officer.

"Trust me, Capitaine; I'm fully tapped into your department and a few others. Would you like to see the results of your last evaluation?" Turning, she saw the shock and disbelief on the police officer's face. Laura almost felt sorry for her, because everything the woman knew and believed in was being turned upside down. With the betrayal of her own people and now this news, Rachelle was probably feeling like someone had kicked her in the gut. She couldn't help remembering how her friend, Janice Williams had felt when her own betrayal came out in the open.

After more than a few long minutes, Laura turned back and returned to the couch. Leaning towards the other woman, she said, "You need to decide what it is you want to do. You can take your chances with your people. I'm sure you have your supporters, but I guarantee they'll demand my head in the bargain." The two stared at each other knowing Laura was right. "But the bigger question you need to ask yourself is why this Minister is so interested in these children? Because if you surrender, you'll be handing those kids over to him to do what he wants to them."

Rachelle bit her lip and looked towards the window where the squeals and laughter still rang out.

Laura gave her all the time she needed to work out the implications of each side of the decision. She had to make her own choice. Laura was banking everything that the Capitaine was more about protecting others than covering her own butt. They both knew there was something big happening behind the scenes and unless they did something, Coutu would get away with whatever he was mixed up in.

That he had personally got involved was extraordinary. Why would he ever take a chance of exposing himself? It had to be desperation or arrogance. For someone in his position, he might talk his way out of some issues, but this had escalated into an international incident. She knew recent history of terrorist attacks throughout France, calling this a terrorist attack would buy him time and resources immediately, but that would only last until the investigation was complete. Eventually he would face some very tough questions; the least being why he was interfering in an area of domestic crime when his portfolio was obviously foreign affairs.

"What do you propose?" Rachelle asked.

"Like I said, we need to find out what is so important about these kids," Laura said. "We also need to find out where they're from. That might give us our first clue."

"Then we need someone who can speak Arabic," Rachelle said and Laura could tell she was contemplating the issue.

After a minute, she looked at Laura and said, "I think I know someone who might speak to the children so we can figure where they're from and possibly what they been through. Before you ask," she said holding up her hand, "Yes, it's someone we can trust."

"'AYUHAAL'ATFAL, MIN yastatie 'an yukhbirani min 'ayn ant?"

Hearing the man's question, the eyes of the children popped open and a couple mouths opened to form tiny "Os" It was obvious to Laura that they understood his words.

A sudden crash of voices filled the room as they all spoke at once, their voices rising as they tried to overcome each other. The huge man's, who Rachelle had introduced as Yusuf Rahal, deep laugher filled the room as he raised his hands over the group like a friendly bear. And he looked the part, Laura decided. Standing over six feet, his arms and chest seem to stretch the fabric of his dark brown jubba dishdasha which hung to his ankles. The well-trimmed beard added to the image, as did the light brown karakal that covered his head.

Rachelle explained that Yusuf was a member of the Muslim community that had tired of those extremist groups that hid behind the lie that they fought for Allah. He and his following had taken a hard stand by offering intelligence, advice and translation services to the police to stop the deadly attacks which did nothing but bring fear and hatred toward his faith. She had worked with Yusuf frequently and trusted his advice and his discretion.

Rachelle had explained the circumstances to Yusuf and he would attempt to extract what useful information he could so they could decide on a strategy. If he had recognized Laura, he had not shown it, only accepting her hand when introduced.

"One thing is for certain," he said looking over his shoulder. "They are definitely Syrian. The rest may take a little longer."

Laura looked over to Rachelle and motioned that she would be outside. On her way out to the courtyard where the last of her wards sat, she made a pit stop in the kitchen to shovel the ice cream that Rachelle had bought into two cones.

She crossed to a swing where Gabrielle sat, her face towards the sun, eyes closed. At her approach, those eyes snapped open; fear flashing across her features.

"Easy," Laura said. "You're safe."

The young girl took in a ragged breath and sat back, accepting the offered cone. The two sat quietly for a while enjoying the sun and the cold treat.

"This is the first time I been able to feel the sun since they took me from the orphanage last year."

"They never let you outside?" Laura asked, shocked.

The girl shook her head, silent tears reflecting the sun. "They only allowed me out on the roof balcony and only at night after the clients left, when no one could see me. My room had no windows, so all I had for comfort was the stars, an old x-box and my books. They learned early that I behaved better if they supplied me with books. It was my favorite escape. When the clients arrived, I retreated into my stories where they couldn't reach me."

This time it was Laura who shuddered. The horrors that this beautiful child had endured was beyond belief. She felt the familiar rage building and part of her wished for a moment she could kill those men again; if anything to pay for the pain they had inflicted on Gabrielle and all the other victims of their trade. Laura opened her arms and after a slight hesitation, Gabrielle leaned in. When Laura's arms came around her, the troubled girl surrendered to the pain and fear, burying her face into Laura's chest. Sobs racked her slim body. Laura rocked her and allowed her to release all the pent-up emotions.

Laura, holding this broken child, suddenly realized what it was she had given up without even being aware of it. Yes, she had lost her best friend and her beloved Canada for her crusade. But she had also given up the chance at being a mother. Holding Gabrielle like this, she felt her own mother's ghost, long gone, beside her, holding her as a child, consoling her or pushing back childhood fears. The most vivid memory was after Susan had died. Although lost in her own grief as a parent, she always had the time and patience to help Laura through her pain. Except for this moment, Laura realized, there would be no one that would rely on her the same way, and it left her empty.

After a long time, Gabrielle whispered, "What's going to happen to me?" She pulled herself up so she could look at Laura for an answer.

Laura paused before answering. The child might be thirteen but she was a lot more mature than others twice her age and would see through empty promises in a heartbeat. "Right now, I can't promise anything except, you won't be going back there while I'm still breathing. There are some powerful people involved in this and once we figure what they are after, we can try to put a stop to their plans and expose them. Once we do that, we can discuss what you want to do with the rest of your life." Laura reached out and cupped the side of the little girl's face. "Maybe a writer," she said with a smile.

The sparkle in Gabrielle's eyes matched the huge smile that creased her face as imaginary characters danced around her that seemed so real that Laura felt she could see them.

YUSUF RAHAL SAT ACROSS from Laura and Rachelle, a cup of coffee balanced carefully on his knee. He looked troubled and Laura wondered what information he had pulled from the children. She sat quietly waiting for him to start.

"The children are definitely from Syria," he started. "From what I could deduce, all of them had been at the Jungle." He was speaking of the huge refugee camp that had been set up in Calais on the shores of the English Channel. For some reason, all the refugees that had struggled across Europe from the civil war in Syria had been brainwashed that entrance to the UK was next to Nirvana. When they hit the coast and could go no further, a huge refugee camp was haphazardly put in place. Make-shift shelters, unsanitary sewage and the lack of fresh water threatened the safety of the refugees and the locals. It had become such an ordeal to the residences and the police services tasked with keeping the peace in the area that the government of France had no choice but to step in and have the camp dismantled. They scattered the occupants across France to wait for the results of immigration applications to see if anyone would allow them to stay in Europe.

"If you remember, there were over fifteen hundred children that had made the journey without families." When the two women nodded, he continued. "These six were among them. They told me there were many others taken, but that someone separated them into small groups of six to eight children and left for parts unknown."

So many!

"Three are from the same family. They watched their father drown as the boat they were on swamped along the coast of Italy and the older boy kept them together." He reached up and squeezed the bridge of his nose as if battling a migraine. Laura recognized it as body language that fought against the horrors he had been exposed too. "The others all have different stories about losing their families during the march, but all talk about the same thing."

"Which is?" Rachelle demanded.

"Once they were taken, they were subjected to a battery of tests by a group of medical doctors and nurses."

Laura saw a look of bewilderment cross Rachelle's face that might have reflected her own, except she was afraid she knew where this was leading. If she was right, then she had stumbled on something much more evil than just human trafficking.

"Were they able to tell you anything more?" Laura asked.

The big man nodded placing his cup on the coffee table, "Someone loaded them onto large buses when the Jungle was torn down. Quite a few of the buses never made it to their intended destination. Instead, they were brought to a huge building that was setup like a refugee center with cots for beds and separated areas for boys and girls. Over the next few days they underwent the medical tests— it almost sounded like a physical, but there was blood work."

"That almost sounds like something the government officials would do to ensure the children were in good health," Rachelle said in defense. "I don't understand why this is an issue."

Yusuf looked from Rachelle to Laura, the fear and disgust clear in his eyes as they glassed over, tears barely being held back. He didn't have to continue. His emotional response told Laura everything she need to know about why the children were so valuable.

"How many, Yusuf? Did they give any numbers?" Laura asked, ignoring the police officer's confusion.

"They told me that there were seven buses in that center. Those buses usually carry forty to fifty people."

"And when were they moved from there?" Laura pressed.

"Yesterday."

Rachelle slapped the arm of the chair in obvious frustration. "Would one of you tell me what I'm missing here?"

Laura look at her newfound ally and sadly nodded. "This is not just about child sexual exploitation, which is bad enough. I think we've stumbled across a human organ harvesting network."

Across from her, Rachelle eyes widen as her mouth dropped open. Laura could see it shook her to the core and looked like she would be physically sick. She rose slowly, wrapping her arms around her chest and moved to the window, keeping her back to Laura and Yusuf.

"There are many, many accounts," Yusuf said, running his hands across his face, "among the refugees about midnight raids in both the camps and on the march across Europe. At first they thought it to be just for the sex trade, but they soon realized that the victims were men, women and children. In fact, they found one refugee alive, but with his eyes plucked out; his assailants wanted nothing else."

"But this is not Africa or China," Rachelle said, spinning around, her skin still pale but a flush of anger tingeing her cheeks.

"Come on Rachelle, you know if there is a demand, then there will definitely be those who will exploit it. It's happening in North America. When a kidney can fetch $260,000 dollars on the Black Market, you know it's going to happen."

"Captain," Yusuf said, "There has never been such a migration of vulnerable people in the history of Europe, nor such an opportunity for those who are involved in human trafficking."

Rachelle's head drooped, and she nodded. "I didn't want to believe this could happen in France. We are civilized and cultured."

"Then help me stop them," Laura said.

The two women stared at each other and Laura was uncertain if the officer could turn her back on the law and allow her the freedom to make the attempt. But after a minute, Rachelle's jaw clenched, and she gave a tight nod.

Yusuf leaned back in his chair with a sigh. "Let me take the children for you. I can easily hide them within my community with people that can communicate with them. I will make arrangements in case you come across more of these lost children."

Laura and Rachelle didn't even have to consult each other. Both nodded their agreement knowing it was the safest course.

"Thank you, Yusuf," Laura said with feeling. "Would you have room for Gabrielle?"

"I'm not going anywhere."

Laura turned to see the teen standing in the kitchen's entrance. She had not heard the girl enter and was unsure how much she had heard of the conversation. Laura opened her mouth to answer but the young girl cut her off.

"Those children will blend in with his people but I would stand out like a neon sign," Gabrielle said her hands on her hips. "It would put both them and me at greater risk. I'm safer here with you two."

"But we won't be here all the time."

"Then I'll wait for you. I can keep the place clean, even do some cooking."

Laura could see the determination in her narrowed eyes. The girl was tough while vulnerable at the same time. Giving her something to work towards couldn't hurt. It would be her contribution against those who hurt her. She looked over at Rachelle who just shrugged.

She raised her coffee cup towards the girl and said, "I like it black."

Chapter Nine

Sporting short, dark wavy curls, compliments of Gabrielle's first dye job, Laura sat across the street from the outdoor cafe she and Aline used to frequent. She was hoping the Parisian prostitute might still keep to her habit of a glass of wine before work. Of course, after the other night, Laura had no idea of the status of the brothel. Rachelle believed the police raided the building and it might still be a crime scene.

Rachelle and Laura had split up to cover more ground. Rachelle would meet with some trusted colleagues for information about Michel Coutu. Rachelle figured it was better to meet her people alone due to Laura's background.

Laura's biggest fear was that Coutu's men had gotten to Aline to find who had talked. She could visualize her friend and her fellow sex workers being tortured. The guilt stretched Laura's patience, and it was difficult to just sit and wait. She had thought about visiting the girl's apartment, but that could make matters worse if her building was under surveillance. At least if Aline visited the cafe, Laura might pickup anyone shadowing the woman.

Sipping on a glass of Pinot Noir while pretending to read, her eyes flicked to every movement on the street, hidden behind dark, large lensed sunglasses. Her ears picked up the click-clack of a pair of high-heeled shoes on the sidewalk and it matched her heartbeat as she glanced up to see her friend skip across the road towards the cafe. Aline greeted one waiter with familiarity, favoring him with a kiss on each cheek and allowing him to seat her at her favorite table. After a brief exchange, the waiter retired to get her order, which Laura knew with a pang of regret, would be a glass of the house white.

She watched all this play out without actually concentrating on Aline. Using her peripheral vision, she watched for movements further down the street in the direction her friend had come from. Sure enough, a tall, thick chested man moving at a slow pace, stopping to view the displays in the storefront windows, before moving to the next. Laura glanced over at the man and his concentration was not on the books displayed on the shelf in front of him, but rather further up; the window's reflection. She almost laughed aloud when the man turned and checked out the cafe where Aline held court as if he doubted the truth in the reflection. When he came even with the small sidewalk cafe which Laura sat in, he took a table against the storefront wall so he had a full view of the opposite restaurant. It also put him behind Laura's position.

Pretending to be absorbed in her book, she sat watching the street to see if he was alone or had another observer elsewhere. After the waiter took and returned with his order, a cup of coffee, she heard a quiet whisper behind her. Turning her head, she saw him talking into a small microphone clipped to his shirt. He clamped his mouth shut and ignored her gaze, looking elsewhere so not to draw more attention. So, this was a two-person team. Question one: Where was the other? Question two: Was he one of Coutu's or was he police?

That was the biggest question for Laura. If this was a police officer, doing his duty, there was no way she would attack the man. However, the gloves were off if he was part of the trafficking group.

From past experience, the direct approach worked best for Laura.

Marking her page in the book with a napkin she closed it. She rose and turned to pick up her purse which hung from its strap from the back of the chair. While she pulled the strap over her shoulder, she allowed her eyes to sweep over the man, memorizing his facial details. He Ignored her, his eyes focused across the street towards Aline, he reached for his coffee and Laura could make out the tattoo stamped on his right hand in the fleshy web between thumb and forefinger.

Got ya.

Leaving her book on the table to indicate her plan to return, she skirted the tables and made her way into the cafe. She moved towards the back of the cafe and seeing the sign showing the washrooms; she entered a narrow hallway. Passing both the men's and lady's rooms, she continued on and pushed through the door at the end of the hallway which led to the service lane for deliveries.

She gave herself a mental pat on the back for having taken the time to explore the neighborhood over the past months. Knowing the lay of the land was a huge advantage. She knew the communication equipment the man must have been using would be more than likely short range, so that his partner had to be close by, especially if they planned to grab Aline. Dodging around shipping crates, she ran to the end of the service lane and slowed as she came to the next crossroad. Circling the block so she came behind anyone waiting out of sight of the cafes, Laura moved at a pace that let her observe the line of parked cars. It was a one-way street so there were cars parked on both sides. Other than a compact taxi that pulled away from the curb before she came even with it, only one vehicle had an occupant. Near the end of the street, hidden from the cafes by the corner of the building, a dark four-door sedan sat idling.

Laura saw the man's eyes flash in his side mirror at her approach. She exaggerated her gait so her hips swayed teasingly and she allowed her purse to swing beside her, imitating the Paris sex workers. Ignoring the mirror, she felt his eyes crawl across her body and brushed off the urge to gag.

As she came even with the driver's door, he said, "How much bi-en-aimee?" He reached out and traced his hand along the curve of her thigh.

Laura took his hand and playfully slapped it. It allowed her to turn the hand and expose the familiar mark beside his thumb. "You know the rules. Money first before you play with the rest." She leaned in, giving him a full glimpse down her top of her blouse, but giving her a chance to view the interior of the vehicle. A small digital mobile radio sat on the passenger seat beside the man.

The man's mouth fell open and pressed hard on his crotch. "Gi—give me your number. I'm working now."

She reached for her purse and pushed a few objects aside while checking the street or anyone near.

Holding on to the offending hand, she said, "Should I write it here?"

The man nodded, her close presence flustering him.

With a quick jab, Laura slammed the pen-looking object into the man's ear. The tool was more like an ice-pick. The front came to a pencil sharp point, the other end rounded to give leverage for pushing. He jerked, and she kept hold of his hand with her left hand so he could not pull away. She used the heel of her other hand to hammer the object through his ear canal and into his brain.

There was only a trickle of blood, which was blocked from view when she rested his head against the driver's door post. She reached in and shut off the engine. Now he looked like someone who was taking a nap while his wife was shopping.

Without looking back, Laura crossed the distance to the corner in time to see Aline leave the cafe and head toward her apartment. The man in the other cafe, jumped up to follow, speaking into the microphone pinned on his shirt. Laura fell in behind him, stretching her stride to gain on him.

Depending on their intentions, there might be another team waiting at the apartment, so Laura decided that she needed to dispatch this fellow before they got any closer to Aline's home. Using her cell phone, she speed dialed Aline's number.

"Hello," Aline said.

"Aline, it's Laura." She watched as the woman stopped and stared at the phone.

"Oh my god, I thought you were dead. Where the hell have you been?"

"I'll explain, but first I need you to listen. Can you do that for me?"

The man, seeing Aline stop, slid behind one of the trees that lined the street. Once again he spoke into his shirt making Laura wonder what he was thinking about the fact his partner was not calling back.

"Ya, I guess so."

"It's very important that you do not look behind you. Just keep walking." She saw the young prostitute stiffen and for a moment thought she would turn around. To her credit, she squared her shoulders and moved forward unsteadily.

"What's going on, Laura?" asked Aline, her voice strained and shaking.

"Everything will be all right, as long as you follow my instructions. There is a man following you, but I will get to him before he can get to you. I need your help to get him off the street. Okay?"

"Y—yes. Please don't let him hurt me Laura."

"He won't lay a hand on you. Now, remember the alley where they found the dead guy in the garbage bins a couple months back?"

"Yeah."

"When you get to the alley, I want you to turn in there. Once you are out of sight, run and hide behind the second bin. Can you do that for me?"

"Wo—won't that put me where he wants me?" Aline said, her breath coming in tiny pants as her panic grew. Laura knew she was close to the breaking point.

"It's okay. I'm right behind him. He'll never get the chance."

Laura was less than twenty feet behind the man. All his attention was on Aline. He hadn't turned around once. Laura's hand was in her purse which was held tight under her arm. She gripped a small, Walther P22 pistol with its threaded silencer. The small caliber combined with the silencer would reduce the gunshot to nothing more than a firecracker being set off. Her fingers moved across the side of the weapon and switched on the laser site for faster aiming.

Aline angled towards the entrance of the alley and the man increased his speed so he wouldn't lose her. Behind him, Laura did the same. For the first time, the guy looked over his shoulder as he somehow sensed Laura behind him. His eyes registered her but there was no recognition that Laura could see. He dismissed her as a threat, turned and resumed following Aline.

Laura blinked. She couldn't believe what had just transpired. She questioned her plan. Was there another shooter out there that she had missed? What else would make the ex-soldier so confident? Or was it because she was a woman? If so, he had made a fatal mistake. Keeping an eye for external hazards she closed the distance and followed him into the alley.

As she rounded the corner of the last building she pushed her glasses up onto the top of her head, wanting nothing to interfere with her aim. She pulled the pistol out of the purse and held it tight against her leg as she advanced towards the man who was cautiously looking around the first garbage bin.

"Looking for something?" Laura said raising the pistol so that the laser sight was centered on the back of the man's head.

"None of your business," he said as his head turned towards her. "Get los—"

His eyes widened as they focused on the weapon being trained at him.

He slowly turned around but tried to radio his partner, his chin lowered towards the mic. Laura realized it must be voice-activated as he held both hands away from his pockets.

She gave him a tight smile, "If you're trying to call your partner, he won't be answering you anytime soon."

His shoulders slumped at the news and his eyes flicked back and forth searching for an escape. With both hands held slightly away from his body he backed away from her.

"Listen lady. I don't know what the issue is, but—"

"Don't bother," Laura said. "I know you're one of Coutu's toy soldiers."

The tightening of the jaw told her she was right. He kept backing up. When he passed the second bin, he must have caught sight of Aline, because he lunged toward her.

Aline screamed as she saw him charging towards her. The first bullet took him in the side and spun him away to bounce off the third bin that lined the building. The woman's cry of terror easily covered the cough of the pistol. While he fell, his hand dipped under his jacket. Before he could extract his own weapon, Laura squeezed off a second round which took him in the back of the head, painting the metal bin in a collage of crimson.

Aline was crying hysterically as Laura jammed the pistol back into her purse. She reached down and pulled the girl out of her hiding spot between the bins. Leaving her shaking and barely able to standalone, Laura grabbed the man's pant legs and dragged him in between the garbage containers so he was out of sight from the roadway. She lifted a bag of garbage and broke the plastic lining so that the refuse spilled over the man, covering him. With luck, no one would find him until garbage day.

With her arm around the girl's shoulder, she told her over and over she was safe, until the hysterics calmed and she got a hold of herself. It took over twenty minutes to coach her to walk normally to Laura's car which was only a couple blocks away. There were a few moments where Laura had to resist slapping the girl to snap her out of the shock, but feared it might make matters even worse. It was imperative they get away from the area before someone found the bodies and the police blockaded the area.

With the late afternoon traffic and a ton of explaining on Laura's part about who and what she was really in Paris for, it took almost two hours to reach Oleans. Along the way, she had Aline copy every phone number she had of other sex workers. Once the list was complete, she had the girl take the phone apart and toss the sim card out the car window. They would drop the phone and battery off in different trash containers at two different rest stops. She checked the two of them into a clean hotel with adjoining rooms under one of her aliases. Armed with two prepaid, clean cell phones, Aline would contact her friends and colleagues she had worked with to find more of the children. She would also warn her friends that Paris might be dangerous for the next while and that a vacation might be wise.

Chapter Ten

Rachelle sat with her back against the rear wall watching the entrance of the small restaurant. She and Laura had agreed to move in different directions, not only to cover more ground but also to deal with the issue from separate angles.

Of all her contacts, Henri Pelletier was not only someone in her agency she trusted, but was someone who held a special spot in her heart.

Her father and Henri Pelletier were partners; detectives dealing with the insurgence of synthetic narcotics in the Paris underworld years ago. During one of their raids, her father took several rounds of automatic fire as they busted into a suspected meth lab. His vest had caught three of the rounds but the last one left a crater where his face had been.

From that point on, Henri had filled that spot, both as a father and as a mentor. He guided her studies and helped with her ascension in the force. He had been a confidant as much as a coach, demanding the best efforts on all fronts.

He walked into the bistro, stopping only to allow his eyes to adjust to the low lighting and to find where Rachelle sat waiting, a tablet in her hand.

As he approached the table, she placed the tablet face down on the table and rose to greet him. He gathered her into his embrace and held her in silence.

"Tell me the truth," he said, whispering into her ear as he hugged her.

"You came alone?"

"Of course," he said as he pulled apart and straddled the high chair that sat beside her table. He settled and looked around the establishment before he turned his attention back to her.

"Talk to me."

She gave him a full rundown of the all that had transpired since they had called her out with her team to blockade a neighborhood to a suspected terrorist attack. She told him of the Syrian children and what they had discovered and about Michel Coutu. For some reason, call it instinct, she held back the name of the Muslim leader who was assisting them. He listened without interruption except to clarify specific details, and afterwards he sat quietly turning the information over in his mind.

"And you trust this woman, this Canadian?" he asked, one eyebrow raised.

Rachelle nodded. "She is authentic. Her only reason for existing is to help children." She leaned closer. "But what she has uncovered is so much larger. Which is why I had to come to you with not only what I know but also what we suspect of Coutu."

Henri covered his eyes and sat quietly absorbing the information and its implication. Rachelle tilted the tablet towards her and watched the video that was streaming. She looked up to see Henri watching her with a sad expression.

"You need to give her up," Henri said. "It is the only way. The force needs to know you have not gone soft. If you do this, they will listen." He watched her eyes for a minute before giving a sigh that was expected to end the matter.

"But my statement..."

"Will not mention Syrian children or Coutu." He put his hands together over hers, holding her tight to the table. His eyes bore into hers. "Listen, we need to make you safe, before we can start a campaign against one of the strongest people in France."

She pulled her hands from his and watched his eyes. That would be the only sign she would get unless she attacked first. Most of what he had said made sense, except altering her statement to exclude the real problem and the enemy. Glancing down at the tablet which displayed the view of the hi-tech hexacopter, hovering at 400 feet, she saw that an entire grouping of anti-terrorist troops were disembarking and surrounding the restaurant she and Henri were now sitting in.

These were her team mates. And he had turned them against her.

A tear escaped her eye and ran down her cheek. She did not bother wiping it away. She leaned across the table with one hand and grasped Henri's hands. The other hand she let drop beneath the table.

"Since before the time of my father's death, you have always had my back and I appreciate everything you have done for me. I just can't understand why you would betray me." She flipped the tablet over so he could see the live video of the building's exterior. Two lines of GIPN officers, weapons held tight to their shoulders, hugged the wall near both of the restaurant's entrances.

She slid a pair of handcuffs across the table. "Put them on Henri." She raised her other hand so he could see the business end of her service revolver.

He closed his eyes and sighed. "They'll kill you the minute they see your gun."

"The cuffs," she said lifting her chin to press the order. "Through the arms of the chair."

He did as he was told. Once secured, she moved around him and brought the butt of the heavy Smith and Weston down hard on his head. He collapsed onto the table and looked like a drunk who had passed out in his cups. Wasting no time, she grabbed the tablet and crossed to the entrance to the kitchen. She opened a door that led to a utility room full of cleaning supplies, with a floor drain for cleaning the gathering of mops leaning in the corner.

"It did not go well," a voice said over her shoulder.

"No, Andre, it didn't," she said blinking her eyes dry. "Thank you so much for your help."

"Be safe, Rachelle."

But she was already climbing the mounted ladder that rose to the roof. Although she had planned this route, she never expected to use it. She had to push Henri to the back of her mind. She couldn't deal with the emotions now. She needed to have her head in the game.

She walked up to a body harness that was laid out on the flat roof and stepped into the two prearranged leg holes and pulled the assembly of re-enforced canvas straps up over her hips. A hard tug on the belt pulled the harness snug on her thighs and butt. She pulled the main lanyard up and attached it to the carabiner that hung from the trolley, hanging from the steel cable that led across the street. With the help of Andre and two of his cooks, it took less than an hour to set it up before first light this morning.

She fished the tablet from her pants pocket and viewed the scene below. The two stacked teams of anti-terrorists were still waiting outside the entrances and she wondered if they were waiting for a signal from Henri. But as she watched, both teams began their assault. They yanked open the doors and tossed flash-bang grenades inside from each direction. Seconds later the double high intensity explosions let go, and the teams entered the building simultaneously. She knew exactly where each team member would be. She had performed countless of these breaches in training and in the field. She pulled up the drone software and hit the "Return to Home" command and pocketed the tablet.

Time to go.

Releasing the brake on the trolley, she took a running start across the roof. When she reached the end, she threw up her feet and allowed the harness to take her weight. The trolley's wheel sang as her speed on the zip line increased. The wind pulled at her hair and she had to squint to keep her eyes from watering, at least she told herself that it was the air stream. No matter how many times she did this, the thrill never let her down. She crossed almost three hundred feet in seconds. She passed in between two neighboring buildings, applied the brake slowly, bleeding off the speed. The end of the cable was secured to a large tree; the wire disappearing beneath the foliage. Fifteen feet before she met the tree, she released the carabiner and dropped ten feet before rolling into a tight ball. The trolley continued, and she heard it clunk against the trunk. She made a mental note to retrieve the trolley after all this was over. The equipment was not cheap.

Not bothering to shed the harness, Rachelle ducked behind the tree, out of sight from the street and made her way through a service alley. She knew the assault team would recognize the zip line setup, but if she could put some distance between her and the restaurant, she should be able to avoid the other units.

She kept her pace steady but without looking like she was running from something. Two blocks further, nestled in between two tenement buildings, she came to a small scooter locked to a gas pipe. It took a second to unlock the back compartment on the bike and pull out a leather jacket and helmet. Once she had donned both, she felt better from altering her appearance. Henri would have made note at what she was wearing and would have transmitted the information to all the other teams. She pulled the cable that secured the bike to the pipe and guided the bike between the buildings to the next street. Ensuring that there were no police cars in the immediate vicinity, she started the bike and left the area as sirens rose behind her.

Chapter Eleven

The return to the farmhouse was bittersweet. Over coffee and sandwiches prepared by Gabrielle, Rachelle filled them on her meeting with Henri Pelletier and the outcome. Laura could see that the man's betrayal had affected the Capitaine more than she was letting on. The dark circles and redness of her eyes told that it was like losing her father all over again. For all her bravado, she was hurting.

"Do you think he was just doing his duty as a cop, or do you think he's mixed up with what we've found?" Laura asked after a moment.

"I'm not sure," she said, her attention on her cup of coffee as if it were tea leaves that would tell everything she wished to know. "The fact that he wanted me to stay quiet about Coutu and the children doesn't sit right, but with the teams moving in, there was no time to pursue that line of questioning."

Laura saw the conflict in the woman and gave her the time she needed. Rachelle would need to compartmentalize the issue before they moved forward. Her eyes swept across the room to where Gabrielle sat quietly, but was following the exchange with intense concentration. She felt Laura's eyes on her and met her gaze with a tight, uncertain smile. Laura returned it and watched the doubt disappear. She needed to know someone accepted and cared for her.

Laura had no idea what would happen to this incredibly strong girl after this was all over. There was no way she could drag her around the world while she continued fighting this battle, but there was no way she would just abandon her to some social worker or foster system. She had been traumatized enough and needed a real support system to help her grow beyond the past. She would definitely have to give it some consideration.

The rattle of a coffee cup on the table pulled her out of her thoughts. Rachelle sat up straighter, her lips in a firm line. "Sorry," she said. "What did you find out?"

"Aline was able to identify at least twelve brothels where the prostitutes have either been let go or told to stay away," Laura said. "I'm guessing more of the children have been hidden in these locations."

Gabrielle rose and picked up the emptied cups, her eyes asking if they wanted more.

Rachelle waited for Gabrielle to leave the room for more coffee before turning back to Laura. "You know this might be a trap?"

"A couple of them might be traps, but not all of them."

It hadn't taken long for Aline to put together a list of the different establishments that had been closed down to the sex workers. Many of the women had turned to the street for work. This allowed for higher returns but there was little to no protection if they ran into trouble. There was always the added danger from the established street workers. No one wanted to lose money to new competition.

Laura had bought a train ticket for Aline and saw her heading south towards the Italian border and relative safety. There was no way she could return to Paris until this was over.

"So how do you plan on deciding which to avoid?"

Laura gave her a wicked smile, "I might not have to."

Rachelle's eyebrows rose. "I'm almost afraid to ask what evil thoughts you're having," she said with a laugh. "But I can't help it."

As Laura explained her plan, Rachelle listened with rapt attention, not even seeing Gabrielle return with the fresh coffee. When Laura finished speaking the three women exchanged looks and laughed.

"Remind me not to piss you off," Rachelle said. "What I don't understand is where you get your information and how you can confirm it's accurate. What you are saying is incredible."

"Let's just say I have some friends who are incredible at finding information others wish not to surface," Laura said draining her cup and putting it down. There was no way she would mention her affiliation with Darren Forbes. She received another information package last night. Although the information was accurate, it troubled her that the CISIS Director would risk so much to help her crusade. He would be destroyed politically and might even face jail time.

She waved no more to Gabrielle who looked ready to jump for a refill. "These are the same friends that helped me tap into your department's system. What they found on Coutu can all be substantiated including an electronic trail of several dummy corporations that separate the criminal elements from those of his legitimate businesses."

Rachelle stared off into space and Laura knew she was turning all the new information around with what she thought she had understood before. She didn't even acknowledge when Laura and Gabrielle rose and left the room.

They deposited the empty mugs into the sink for later cleaning and retreated to the bench out under the trees. The young girl stretched out her legs and raised her arms over her head like a contented cat ready for a nap. She squinted as she lifted her face to the sunlight.

"So," Laura said, "Do you think you could play your part of the plan?"

"Are you kidding?" Gabrielle said sitting up and turning to Laura. Her eyes flashed hot anger. "It's not like I have to act. Those things have happened to me. The only lie is that I worked at all these different brothels, but it makes sense they might move the younger ones around."

"But this," Laura said waving her hand across the young girl's face, "this anger and strength I see in you right now tells a different story. You need to look scared to death, unable to trust anyone, including those that try to help. It will paint a powerful picture while making them want to act immediately on the information you bring them."

The girl nodded, allowing her eyes to squint and lower to the ground. Her bottom lip quivered, and she looked lost and broken. Laura marveled at the transformation. She released a laugh at the girl's antics, its loudness bouncing across the small courtyard.

"What kind of monster am I creating?" she said, pulling the girl into her in a huge hug. "I think you'll end up being a world class con-artist or make millions as an actress."

FOR ALL HER BRAVADO with Laura, now that Gabrielle was here in one of Paris's largest newspaper's offices, picked because of its rivalry with Coutu's paper; the fear was real and she could smell the rank sweat that oozed from her body. She forced herself to put one foot in front of the other, keeping close to one side of the hallway both to avoid the foot traffic and for her own security. The cool granite wall helped center her, but she felt her stomach doing flip-flops.

To make the disguise more convincing, Laura helped her rub dirt into the skin of her face and hands. A jagged rip in her jeans and another across the back of her shirt suggested a fast moving, tight squeeze. She hadn't combed her hair this morning and the film on her teeth that she could feel under her tongue disgusted her.

Rachelle and Laura had coached her late into the night on what to say and how to present herself for the best effect. She allowed her mind to replay those lessons to help settle her nerves. She lifted her eyes in quick flashes, always dropping her gaze back to the ground like a scared rabbit.

She'd taken the stairs up to the fourth floor as Laura had coached her. She glanced up and read the hand-painted name on each door as she made her way down the busy hall. People all seemed to be in a huge hurry, running breathlessly for a multitude of unknown tasks. When she finally came to the door with Editor stamped across the frosted glass, she closed her eyes and took a deep breath. She opened the door and slipped in, her back to the wall, ready to bolt.

The room was a large reception area with a round desk that housed a middle-aged woman who had multi-color hair in an attempt to look younger. She wasn't fooling anyone. Gabrielle waited quietly until the woman looked up and noticed her.

"Are you lost?" the woman asked her eyes taking in the dirt and shabby clothing.

Biting her lip, her eyes threatening to spill over, Gabrielle shook her head and dropped her gaze to the ground.

She heard the woman rise and move around the desk. She bent down in front of Gabrielle and raised a hand to her face.

"What's wrong?" the woman said in a soft, worried voice.

Thinking about the real times she had been scared and hurt in the past, Gabrielle easily tapped into the feelings that generated real tears. She opened herself to those feelings and began to cry, her shoulders shaking under the woman's startled hands. She allowed someone to guide her to a chair and heard the woman call out for assistance. Through her tears, she sensed more than saw different people come into the reception area. Concerned voices filled the space. With real effort, she dragged the door to those hurtful memories closed and allowed herself to calm.

"I don't... I don't know where else to go," she said her voice cracking with emotion.

"Tell us what's wrong, sweetheart," said a man with a strong authoritative manner.

"I escaped," she said wiping her nose with the back of her hand. "But my friends are still there." She bit her lip and let fear fill her expression. "And they will hurt them."

"You escaped?" the man said. "From where?"

"A... a house of prostitution," she said and cupped her hand over her mouth as another torrent of tears slid down her cheeks.

There were gasps in the room and a muttering of whispered curses. A few of those standing by, stepped back as if she was unclean and she felt shame well up in her chest.

"Cheri, can you tell me where the house is located?"

She nodded and dug a hand deep into the front pocket of her pants and pulled out a wrinkled wad of paper. She carefully pulled the sheet apart and in between sniffs and shuddering heaves, she said, "Before we ran, we put together a list of the different houses we had stayed in so maybe someone could help the other kids."

"How many others are there?" the man asked gently, taking the limp sheet of paper.

"Normally, there are one to two in each house, but they are bringing in a lot of new kids, which is why we were moved together. They brought nine new kids to the house I was in."

"There are twelve addresses on this list? Are you say each building is holding that many children?"

"I think so." Gabrielle grabbed the man's hand in desperation. "Save them. You can't let them suffer the same things I did." She squeezed him hard. "Please."

The man nodded and said over his shoulder, "Sylvie, call the Police."

"No!" Gabrielle tugged hard on the man's jacket. "Some of these people *are* police."

WITH THE EFFICIENCY of a military general, the Editor of the Paris Daily gathered a large crew of photojournalists and assigned them to the different addresses listed on the sheet. He ordered his people to record anyone entering or leaving the buildings and to keep special attention to the activities of the Police during the event.

Although he had explained his plan to Gabrielle in simple terms before calling in his people, she watched and listened with rapt attention. Many of the reporters glanced at her during their briefing, understanding there was more at stake than just a good story. One person took a picture of her only to be chastised by the Editor, due to her being a minor. She kept her head down with a scared demeanor.

The man made a fast apology to avoid a worse grievance from the lead newspaper man.

Within minutes of giving final instruction to the gathering, the group was gone, leaving Gabrielle and the Editor sitting together in the massive boardroom.

"As I explained, we will give them an hour to get in place and then I'll call a special contact I have within the department and tell them that one of my trusted sources had brought forward information of a huge hostage situation. I will suggest that it might be a terrorist issue so they will take it seriously."

Gabrielle nodded. "I think the new children may have been foreigners. Some of them had darker skin, and they didn't speak French. None of us could understand them."

The man studied her for a moment and she lowered her gaze subconsciously.

"Where are my manners?" he said his expression lightening up. "You must be starving. When was the last time you ate anything?"

She allowed her eyes to grow large and placed a hand over her stomach. "I *am* starving."

"I'll get Sylvie to order something in for you. You can relax here now. You're safe here. I promise."

Biting her lip, she looked up. "Thank you."

Good to his word, Sylvie arrived with pastries by the boxful and sweet fruit juices that Gabrielle dove into with enthusiasm. The editor came in later and smiled at her sticky face.

"I have calledthe Police in. I've explained to them that my people are on location, so there should be no funny business. I am hoping your friends will soon be safe."

Blinking back fresh tears, she said, "Thank you so much, monsieur."

The next time the Editor came to look in on her, he found only an empty room and a half-eaten collection of sweet treats. No one had seen her leave.

Chapter Twelve

Laura and Rachelle stood before a set of garden doors that led to a small balcony, both with a set of high-powered binoculars pulled tight onto their faces. They were two streets away from one address that Gabrielle had supplied to the newspaper; close enough to view the show, but far enough not to be in the working zone of the elite RAID and GIGN attack teams.

Behind them on the hotel's queen-sized bed, Gabrielle lay moaning about her stomach ache. She wasn't getting much sympathy from either woman. Her over-indulgence with the rich French pasties was her own doing.

Laura had been waiting exactly where they had planned and Gabrielle had dove into the rear of the vehicle, keeping her head down as she crowed at her accomplishment. The cheering had been short-lived when her stomach pushed back from its most recent attack. Laura suppressed a grin as the girl moaned behind her. Hard lessons were lessons learned.

Laura felt Rachelle's hand on her arm and focused on the scene down range.

"They are beginning their assault," said in a neutral, professional voice similar to an experienced pilot who radios that he is about to crash in a calm, matter-of-fact manner, devoid of emotions.

Raising the optics back in place, she toggled the focus setting, bringing the distant vision into sharp detail. From behind one of the armored personnel carriers, a line of soldiers marched in a tight line, covered by two ballistic shields held by the first two soldiers in the line. There had been an attempt at negotiating, but a shot fired from inside the house at one of the police officers had determined the next level of force.

A second-story window slid open and under her breath, Rachelle said, "Gun." She needn't have worried. Before the assailant could point his rifle at the line of advancing soldiers, the heavy crack of a high-powered rifle announced a police sniper. It blew the figure in the window backwards and out of sight.

The column of assaulter's came to a sudden stop as two other weapons opened up. Even through the thick, sealed glass of the hotel window, Laura could hear the unmistakable report of automatic fire. She felt Gabrielle stand beside her and watch the gun fight. The two soldiers knelt leaning into the heavy shields as round after round peppered them. Those at the rear stayed behind the armored bulwark, leaning out only to return fire before ducking back.

One soldier stationed behind an armored car, pulled a weapon to his shoulder and fired several rounds high into the air towards the building. Laura recognized the RBG 40mm Grenade launcher by the heavy 6-round drum. Rather than heavy explosive grenades, he walked a line of smoke grenades across the front of the building. In seconds the house disappeared from sight, but with their thermal optics, the soldiers were unimpeded by the dense smoke. She watched as the tail of that highly skilled anti-terrorist squad disappeared into the white fog.

There was a salvo of gunshots with the familiar sound of flash bangs mixed in; followed by an unnerving silence that seem to last an eternity.

"As a commander, this is the time I hate the most," Rachelle said. "Even when you have radios, you don't know everything they have found or run into."

"I'm guessing we found the one trap we were discussing." Laura said, her eyes still watching through the binoculars. "What I can't understand was why they didn't just give up once the police arrived?"

"Maybe it was a holding pattern to evacuate the children and the bulk of the force through a rabbit hole, like the one you escaped through with Gabrielle."

Laura lowered the field glasses and looked over at the officer. "We should know soon. They won't leave the children in the building while they go over it."

Rachelle shook her head. "No. They'll have them checked out medically under guard, while the investigators deal with the residual evidence. Statements will come later." She snorted and gave Laura a knowing look. "If they are Syrian, like the others, they must deal with translators and community leaders."

"And this is only one building," Gabrielle said still holding onto her stomach.

Laura absorbed the information. She handed the glasses to Gabrielle and walked over to one of the hotel room's coffee table. Picking up the television's remote, she turned on the set, surfed until she came across a twenty-four-hour news channel. The large-scaled raid on suspected brothels around Paris was the top story. The press almost had too much live footage as they flicked from building to building. Raising the volume, they listened to a mannequin anchor-person express shocked horror at the number of children the police could rescue, citing an anonymous source.

"Laura," Rachelle called over her shoulder, the binoculars still held to her face. "No children."

Even without the magnification, Laura could see the soldiers leaving the building; the fog from the smoke grenades already dispersed and them stripping down some of their heavy ballistic armor.

"You're probably right. They must have had an escape route," said Laura.

They continued to watch the scene and the newscast for over an hour. Gabrielle lay on the bed, her stomach growling. She sat up during a press conference with police. The spokesman confirmed there was a surprising amount of defiance and fifteen suspects were fatally shot and another six in hospital with a variety of wounds sustained in the twelve raids. The attacks also injured two police officers, who were in stable condition. Of the sites targeted, all but two had children being held in captivity in what police were calling a human trafficking operation of an unprecedented scale. They had rescued forty-six children, most of Syrian descent.

Laura winked conspiratorially at Rachelle and plopped on the bed next to Gabrielle. "Forty-six kids. You did that. You saved those kids."

Gabrielle blushed at the unexpected praise, even more so when both women clapped.

"You know what this means," Laura said to Rachelle.

The Capitaine nodded gravely.

Gabrielle looked from one woman to the next, now wary. Worry lines creased her brow making her look even younger than she was.

Laura awarded her with a blinding smile, her eyes twinkling in mischief. "It means we need to celebrate," she said slapping the girl's thigh. "This calls for cake! My treat."

Gabrielle's face lost all its color as she absorbed what Laura suggested. Her stomach rumbled in protest and she bolted towards the bathroom, laughter following her.

ARMED ONLY WITH HER new hair color, Laura walked through the large doors of La Verite, another rival press of Michel Coutu's. Crossing to the reception desk, she waited until the twenty-something who was refreshingly not wearing any makeup, finished with a phone call.

"Good morning," said the girl with a genuine smile as she replaced the phone in its cradle.

"Hi," Laura said returning the smile. "Someone asked me to drop these files off." She handed a thick manila envelope over to the girl who browsed at the address, which signified the Editor-in-Chief, Gaetan Blais.

"Can I ask who they are from?"

"I'm sorry. Some guy outside gave me 100 Euro to drop them off and say it had to do with the raids on the brothels yesterday."

"Oh, those poor children..." the woman began, again with genuine feelings. Laura could not help but like the woman.

"At least they're safe."

"Thank God."

Chapter Thirteen

Michel Coutu threw the large brandy snifter at the fireplace. The contents shattered violently into the open flames, burning off with a massive roar and a light that pushed back the shadows of the dark room.

"Fils de pute!" he screamed, his vision going black for a moment as his anger consumed him.

None of the other men in the room moved. They didn't dare. They kept their eyes averted from their overlord, studying different aspects of the room as if they were historians in a museum.

He wheeled around towards Antoine who stood patiently, his hands behind his back. Coutu's finger stabbed the air towards him. "Any idea who that was?" he spat. "That was my good friend, the President, who called me personally to inform me I am under formal investigation and that until further notice, I am on leave from my duties as Minister." He stomped across the room trying to bleed off the fury that threatened to overwhelm him. He needed to keep his cool so he could think straight.

"Someone has sent Information to the Editor of La Verite, the Leader of the Opposition and the President's Office. From what little he divulged, the information could only come from someone inside the organization. I want you to find the leak and to plug it permanently." He moved towards the huge ex-soldier so they were face to face. "I also need to know what information was released so we can try to limit the damage."

"Yes, Sir."

He stared at the ex-soldier for a moment to ensure the man re-alized what this development could mean. Not only for Coutu, but Antoine would suffer as well. Of course, he reminded himself, if it were to go that far, investigators would attempt to have his main en-forcer turn on Coutu. He was after all the *prize*, not just some soldier who followed orders. He had people within the Police as he did in so many other areas. He would have to keep a close eye on this in-vestigation to see where it went. He would not hesitate to eliminate anyone who might pose a threat; even Antoine.

Losing his number one man would be a hard blow. They had been together for so long now. He had rescued the man from a prison in the Congo over three decades ago and made him rich beyond his expectations. All he expected was complete loyalty. There had never been a time where he had to concern himself with the man's fealty. But this is the first time that the organization had ever been compro-mised.

"What have you discovered about the other matter?"

From the breast pocket of his suit, the huge man pulled out a notebook and snapped it open with a flick of his wrist to a page that was earmarked. "We lost two men who were trailing one whore from the brothel that this Laura Amour attacked. Aline Moreau. This is more than likely not her real name. She's completely off the grid, al-though we have feelers out," he said looking up from his notes. "We know that she contacted several other women and was looking for those houses we had closed up to house the children."

"So to avoid our trap, Amour sends in the police to do her work for her. She's definitely someone not to be underestimated."

The soldier nodded. "The original information was brought to the Paris Daily by a child who has been described as one kid that worked at the brothel Amour had attacked the other night."

"So," Coutu said his eyes unforgiving and the skin clenching at the jaw. "She has recruited our own people to help her. I want examples made."

"It's already happened. I have dealt with the women who spoke to this Aline Moreau."

Coutu nodded. At least he could trust the man to act on his own.

He froze. The suddenness of the thought was like a blinding flash of sheet lightning. Could the leak be Antoine himself? With the chaos of the Amour attacks, a hostile takeover would be a fairly simple maneuver for someone who knew every aspect of the organization and who had the nerve and audacity. The man had plenty of both.

He purposely turned his back to the man and sank into his chair, eyes on the fireplace but not seeing it. He would have to plan for every contingency and lay a couple of traps of his own. He forced himself to be calm. He did not want to react out of fear or uncertainty. That would only lead to disaster. The plan he had to trap this Amour was now a waste of time. She was moving too fast for him to do anything but react and even that left him wanting.

He could hear the shuffling of feet behind him as the men wondered if he had dismissed or not. They would take their cue from Antoine and he knew from experience, the man would stand there all night until Coutu gave him the sign.

Loyal dog or sly cur?

"Ensure we react accordingly regarding Amour. Move no more children. The facility has no link to any of our subsidiaries, so it should be safe." He paused to consider his words, so he didn't expose his thoughts on the matter of loyalty. "Our main priority is to unearth what was leaked, followed by containment. The information might lead us to the who."

"And our clients?"

"Ensure them we are actively looking for replacement of our stock. If this is impossible, we will reimburse them for the inconvenience and assist them with contacting one of the other organizations."

"Very well."

"And Antoine," he said as a matter of dismissal. "Have the guards posted outside of the door removed. If Amour or anyone else attacks, two extra guards will not make a difference."

"Yes, Sir."

He listened as they trailed out of the room, the closing door once again throwing the room into shadows interrupted only by the firelight. He rose and took another glass, filling it with a healthy amount. Allowing the leather chair to enfold him in its embrace, he sipped the fiery liquid.

He reviewed all that he knew and those he suspected. Just because a bush moves, doesn't mean there's anything worth killing in it. A wasted shot can also tell the prey of your intentions. Better to plan and wait until you had the perfect kill shot. It would be a total waste to take out Antoine if he was actually loyal. It would be like cutting off one of his arms.

He needed more information before he could act. But when he acted, it would be decisive and without mercy.

Chapter Fourteen

While Laura and Gabrielle moved from the farmhouse to another safe house closer to the city, they decided that with her investigative skills, Rachelle might have a better chance to identify the tattoo that some of Coutu's men wore. That it might be an offshoot of the French Foreign Legion, no one was debating. It was close to the official symbol. The stylized fleur de lis with the ring was commonplace. Most soldiers would add a number within the ring to signify which battalion they served with or the year. The crisscrossing lightning bolts within the ring was something she hadn't recognized and due to all the ex-Legionaires that ended up joining the police force, she had seen many.

Laura had emailed the photos she had taken off the men in the tunnel to Rachelle so she could include those from the men who ambushed the ambulance and killed Andre. Armed with the photos, her first stop was at a Military Museum. The curator was an old soldier with faded tattoos that were covered with age spots. Although he looked frail, the width of his shoulders spoke of a day of what he might have been. When he saw the photo of the tattoo, it baffled him. It was obvious that the photo was taken of a dead man and when he first looked at it with suspicion; she flashed her badge and explained she was following up on the tattoo to identify the man. Contented with the explanation, he studied the photo carefully.

"Of course, there are several variations," he said as they walked through stacks of books. It took him minutes to find the book he was searching for and laid it across a reading table for Rachelle's benefit.

Flipping to a page that held a collage of images, he pointed at one in particular.

"This is the official logo of the Legion," he said. "You can see the stylized fleur de lis and the ring. If there is any kind of wing, like this one," he pointed at an image with a fancy wing of open feathers with the fleur de lis to one side holding a dagger or bayonet "is a part of an airborne regiment." He continued to flip through the book, but could not find anything similar to the tattoo.

Shrugging he said, "Maybe this guy saw a real tattoo and thought it looked cool. There are many people who have similar ink that have never seen active service, or he merged two different images."

Rachelle wasn't buying that. If it was only one person with this particular body art - maybe. But there was a group of connected people. "Could it be a special ops team symbol?"

He raised his hands to indicate anything was possible. "I only can tell you about what I know. I'm sorry."

Nodding her head, her mouth in a tight line of frustration, she thanked him for his help and ensured the photos were secured in her purse. She was almost at the entrance to the museum when he called after her.

"I'm not sure it'll help," he said as he tried to catch his breath, "but there are several places that ex-Legionaires and those on leave frequent and if I remember right, there are three or four tattoo shops in the same area."

"Where is it?"

His eyes narrowed, and he raised a finger. "It's in the red-light district and you better be careful. That badge and any gun you might carry won't scare that crew. There are some messed up people who hang around that crowd and they'd gut you if you look at them wrong."

RACHELLE LOCKED HER vehicle and adjusted the holster in the small of her back, concealed by her jacket. Her backup was a lethal fighting knife that Laura had pressed on her, strapped to her calf. Looking up the street where the first of three different drinking establishments controlled an intersection, she could hear the odd yell, laughter and curse over the din of three different music genres.

From her vantage spot, she spied two of the tattoo parlors easily, with their street facing picture windows that were plastered with collages of the popular body art. A flashing sign pushed away from one wall to announce that body piercing was also a specialty.

Taking a deep breath to center herself, she walked purposely towards the closest tattoo parlor. She took a moment to study the different artwork posters, some of them hideous with skulls and death-dealing images while others were graceful and multi-colored. A few were quite appealing. She had never considered getting a tattoo, but there were a few she saw that might convince her to try one.

Stepping inside the shop, she faced the back of a huge, bald tattooist bent over a customer partially exposed, whose bare ass to allow the artist to drag some scroll work below the panty-line. Careful to pull the needle away from the client's back, the head swiveled to inspect her image in the window.

"Looking to get some ink?"

"Might be if I can find something suitable," Rachelle said.

"You can look around and there are a couple of catalogs on the table near the back of the room. If you find something, we'll have to set up an appointment. As you can see, I'll be here awhile."

"Thanks," she said and moved across one wall, checking out the different patterns and stencils. On the back wall there was a scattering of the now familiar Legion symbol, many she had seen at the museum or sported on the arms of her fellow police officers.

"Are you looking for anything in particular?" asked the artist over his shoulder. There was no interruption of the hum of the electric needle machine.

"My boyfriend was in the Legion and I thought I might get one for him for our anniversary," she said. "He saw one he really liked, but I don't see it here."

"What did it look like? I do damn near everyone out there."

She put her finger on one image tacked up on the wall. "It was the regular fleur de lis with the ring, but instead of the Battalion number, he said this one had crisscrossing lightning bolts in gold."

The machine slowed to a stop as he took his foot off the foot pedal and turned to her in a slow deliberate manner. His eyes narrowed as he studied her face for a moment then shook his massive head, "Never heard of one like that. You can check the other shops in the area, but we all do the same patterns."

Turning back to his client who was stretched across the length of a weightlifting bench, he said, "Sorry, I can't help you."

To Rachelle's ear, it was more dismissal than regret.

THE LAST TWO PARLORS had offered no leads either although neither of those two artists had reacted so suspiciously about the description of the tattoo. Her gut was telling her that the first fellow knew a lot more than he was letting on. If she found nothing in this last shop, she would make a return trip.

A bell tinkled above the door as she entered the storefront. The room was narrow with a counter running down one side of the room and a closed door at the rear of the room. There was no one present she could see, but the whine of a security camera explained why.

Moving along one wall, she studied the dozens of different shots of proud owners of new ink. There were people from every walk of life as body art became more popular and accepted in today's society. There were always the extremists with piercings and tattoos in places or numbers that shocked the average person, but with the advances in technique beautiful art was being created. She remembered seeing one that allowed it to play a voice clip, like the voice of a dead parent.

The door at the back of the shop opened. Rachelle turned to look and was surprised to see a beautiful woman walk through the door. She had been expecting another muscle bound guy with a variety of tattoos and piercings like she had met in the other shops. Other than the green hair and a diamond piercing on the right side of her nose, the woman was an example of simple beauty. No makeup shadowed her near perfect, porcelain skin. There was no need.

Her arms were also clear of ink, which in Rachelle's eyes would have taken away from the woman's girl-next-door appeal. She loved the concept of Ma, where the pure, essential things stood beyond the everyday things and routine.

The woman moved through the shop with a relaxed pace that seemed to show that she was where she should be. Without saying a word, she gazed at the photo that Rachelle had been studying before she had entered.

"We do not judge here," the woman said with a velvet voice.

Rachelle looked at her with a touch of confusion.

"There are some who have demons within that drive them to make extreme statements, while others hide the stamp of independence behind an earlobe or in an armpit."

"I suppose we each have our own demons," Rachelle said with a sigh.

"Any idea what you are looking for?"

"I'm looking for a specific Legionnaire tattoo," she decided to play it straight with the woman rather than pretending it was for a friend. She pulled the photo of the dead man's hand out of her pocket and passed it over. "I'm trying to identify the individual, hoping it might lead me to who killed him."

The woman examined the image, and it surprised Rachelle that there was no shock or unease at the fact she was looking at a dead body. Looking up, she locked eyes with Rachelle and stared with an intensity that was almost unsettling.

"I have seen it."

"Where?" Rachelle asked trying hard not to seem desperate.

"Here. That is one of my designs."

"Do you happen to know the individual you did this for?"

"There were several of them. If I remember right, they were all from the same unit." She used her thumb to indicate the back room. "I can check my files for you, if that will help you?"

"That would be a huge help," said Rachelle relieved that there was no necessity for a warrant. Because of her predicament, attempting to gain one would have her arrested before she reached a court official. Of course, Laura would just take the files she needed, but Rachelle didn't want to cross that line. The law wasn't perfect, but it was something she believed in.

The tattoo artist led her to the back door, opened it and stood aside for Rachelle to enter. She saw a flash of movement to her right and began to turn towards it, her instincts making her hand reach for the weapon in the small of her back. Before she could grasp the pistol grip, someone slammed her into the wall, effectively pinning her arm behind her back. Her head hit the wall, dazing her enough that her assailant could disarm her. She blinked away the flashing stars that cascaded across her vision, she heard a key turn in the door lock and she knew she was trapped.

Raising her head, she came face to face with the brute that held her. He smiled a wicked grin at her, his lips twisted because of a knife scar that dug in below his left eye and ended at his chin. His eyes twinkled with joy at the violence and fear he had brought her. He was enjoying this. With extreme effort, she suppressed the shudder that threatened to rake her entire body.

"Hans," A deep voice said from further into the room, "Be nice to Capitaine Rachelle. If you want her to cooperate, you must treat her with respect."

The pressure on her chest and neck relented as the huge German stepped back. From his expression, Rachelle could tell that he was not pleased to be denied his new toy. He stood ready and the glitter in his eye begged her to disobey his master. Looking beyond him, she could make out another large man, the width of his shoulders and the tightness of his chest proclaimed him to be ex-military or a clone of another famous body builder turned actor, turned politician, turned actor again.

"Please," the man said pointing at a central chair which had hard arms that could be adjusted to different angles. The seat even reclined like something you would sit in to watch the television, but with extensions that would allow turning or twisting the legs. Rachelle realized this is where the tattoo artist plied her trade. Beside it was a bench similar to a weightlifting bench where the client could lie while the artist worked on their back.

The German walked her to the chair, his hand completely wrapped around her arm. She had no real choice. Her back slammed into the back of the chair and Hans closed both arm rests to ensure she was, if not trapped, at least encumbered by the seat.

The other man, his suit fitting him as if it had been hand tailored, stood like a soldier at ease; feet apart, hands clasped behind his back. He stood like he was on the parade ground just waiting for the command to stand at attention. Relaxed, but with so much kinetic energy you could feel it vibrate from him.

"My name is Antoine. I too, held the rank of Capitaine when I served in the Legion. From one officer to another, I hope we can make this exchange of information courteous and professional."

"How do you go from an honorable position within the Legion to that of a hood that does all Coutu's dirty work?" Rachelle spat. She didn't see the blow coming, but the stars returned as her head rocked forward.

Meaty hands gripped the back of her neck and the big German whispered into her ear, "Watch your mouth, bitch."

The man who identified himself as Antoine, came closer, dropped into a crouch and sat on his heels. She noticed that he kept himself far enough she could not kick out at him. "You see Capitaine, we can do this civilly or if you prefer, we can do it Hans' way. Believe me, the results will be the same."

"What do you want?"

"The children," he said casually as if it was nothing of consequence. He might have been talking about the price of a cup of coffee. It meant that little to him.

She decided to tell him. She would not reveal Yusuf's identity, but would give them some bogus name. The best lie had to have a foundation of the truth. If they thought the children were out of reach, they might stop any search that was happening. She didn't give her own chance of getting out of this in one piece, so if she could mess up their plans, she would take that as a win. At least, Laura would avenge her. For once, she saw a good reason for working outside of the law.

"They're gone. There's no way you'll find them."

"Humor me," Antoine said his voice still soft like he was speaking with a child, but his eyes told another story. They drilled into hers looking for any sign she was lying.

"They're back with their own people. The Muslim community," Rachelle said. "By now, they'll have been spread all over France and any attempt to take them will open a political and cultural war on Coutu's head."

His eyes widened as he realized the implication of what she revealed. He stood to his full height and glanced at his partner before returning his attention to her. "That was actually brilliant. Unfortunate from a business point of view, but quite ingenious." He studied her for a minute until she felt uncomfortable. "Was this your idea or did it come from the Canadian terrorist you have allied yourself with?"

"Laura is no terrorist."

He smiled a tight grin, his lips arching over covered teeth. "Your loyalty is admirable, but the country has mounted one of the largest ma- sorry, woman-hunt since the Paris attacks. In fact, you are also being sought. You not answering the original question, tells me so much." He crossed his arms in anticipation. "So, the next question is where is Laura Amour?"

He glanced at his German companion and she felt his arm and hands hold her tight to the seat. From a small, wheeled cupboard, Antoine lifted a syringe, its contents a pale yellow and explained, "Sodium Pentothal or as it is more commonly known, the truth serum."

Rachelle tensed up under the iron grip of Hans, her heart racing as she realized what they planned on doing. The rational side of her knew the drug didn't work as well as it did in the movies. It caused the patient to not only answer questions but to exaggerate, lie and embellish information so that the questioner couldn't know what was real and what was made up. The flip side of the coin was that she might divulge information that might compromise Laura and Gabrielle or even the other children. That and the fact that Antoine was putting some chemical into her bloodstream was terrifying.

"Now hold steady. The last thing I want to do is break the needle off because you struggled."

As the sharp end pierced her skin, she imagined the liquid burning her arm as it spread through her body and began to shake uncon-

 DAVID WICKENDEN

trollably. She felt warm, but could feel the heat coming off the huge German who held her secure. Within seconds, she felt a wave of fatigue wash through her and her head drooped onto her chest. Her captor released his hold on her and she would have fallen if not for the chair's arms.

Antoine's face seemed to swell in front of her and she had a hard time focusing on him. His voice, when he spoke felt like he was talking through a tunnel across a fair distance.

"Almost there. A few more minutes and we'll see what you know."

Chapter Fifteen

Gabrielle leaned over the tablet screen that showed the view that Rachelle's hexacopter was transmitting. It transposed the night scene into different shades of gray thanks to a powerful night vision lens. Occasionally, she called out directions as the vehicle they were following altered directions. The true beauty of employing the drone was that Laura could stay far back so not to arouse suspicion. Even then, the car did more than a few counter-surveillance tactics hoping to spot a tail. Having the eye in the sky allowed her to avoid those maneuvers with no risk.

But, Laura had to admit, the suspicion displayed by Rachelle's superior, Henri Pelletier, did not reflect well on the police officer. What was he involved in that required this kind of paranoia?

"He's slowing down again," Gabrielle said. "He's backing into an alley beside a large building. Okay, he's killed the engine. I will go high and pull back so he doesn't hear me."

Laura could only see the top of Gabrielle's head in the car's shadowy interior. Having seen the girl manipulate the flying machine's controls, she knew her fingers were pulling back on the toggles, even as she used the camera's lens to pull in closer to Pelletier. She smiled. Who says you learn nothing playing video games?

"Do you think he's waiting to see if anyone is following him again?" Laura asked, ready to pull over to the side of the roadway.

"Maybe-no, he's getting out of the car and heading around the back of the building. Let me circle around."

"No Gabrielle, pull back, but keep the building in sight. I don't want to tip our hand," Laura said, pulling the vehicle around a corner and off the main road. Shutting the engine off, she turned toward the girl in the back seat. "I'll approach on foot and you let me know through the radio if you see any threats. Keep the drone as far back as possible but position yourself so you can see at least two sides of the building, okay?"

The girl nodded and turned the tablet so Laura could see the building in question. "We're here," she pointed at the screen, "and his car is parked along the side here."

Laura studied the aerial scene, memorizing the layout of the streets and possible cover. "Can you zoom in on the sign on the building?" With a quick dial of the controls, the building seemed to race towards the screen. When the focus sharpened, she could read, Importation Alpha. With a quick wink at Gabrielle, Laura pushed the earpiece in place, touched the pistol that rode in the shoulder holster under her dark jacket and exited the car. She had pulled the light bulb out of the car's interior dome light so she would not give herself away when entering or exiting the vehicle. The street lights were all on her side of the street, so after casting a look around, she angled across the street and into the shadows of the opposite side-walk.

She had the street to herself as the old district had been reverted to warehouses and businesses. Schools, long ago shut down, were pressed into service as offices and even they seemed to be on their last legs. The area did nothing to enhance a business brand or encourage growth. Like old neighborhoods around the world that fell apart, the area would soon revert to a place where addicts frequented in crack houses or piaules, for cheap sex in exchange for cheap highs. And unless some conglomerate bought the whole area and re-purposed it, the area would slowly disintegrate into itself.

She pressed her throat mic and said, "Any change?"

"No movement on the side or rear."

"Does your thermal show any heat signatures that might indicate cameras?"

There was a minute of silence and she could imagine Gabrielle, manipulating the controls and glaring into the tablet screen. Laura continued to the corner of the block, but held up before exposing herself from the safety of the shadows. She waited patiently, not wanting to push her young protégé at the task she was working on.

Since becoming involved with Laura's schemes, the young girl had blossomed in a way that surprised both Laura and Rachelle. They had seen her strength, but the sharp analytical mind she seemed to approach any new idea or skill set with eclipsed this. While the two planned their different strategies together, Gabrielle spent most of the night practicing take-offs and landings with the drone and putting it into every conceivable maneuver she could think of until it had become an extension of her. Laura couldn't help wondering how the young girl might do under a formal education.

Regardless of the feelings she felt forming for this tough kid, she knew this was not the life to raise a child. It was neither safe nor appropriate. She was keeping Gabrielle close so she could better protect her, but eventually she could be compromised and used as bait or as vengeance against Laura.

The girl's hollow voice in the earpiece interrupted her thoughts. "Each building corner has a rotating camera and there is one stationary, directly over the loading doors in the rear of the building."

"Got it, thanks."

Rounding the corner, she quickly crossed the street so that the building would be on her right. It was lost from sight because of the neighboring complex. When she approached the alley where Pelletier's vehicle was parked, she could hear the whirl of the rotating camera in the quiet night air. Chancing a quick glance, she saw that approaching the building unseen by the monitors was impossible as they had designed the coverage to overlap each zone. If anyone was monitoring the video feed, they would see all movement around the building. There were electronic tools that could temporarily interfere with the feed, but Laura wasn't prepared for that kind of infiltration. This was only a recon to find how it involved Pelletier.

Taking in the business beside her target, she recognized the logo over the front entrance as a mobile phone company that controlled the bulk of the cellular networks in France, if not most of Europe. On impulse, she followed the driveway behind the complex and discovered not one, but three towering cell towers. One was a hundred foot mast with an array of receptors that faced outward while the other two were two hundred foot lattice frame towers with three sides. There were a variety of receivers on these two including the familiar round microwave receivers.

It would do.

She jogged over to the nearest lattice frame and climbed the aluminum structure, keeping an eye on the opposite property for anyone who might see her. The dark clothes helped conceal her, but movement could easily mark her to an observant guard. She reached higher and was rewarded with an almost unobstructed view of the neighboring grounds.

Once she was about thirty feet above the ground, she wedged her body between two branches of aluminum that formed a 'V' and studied the opposite property. There were three large loading doors spaced evenly across the rear of the structure. Parked up close to the middle door was a white van with a logo she could not identify because of the distance. She looked over her shoulder into the night sky needlessly, knowing she would not see the drone and pressed her transit button on her throat mic and said, "Zoom in on the van and take a picture of the advertisement on the side."

Two clicks in her ear piece told her that Gabrielle understood.

As she watched, the middle loading door rolled up, the light from inside bathing the loading area brightly. A man in what looked like a painter's outfit emerged and unlocked the rear compartment of the van. Two other men, both armed with silenced automatic rifles slid out the door and spread to either side of the van and away from the light. A fourth individual, also in the painter's suit, rolled out a large, flat loading dolly with several crates piled three high. Each crate was about five feet in length and about two feet in height and width.

The two loaded the crates into the back of the van and from the noise being carried across the yard, they were not being gentle about it. Wood slamming into metal and wood against wood told her that whatever was being shipped was not delicate. Once all the crates had been loaded, they slammed the rear doors shut and re-locked them. The two painters unzipped their suits and allowed the top section to sag from their waists and joined each other in the van's front. They waited while the two armed guards moved to a dark sedan that Laura had not noticed until now.

From the doorway, Pelletier walked out with two others. She was too far to get a good look at his companions but hoped that Gabrielle might have taken photos or recorded that activity. The trio shook hands and Pelletier walked back to his car which blocked the other vehicle from leaving. The rear door came down and the interior of the building slid from view.

Laura dropped to the ground as quickly as she could and ran down the driveway toward the roadway. Pressing the throat mic, she said, "Keep the van in view, I'm on my way."

At the corner of the building, she had to wait until the small convoy turned into the roadway and then up the street where Gabrielle lay hidden in their own vehicle. The van slid by and she read the logo on the side, Crematorium Pere Trembley. She gasped as she understood what was happening. They were getting rid of evidence. If the evidence was what she thought it might be, someone would pay heavily.

"Gabrielle, get down. They are headed towards you," she said in a panic before realizing the girl would have seen Pelletier and the line of cars through the drone's lens. Relief swept through her as she heard the double tap of the transmission button.

Keeping to the deep shadows alongside the street, Laura ran like the wind. She watched as Pelletier signaled a left turn, followed by the other two vehicles. When the sedan carrying the two armed guards disappeared around the street corner, she ran for the car, remotely unlocking the vehicle with a wave of her fob. In seconds, she whipped the vehicle in a tight, tire squealing turn and eased into the main road.

"Pelletier is turning off, while the other two are continuing straight," Gabrielle said tensely.

"Okay, I think he might look for a tail. You follow him and let me know. I have the other two in sight."

It was a tactic he had used earlier this evening, where he would circle around the block, first to see if anyone followed but also to come up behind anyone that was trailing behind. But with the eye in the sky, he could not catch them by surprise. It was child's play to avoid detection.

Minutes later, Gabrielle said, "You called it. He's circling around the block and he's picking up speed."

"Get after the van," Laura said taking the next left. Right on cue, Pelletier's car came tearing around the next intersection heading toward them. Laura had to squint to avoid being blinded by his headlights, but knew there was no way for him to identify her either. She allowed her car to slow as she approached the same corner and watched as his tail lights turned back on the main roadway. She continued around the block and came back on track behind him.

"We have about five more minutes of battery time," Gabrielle informed her. "We should look for a place to change batteries."

"Okay, try to put yourself ahead of them and land wherever you think is safe. You guide me to the unit and we'll swap batteries and be back on the road as fast as we can."

"No. I'll grab the unit and change the batteries as you drive. If they hit the highway, the drone will never keep up and we'll lose them anyway. Better to launch once they reach their destination."

Laura glanced back at her young ward in the rear-view mirror, impressed with the logic she brought to the discussion with so little effort. So much potential.

Minutes later, Laura closed the distance between the convoy. She signaled and turned into an empty church parking lot and Gabrielle hit the ground running for the drone before the vehicle had stopped moving. She scooped up the flying machine and hopped back into the rear seat; the door slamming from the quick acceleration as they rocketed back onto the roadway. In the distance, she could still see the taillights of those they pursued.

Twenty minutes later, the three vehicles slowed, then pulled through the stone and wrought-iron gates of a large cemetery. Laura kept her speed steady and drove past the place until it was long out of sight. She took the next road and parked the car beside a row of trees that separated the graveyard and the next farmer's field. North of her position, the bright lights of Charles de Gaulle Airport lit up the night sky and all the surrounding area. Looking back towards the crematorium, she saw the funeral home on the hill overlooking the masses of tombstones, but could not discern where the vehicles were. She slid out her new phone and pulled up Google Earth and typed in the business name. In seconds, a map showed the property and the road system in the area.

"I will try to bring us around to the far side so the lights from the airport don't give us away," Laura said over her shoulder. "You must keep fairly low with the drone so it doesn't interfere with any air traffic."

"Got ya."

"Same rules. You keep down and out of sight. And no leaving the vehicle for any reason."

"How about if the guy has a gun?" Gabrielle said her voice dripping with sarcasm.

Laura glared at her in the mirror but the kid was grinning from ear to ear. Shaking her head, she shifted the car into gear and drove.

Minutes later, Laura allowed the quadcopter to rise into the night, before giving her accomplice the thumbs up and making towards the line of trees that marked the cemetery's boundary. She squeezed between two trees and pulled her revolver from its shoulder holster. The sound of the drone faded in seconds and she was alone in the darkness.

Her ear piece crackled. "One vehicle is just inside the entrance gates. I only see one guy though."

"Pelletier's car?"

"I don't think so. Looks bigger."

"Okay, keep searching."

Keeping low and moving from cover to cover, Laura closed the distance to the large building on the hill. From her peek at the satellite imagery on the Internet, she knew there were several buildings behind the main building. She expected that the crematorium and other utility buildings to be hidden from view from the main entranceway. Making her way through the rows of tombstones, she saw that the new sections of the graveyard held circular tiers of columbariums for the interment of ashes as this was becoming more popular and less expensive.

"The other two vehicles are outside a two-story building behind the main building. It's situated right beside a large garage with... five bay doors. Only one person standing outside. He's armed."

"Good, keep Overwatch, but watch your own back."

It was time to get some answers.

Chapter Fifteen

Bent over, Laura kept trees or tombstones between her and anyone that might be watching her approach. She closed on the area behind the big mansion which she suspected was the funeral home. It was a massive three-story stone building that might have been over a hundred years old if the style of the building was any indication. The lawn sloped in a shallow grade towards the rear of the property and she slowed her pace. She saw the roof peak of the out buildings first and slowed herself. Even in the dark, movement was her enemy. What made it worse was the lights from the airport had taken the edge off the blackness. She would have to be careful that it didn't highlight her.

She crept from row to row, always keeping some kind of cover between her and the two buildings. Halfway down the slope, she crouched down to one knee and allowed her eyes to scan across the distance, searching for the guard that Gabrielle had spotted. She could see the white van parked up against the loading dock of a two-story building. A tall brick chimney rose high off the back peak of the roof-line. Pelletier's vehicle sat on the far side of the van, its interior dark. If he was sitting in the driver's seat, she could not make him out. From the angle, the drone's thermals should have picked up his heat trace if he was in the car, but she couldn't chance it. No shortcuts.

She continued to use the gravestones as cover as she began a slow circling of the area. She paused as her ear piece crackled.

"The guard is in between the two buildings. In the shadows."

She double tapped her throat mic; glad she had her own eye in the sky.

The lush lawn made her approach as silent as a breeze. She rounded the nearest building, the garage and approached the gap. She leaned her head past the corner and could see the slight outline of the guard against the lighter background. He was leaning against the crematorium wall, both arms crossed in a bored manner. His weapon dangled from a shoulder strap. Laura aimed her weapon at the man's head and carefully moved forward, easing each foot down after feeling for any obstructions. Fortunately for her, the groundskeeper was meticulous and there was nothing to trip her as she closed on the guard.

Although she had her suspicions who this person worked for, she couldn't take the chance he was not one of Coutu's hired mercenaries. He might actually be a member of Rachelle's team. Until she knew for certain, there was no way she would kill the man. She raised her pistol just as some inner sense spoke to the man. He tensed and began to turn towards her when she brought the butt of the pistol against the side of his head. He dropped without a sound and she had to jump back so he didn't fall across her legs. Threading the sling over the man's arm, she slung the automatic over her neck, so that the weapon hung down her back. Tense, she listened to the night to see if anyone had heard the encounter and was moving to investigate.

After a few moments, she resumed her circle of the area, positioning herself so she could see if anyone was in the police commander's vehicle. Confirming it was empty, and she was alone in the night, she retraced her way back in between the two buildings. Shielding the glow of a small penlight, she checked the man's hands and found the familiar tattoo on his left. So be it; if push came to shove, she'd show no mercy.

With the silenced pistol leading the way, Laura inched around the building and pulled up beside the building's door. Keeping to one side, she reached over and tried the door latch. It was unlocked. She pulled the door open a crack and peered into the room. Squinting at the harsh light, she saw that the room was a basic loading dock with a couple of folding carts to move caskets from the dock to the interior of the buildings. The rear of this room opened to a larger area and she could see shadows dancing across the distant wall. She tensed, waiting for someone to come through the opening, but realized that it was a just a reflection of the movement of the individuals within the back room. They weren't coming towards her.

She pushed the door open just enough so she could slip in and eased the door close behind her so it made no noise. She surveyed the room for movement, and other entrances. Seeing none, she debated locking the door behind her. It could hinder her if she had to make a run for it, but it would stop someone from coming at her from behind. She decided to keep it unlocked, trusting Gabrielle to warn her of any movement outside the building.

Using a technique learned from one of the Canadian soldiers of the 427 Special Operations Aviation Squadron, she placed the outside edge of her foot down and allowed the foot to roll to center. This avoided any noise made by her shoes. In the bush it also allowed the individual to feel hidden branches which might snap once weight was applied. She glided silently across the concrete floor and sent a mental nod of thanks to a certain Master Corporal.

Crouched against the wall, she pulled out her endoscope, attached it to her phone and powered the unit up. Straining to hear if anyone was approaching, she pushed the small camera around the corner of the wall, low to the ground. The phone's screen gave a distorted view of the room. It was like looking through a fishbowl, with the picture stretched in a wide lens view. The two men in the chemical suits sat off to one side, their body language telling Laura that they were bored with the wait. Pelletier stood with another man in a dark suit. This new person was an older man with a shock of white hair. She assumed he worked for the crematorium, but was unsure.

There were four large, stainless steel ovens, each with a gravity conveyor roller to help move the coffin into the oven. The huge units stood from floor to ceiling with a large control panel protruding to the right of the unit's single door. The lights of all four ovens showed they were in use.

Pelletier would be armed she knew. Now, like earlier, she could see no sign of the men in the chemical suits being armed but even if they were, the coverall suit would slow them. With the one guard at the entrance and the other unconscious outside, everyone that came from the warehouse was accounted for. This older person was an unknown as was anyone else that might be in another room. It was always the unknowns that bit you in the ass, but it was a risk she had to take, especially if the boxes contain what she suspected.

Retracting the camera and putting everything back into her thigh pocket, Laura slipped the safety off her pistol. For Rachelle's sake, she would not kill the police officer even though she knew he was as dirty as hell, but that was the only concession she'd give him. Hopefully taking out the group's leader would take the fight out of the others.

With a sigh, she turned the corner, the sights of the pistols tracking the surprised look on Pelletier's face. His hand was half raised as if he could stop the bullet she sent his way. The projectile took him in the lower thigh, just above the knee, knocking his leg backwards so he plunged face-first into the floor. The roar of the ovens and the high intensity exhaust system muffled the silenced shot so the other three men looked on in confused shock at Pelletier's distress.

The two in the chemical suits stood and were moving towards the stricken man when Pelletier finally found his voice and screamed in pain. The older man stood rooted in place as he stared in confusion at the widening pool of blood. Obviously he was not used to the violent end of the business. The other two became aware something was wrong and slowed their pace when they caught sight of Laura, the pistol pointed towards them.

"Easy," she said. "I think you know I won't hesitate."

The two men looked defiant, but both nodded.

"Hands behind your head," she commanded. "Now, on your knees."

The one man dropped instantly to the ground while his partner made no move to follow.

Moving sideways towards where Pelletier withered on the ground, she indicated the police officer and lowered the aim of her pistol at the defiant white clad man.

"I can take your knees out like I did the good Commander here. Your choice; it matters little to me, especially if those crates contain what I think they do."

His narrowed eyes and flaring nostrils told Laura that she might just have to shoot the man, but the helplessness of his position finally sunk in and he slowly dropped to his knees.

"Keeping your hands behind your head, lower yourself to the floor and cross your ankles." Keeping her eyes on the two men, she pulled the older man towards her and said, "Who are you?"

He cringed as she touched him, the horror in his face told Laura volumes. Even before he finished stammering he was the funeral director, she had shoved a handful of tie wraps into the man's shaking hands. "Secure their hands behind their backs."

"But—"

"Now!" she said pushing him towards the two prone men. She dropped her eyes for a second then reached for Pelletier's service revolver and tucked it into her pant pocket. With her knee pressed hard into his back, she kept her attention on the actions of the old man and her two captives. She quickly frisked the officer to ensure he had no other weapon. From the inner breast pocket, she pulled out his cell phone and confiscated it.

Risking another look, she realized the man would bleed out if she didn't do something. He was pale and semi-conscious, his cries of pain reduced to low moans. She must have hit or nicked an artery. Taking two tie wraps, she put them together and then circled his upper thigh. With a savage tug, she pulled the plastic strap tight like an improvised tourniquet. Hopefully, this would keep him from bleeding out until he could get medical help. She had promised Rachelle that she would not kill the police officer except in self-defense. Although she was a criminal being sought by police agencies in multiple jurisdictions, she knew the fact she hadn't attacked police worked in her favor. Although Pelletier had crossed the line, she would let the system take him down.

The old man was just standing from his task when Laura said, "Now their feet."

His shoulders slumped in surrender and he secured one and then other man's feet at the ankles.

As the director finished, she used the pistol to guide him towards the pile of crates that stood waiting their turn before the ovens.

"Do you know what's inside?" Laura demanded.

"I'm guessing a body, but they never told me."

"So you just do as you're told, is that it?"

The old man's eyes dropped to the floor and his hands shook. "I had no choice," the man sobbed. "They had... have photos of my granddaughter." His shoulders trembled as he tried to suppress his fear and pain. "They told me that if I didn't do as they wanted they'd take her and sell her to the highest bidder," he said in a rush and completely broke down. He leaned against the wall and slowly collapsed to the floor, his body wracked by his weeping.

Laura felt a mixture of sympathy and anger fill her stomach in response to the old man's story. This was a story as old as organized crime. They found something you loved and used it against you. She looked over at the two white-covered thugs and part of her wanted to take out that anger on them, especially the one that had been all tough and defiant. But it would do no good. Someone else would replace them. Besides, she had to move if she was going to get the medical help for the commander so she didn't break her promise to her newest friend and ally.

She pulled out a combat knife and used it to pry on the top of the crate. Working the blade up and down until it gave her some purchase, she walked the knife along the edge of the crate. Once one side was loose, she grabbed the top with both hands and yanked hard at the wooden top. The tight press board groaned as it pulled at the remaining nails before finally coming free. She laid the top against the wall.

As she suspected, the crate held a body. They had wrapped it in a bloody hospital sheet and she could smell stale disinfectants even before she pulled back the sheet. She reached forward and took a deep breath before dragging the fabric towards her. She gasped. Even knowing what she would find, she was unprepared for the horror before her.

The bone white corpse of a young teen girl looked like they had drained it of blood. The typical "Y" cut of an autopsy incision was efficiently and professionally done, except that unlike a legal autopsy the opening had not been closed. The flaps had been left to fall into the stomach and chest cavity to show a dark, bloody hollow. Her hand over her mouth as if she would hurl the contents of her own stomach at any moment, Laura tried not to breathe. The image of this broken discarded child would stay with her forever; she didn't need the olfactory memories that would accompany them.

She staggered back, putting as much room as she could between the pile of crates and herself. She felt the familiar anger rise, but this time it had an edge to it. She fought to contain it, because she feared that if she let it consume her, she would go on a killing spree that bordered on madness. There were other children out there, including Gabrielle, who were counting on her. She could not allow herself to lose control.

The old man, seeing her bolt away from the makeshift casket, came to his feet and leaned towards the open box to see its contents. His reaction was not as strong and Laura figured that it was because he was so experienced with dealing with the dead, but he was taken back. He looked at her and she saw that he understood finally what they had involved him in.

"Can you stop them?"

She nodded. "Even if it kills me."

Chapter Sixteen

Laura and Gabrielle watched the kaleidoscope of lights that centered on the crematorium and funeral home in silence. The young girl seemed to instinctively know Laura needed time to deal with what she had experienced and for that she appreciated once again how special her new ward was.

The first call she had the funeral director make was for an ambulance to deal with Pelletier. She had released the tourniquet for a few minutes but then reapplied it as the bleeding continued. He might lose the leg, but for his part in this sickening affair, he's just fortunate that she had promised Rachelle not to kill him. He would not get off that easily though, because now he was implicated in a human trafficking ring that dealt with organ harvesting and of course, murder. A former cop wouldn't fair well in prison.

The next few calls went to the members of the Fifth Estate with a condensed version of the facts and that the Commander was heavily involved. There was no doubt to whether they would attend the cemetery.

Wanting to ensure that the Press arrived before the police, she held off reporting the incident. She used the time to gather everything about the funeral director's granddaughter and sent it off to her computer friends with instructions to find and destroy any information that might be used for blackmailing others from Coutu's server.

With a sigh, she started the vehicle and drove away from the cemetery.

"Ah... You okay?" Gabrielle asked in a soft voice beside her.

Laura looked across seeing only the outline of the young teen. The silence extended while she gathered her thoughts. She took a shuddering breath and said, "It's what we had suspected. The crates were filled with bodies of children; minus their organs."

She heard Gabrielle take a quick breath. Suspecting something was so very different from knowing it for a fact. Fortunately, she would not have the images stamped in her subconscious forever as Laura would. Of course, she had her own nightmares to deal with and no matter how strong she was, it would take time to put those horrible experiences behind her; if she ever did.

For Laura it was different. She was able and willing to strike back and make those involved in these vile acts pay for their sins. It was all the therapy she needed. There was no way she would take the chance and hope some benevolent supernatural Deity would rain hell and fire over these people. For all she knew, they were all worm bait after death, anyway. She could stop them from hurting more people. More children. The argument that if she took these criminal monsters out, more would take their place was a copout to her. She would gladly come back and do it all over again until they thought twice about testing her resolve. That strategy had worked in Canada to where child abusers were terrified to leave the relative safety of the Canadian Penal System. She was sure it would work anywhere.

Her shock and revulsion were slowly being replaced by the familiar heat of anger. She reached out a hand to her young ward and said, "Thanks for your help. It was good knowing someone had my back."

"I was happy to help you, Laura," she said with emotions that the darkness couldn't hide. "So, is it over now that the police have found out about the organ harvesting?"

"I'm afraid not. I'm sure they'll end up following the trail to Coutu, but that could take months if not years to build a case strong enough to charge him, let alone convict him. He's a powerful man with powerful friends. I'm sure that he'll be looking to derail any investigation; legally or otherwise."

"So, he wins."

"No," Laura said with a tight smile. "He still has to answer to me and I won't let him get away with these crimes or hide behind a bunch of high-priced lawyers."

"Thank God. I'm still terrified that he'll find me and drop me back in that hellhole."

Laura could understand the girl's fear. Having lived so long in the brothel with no chance of ever escaping, her newfound freedom was as precious as it was precarious. The sooner they could put this whole sorry affair behind them, the faster Gabrielle's recovery could begin. A glimmer of an idea for the girl's future was forming, but she would have to make some inquires before voicing it. There was no reason to build false hope at this point.

"I will never allow that to happen. I don't care if he has the entire French Foreign Legion on speed dial."

THE DRIVE TO THE NEW safe house took over two hours because of having to skirt the city of Paris and head east. Leaving Gabrielle in the vehicle, she checked out the small cottage nestled in a vineyard that housed the migrant workers brought in for the harvest season. In the off season, they rented it as a retreat from the city or a lover's nest. It served her purpose because it was secluded with no noisy neighbors. Once cleared, Gabrielle setup the charger for the drone batteries while Laura carried several grocery bags in from the car.

After putting a dozen eggs to boil, Laura texted Rachelle to see if her investigation had borne any fruit. That there was no quick reply didn't alarm Laura. She usually kept hers off, so she wasn't distracted at an in-opportune moment. Rachelle would contact them once she stopped to check her messages.

The stress and excitement of the evening had exhausted both, and they stretched out after a light meal; Gabrielle in an upstairs bedroom while Laura took the main floor couch. She didn't expand on the fact it was so she could cover the entrance in the event Coutu's men had discovered their whereabouts. The odds were next to impossible as only Laura knew the location. Even Rachelle didn't know where to find them as Laura had been unsure which of her safe houses she would use when they separated. She planned to send the coordinates when the police officer contacted her.

Before surrendering to the night, she sent out the first inquiry that might give Gabrielle a fighting chance for a new life. She struggled to convey the need and what the girl had gone through. She knew what she was asking and it wouldn't be cut and dry. The acceptance of this 'favor' would be life altering for both the recipient of the email and the young girl.

Sometime through the night, she awoke to the sound of Gabrielle crying. With her pistol at the ready, she took the stairs two at a time. There was no creeping up the old staircase as it moaned under her weight. The girl's bedroom door was ajar and Laura pushed the door open, sweeping the room with the gun. Once she saw there was no intruder, she approached the girl who lay rocking herself as her sobs continued. Laura laid on the bed and held the tortured teen close. Whether from a nightmare or waking scared in a strange environment, she would never know but her closeness calmed the teen and before long her breathing became more regular as she fell back to sleep.

The following morning, Laura eased herself out of the bed and covered Gabrielle with a blanket. She stared at the girl surprised just how attached she had become. This was getting out of hand. If she didn't control herself, it would kill her to let her go. And she had no choice but to let her go. This was no life for a kid. She needed a home and a family she could count on. She should be at school, doing things normal teens did; not hiding out in fear of a monster who only cared about how much money he could make off her.

While the coffee brewed, she checked her phone and saw that Rachelle had not answered her. She felt a tinge of worry run through her. She knew the woman was a highly trained professional, but even the best can trip up. Not wanting to think the worst, she gave it more time, although she checked her location through the GPS link they shared. She hated to wait but concluded that she had to give the woman the benefit of the doubt. If she heard nothing by this evening, she would take a more direct approach to Coutu and his people.

BURNING LIGHT SCALDED Rachelle's eyes, and she tried to squeeze them tightly closed only to find that they wouldn't cooperate. She tried to raise her hand as a shield only to find that both her arms were restrained somehow. Part of her felt a sense of panic deep within her, but another part didn't care. She mentally groped for an explanation but could not comprehend where she was or how she came to be here; wherever here was. The thickness in her mind suggested drugs, like when she had undergone surgery as a child. That groggy, floating sensation that made it hard to think let alone move properly.

With her head clamped in an awkward upright position facing the harsh brightness, she could see nothing but whiteness. It was so close she could feel its heat on her skin and the dryness of her eyes begged to blink. On both sides of her face, tracks of dried tears signaled where the moisture led.

Behind her somewhere, she could hear a steady beep like you see in those hospital movies to show that the patient was okay. She tried to concentrate on the sound, the rhythm speeding up. Was that good or bad? She couldn't remember and didn't know why she cared. The beeping faded into the background as she heard a door open and footsteps moving towards her.

The light mercifully was pulled away but the flash globes floated in her vision so she could not make out any details of the room.

"The effects of the drug will wear off momentarily," said a man's voice from behind her. "I am adding drops to help lubricate your eyes before I take off the tape which is holding them open. It was an unfortunate but important part of the interrogation, Capitaine Deschamps." A hand holding a small bottle tilted over one side of her and then the other. She felt the squirt of the solution as it coated her eyes and it was like she was swimming with her eyes open. What she could see was blurry. A sudden tearing pain pulled at her right eyelid followed by the left.

"I apologize for that. It was unavoidable," said the voice heavy with genuine regret. "No real damage was caused though. Neither will the headache that will replace the fuzziness. Someone has told me it from staring into the light for so long, but that too will wear off in time. We'll talk after that."

She heard his shoes on the floor and the door open and close as he left. She still did not understand who he was or what had happened.

With a sigh, she closed her eyes, but it was like rubbing sandpaper over her corneas. She blinked at the pain only then realizing that she actually had use of her eyelids. The dryness mixed with whatever solution he had administered got her own tear ducts working and slowly the pain subsided only to be replaced by the excruciating pain of a migraine the likes she had never known.

WHEN NEXT SHE OPENED her eyes, Rachelle knew exactly where she was. The confusion had left her, and she recognized the back room of the tattoo parlor. How long had she been here? It felt like days had passed.

Still tied to the damn chair, but at least now her head was free and she could look around. While she surveyed the small studio with a number of highly detailed drawings on the wall, she looked for anything she might reach to either free her or that she could use as a weapon against her captors. A small paring knife stuck out of a chunk of cheese nearby but was unless she could release her bindings, it might as well be ten miles away instead of ten feet. Pulling on her bindings, there was no give and she could feel some kind of strap bite into her flesh. She was not going anywhere.

Behind her, she heard a grunt as someone stood and walked to the door. She had sensed no one there. There was a rap on the door and a few moments later another person joined the first. She kept her head faced forward and refused to look over in panic or fear when they rounded the chair. It may have been a small gesture of bravery but it was all she could offer.

With his hands behind his back, Antoine studied her. "I'm sorry you had to experience that, Capitaine, but my employer expects results and you were impeding my ability to produce those. Although you have given us a fair amount of information during our session, it will take time to substantiate it. Time I do not wish to waste, so I will ask you one last time if you would be willing to offer anything else?"

"I've already told you. The kids are in the wind and I don't know where Laura is. We split up to investigate different avenues of Coutu's operation."

"But there had to be a way for you two to meet up?"

"When it was time to meet, she would send me the GPS coordinates."

He stared at her as if wondering just how much he should believe. After a moment, he turned and walked to a table she had not noticed before. She recognized her revolver secure in its holster and a number of other items. He picked up her cell phone and hit the power button.

After a moment he looked up and said, "Password."

She allowed her gaze flicker between the two men, hoping they took it as uncertain hesitation. This might be her only chance to warn Laura. "24Aug44."

"How patriotic," Antoine said with a smirk. "The liberation of Paris by the Allies."

Hans let out a harsh bark that could have been laughter or a curse. He pulled out a wicked-looking dagger and twirled it expertly like a deadly baton. What Rachelle thought strange about the knife was it had a button near the base of the blade. She had never seen a setup like it, but knew if this psychopath was carrying one, it didn't bode well for whoever was on the business side of the that lethal tool. She didn't have to pretend to be nervous with him around.

He typed in the password and then punched the screen with his manicured fingers. She watched as his lips tightened as he found the text he was looking for.

"She's inquiring how your investigation is coming along?" He looked up from the phone and said, "How would you like to answer?"

Rachelle could not get over the surreal conversation she was having with this known killer. He sounded like a true gentleman but she knew he would snap her neck, or more than likely get the ape-like German to do it for him. He wouldn't want to wrinkle his fancy suit.

"Will talk soon. Where's home?"

Once again, he stared hard at her. She knew he'd be suspicious at her cooperation. Did he sense the trap? She was betting on the man's arrogance that she feared for her life. She allowed her eyes to bounce again between the two soldiers, hoping he saw fear in her expression. She held her breath as he typed the message and forced herself to watch Hans using the knife to clean his fingernails with a bored look on his face. She could feel Antoine's eyes on her, but kept her attention on the German.

"Okay," said Antoine. "Now we have to wait for her reply. You have done well Capitaine. I hope you have not wasted my time or else Hans will get a new playmate."

The ugly soldier blew her a kiss, and she shuddered at the thought of being alone with him.

Two hours later the phone vibrated and danced across the table. Antoine looked over at Rachelle before reaching for it. He retrieved the message and smiled. "Capitaine, you have my gratitude. I wish I could reward you, but you understand that this exchange never happened."

The coldness in his voice struck her as the huge German stood up and stretched his muscle bound arms over his head, like a lion would stretch before it went hunting. She panicked, and the terror was no longer an act. She pulled savagely at her bindings knowing they were secure, her eyes almost bulging from their sockets at the strain.

"Hans," Antoine said fingers raised to accent the point. "Five minutes. No more."

Rachelle's eyes snapped to the brute that walked towards her, pulling the knife out of its sheath.

"Wish we had more time Fraulein, but orders are orders." He waved the knife in front of her eyes with flare. "Do you like my new toy? They call it a Wasp. It has a CO_2 cartridge in the handle and when I push this button, it releases compressed air from this hole in the blade's tip. I've tried it on a melon and it blew the thing all over the room. Made a big fuckin' mess, it did."

He slid the blade up her cheek like he was giving her a shave with a straight razor. His touch revolted her, but she did not dare move or the edge would slice deep.

"My problem is that I have not had the opportunity to try it on a real person." He smiled at her watching the fear grow inside her. He was like a cat toying with a mouse. He enjoyed tormenting. Probably more than the actual kill. "Until now."

He put the point of the knife just under the center of her rib cage and looked her straight in the eyes. With deliberate slowness he pushed the blade deep into her chest cavity. She shuddered as the pain registered and grew to where it was all-consuming. She could not breathe. She could not think. All there was, was pain.

"Now let's see what happens when I press this button."

She heard him, but had trouble understanding him.

Suddenly, she felt a violent pressure tear through her chest, cracking her ribs outward. It was like a party balloon exploding inside her. The pain was a whiteness that lasted mercifully quick.

The whiteness faded to black.

Chapter Eighteen

"Grab your stuff, Gabrielle," Laura yelled.

"Wh-what's wrong?" the girl said as she ran breathlessly down the stairs her tight braids bouncing as she descended; a pack sack over her shoulder. Her eyes were large with nervousness, but she held the pistol that Laura had entrusted to her with calm authority.

"Rachelle just texted and something is wrong. We had worked out a simple code in case either of were compromised. When she needed to find us, she would ask where we were nesting if all was well, but if she asked about home, then I would know she was in trouble."

"So she asked about home?"

"Yes. I linked our phones while they are on through a GPS tracking App. I know where she is so whomever has her might know where we are." She headed for the door. "I'm not taking the chance. We'll head to that location and then I'll send them the coordinates for this place."

Laura took the heavy bag that contained the drone's charger and spare batteries. They were fully charged now. It was a handy tool, but she once again felt the need to find a place safe for Gabrielle. Things could go critical at any time and she needed to know she was out of harm's way.

Checking the surrounding yard for threats, the two made a dash to the car and put the cottage behind them.

It was all Laura could do not to punch the gas pedal through the floor, but the last thing they needed was to attract the attention of the police. She kept her speed even with the pace of the other traffic.

When they approached the city, they noticed a heavier police presence which comprised spot checks on those roadways leading from Paris.

"Do you think they are looking for us?" Gabrielle asked as her head turned with the threat as they continued with the flow.

"It would be a good guess. I would have been surprised if they hadn't checked outgoing traffic. Had we not gone around the city last night, we might have encountered one."

A look of worry creased the young girl's features. "Will we be able to leave the city?"

Laura grabbed Gabrielle's hand and gave it a squeeze. "They can't watch every road in or out of Paris. They don't have that kind of manpower, but they'll be using facial recognition on all the traffic cameras, so we have to keep altering our appearance."

Her assurance helped the girl relax, at least visibly, but it was a reminder to Laura that this was no situation for a young teen. She also knew she'd have a fight on her hands when it came time to leave Gabrielle. It would be a two-way fight. The girl would not want to leave Laura, but Laura didn't want to lose the only person that gave her a sense of normality. If she were to have a daughter of her own, she could not ask for anyone better than Gabrielle. She blinked back the sudden stinging in her eyes, surprised at her own raw feelings. She had never imagined a time where she would even want or need a family. Her friend Janice had filled that void in the past. Her career as a psychologist and international champion of PTSD treatment, not to mention the crusade she embarked on against child abusers made no room for a normal home life or family. And she had been okay with that until she met this brave young lady.

The fierce need to strike back rather than curl up in a ball and hope for the best was so alive in the girl. It reminded Laura a little of herself, but also a lot like Janice. She too had been abused but fought back and would not allow the animals to have free reign.

Laura did a drive past the coordinates the GPS signal had identified as the location where Rachelle's phone was last used. She had known the police officer was investigating the origin of the tattoos in case it led them closer to Coutu's main enforcers. while she drove through the area, Gabrielle lay in the back seat, in case one of the ex-soldiers they were looking for recognized her.

The collection of the parlors so close together didn't surprise her, having seen similar back home. What came as a shock was the condition of the neighborhood. The entire area had a rundown, tired look to it, like a cancer patient who just wanted to let go and die. Many of the storefronts were boarded or someone had pried the sheets of plywood open to allow access.

The vacant buildings were more than likely flop houses for the homeless. She shuddered at the thought of all the used condoms and needles that would have littered the floors. It didn't matter which city or country you went to, the squalor of the poor and the hopeless lived in was revolting to the uninitiated. She knew from past experience that fire departments had safety policies in place for these types of drug houses which did not allow interior rescue due to the high chance of injection of hepatitis C and HIV infected syringes.

The lane ways were even filthier than the streets as if the city had also given up trying to clean the area. Eying the older prostitutes on each corner, she was sure some residents were fine with the lack of official presence. Even the police would think twice before entering the district.

As she drove past the building in question, she spotted a heavy sedan parked alongside with one occupant sitting low in the driver's seat. His eyes followed Laura's vehicle as she drove past and she felt him watching until she was out of sight. Because she was dealing with ex-military, she took it for granted that if there was a visible guard outside, there were probably a couple of unseen over watchers. Before making a move, she had to find these guards.

Pulling back two streets, she backed her vehicle into the shadows of a three-story tenement that had seen better days decades ago. While Laura took the drone out of the trunk, Gabrielle booted the laptop and did a system check on the flier.

"Remember, keep the doors locked and the pistol out of sight but at the ready. You don't know who's packing in this kind of neighborhood. Keep high and use the telescopic. We don't want to give them any warning."

Gabrielle gave her an annoyed look from under her brows, "Yes, Mom."

"Smart ass!" she got back with a smile and a light-hearted swipe at the girl's shoulder.

The quad-chopper rose gracefully and then glided behind the tenement before rising. Laura watched the live video feed as the flier pulled high over the suburb. The little unit slowed and became stationary and its pilot closed in with the zoom lens. She pointed out the tattoo parlor that the coordinates had identified and the vehicle they had spied during the drive by.

"Okay, so concentrate on the roof tops first," Laura said, as she placed the earpiece in place and turned on the portable radio. "That's the first place I would setup."

After a test of the communication, she tucked the radio into a leg pocket and continued checking the readiness and placement of her gear. She realized that she might be walking into a trap, but the police officer was relying on her for help. Once she sent the GPS coordinates for the farmhouse, she would have to shut down her phone so whoever was in there could not track that she was just outside the building. How they reacted would determine the next course of action.

It would either be a rescue or a recovery.

"Found one," Gabrielle said pointing to the screen. It was as she had expected, a lone gunman lay tight up against the chimney overlooking the building and street. The shooter was on a two-story business so it put him approximately twenty feet over the street and about two hundred yards from the parlor. An easy shot for any half-ass shooter as long as he took in the angle into his shooting calculations. For a downward shot, the bullet would usually hit higher and this had to be taken into considerations, but due to the short-range distance, it would be minimum.

Laura turned on her phone and texted Rachelle the GPS coordinates and then pried the phone apart to pull the battery and sim card out. Now there would be no way to track her.

Noting which building it was and the access points available to her, Laura tapped her ear as she closed the door to the car. Her young protégé nodded and focused back on the computer screen, her body already sliding out of view on the car seat.

Laura weaved through the rundown yards to the two-story. At its base, she looked around to see if she was being watched. Seeing no one, she grabbed the steel wire conduit that carried the electrical cables from the roof to the meter and climbed the wall of the building, both hands and feet moving in smooth movements. She double tapped her transmitter as she neared the top,.

"All clear," came the whisper through the ear bud.

Taking a deep breath, she slowly pulled herself even with the roof. A quick scan saw the sniper on the opposite side. He was in a prone position scanning the street, his back towards her. She pulled herself onto the gravel and tarred surface, her muscles burning as she controlled her movements to make as little sound as possible. This high up, there was a slight breeze that crossed between her and her target. It was not enough to muffle any noise so she would have to be extra cautious. Drawing her weapon, she disengaged the safety and took a bead on the back of the sniper's back. He might be wearing body armor, but if needed, a double tap would still incapacitate him while she closed in. Almost like a funeral slow march, she placed one foot carefully ahead of the other while crouching low, ensuring that she didn't scuff or kick any loose pieces of gravel.

She was halfway between her antagonist when she was startled to where she almost pulled the trigger.

"Down!" she heard Gabrielle scream.

She dropped to the roof without hesitation as a bullet snapped the space where her head had been. There was no rifle report, so she concluded that the killer was using a silencer. Not knowing where the shot had originated, she kept her aim on the man in front of her. He turned at the noise of her hitting the roof and she squeezed off a trio of shots that took him in the side, the back and the base of the neck. He slumped noiselessly over the rifle now wedged under him.

Rolling to a cluster of vent pipes that was the only cover nearby she heard Gabrielle blurt out, "He's moving to get a better angle. He's almost across from you behind the parlor."

Looking across the span of buildings, she saw a figure run and jump across to an adjacent building. He skidded to a halt and threw a rifle to his shoulder, aiming it towards her position. Laura didn't waste time letting him get a bead on her, but rolled towards the edge of her own rooftop. If she could get behind the chimney, it would at least give her some cover from the sniper. However, if he had had communication with the others inside the parlor, it wouldn't take long to have her boxed in.

"Hold on," the voice in her ear advised her. "I have an idea."

"Stay in the car," Laura said desperate that the young girl would either get hurt or captured.

"I am. Don't worry."

"Then what are you doing?"

"Would you just trust me?"

Laura was surprised at the harshness of the girl's reprimand. It might have come out because of the high stress of the situation, but she wasn't sure. She was only a kid, but the steel she had sensed in the girl was not just for those that hurt her. It was also to assert herself as an individual. She had no choice but to wait and see what Gabrielle had planned, especially being pinned down by a guy with a high-powered rifle.

Minutes, that felt like hours passed before a very subdued voice said, "Clear."

"Gabrielle, what happened? What did you do?"

"I dealt with it. The guy is no longer a threat." An ominous silence followed the dead panned voice and Laura knew something traumatic had happened, but she couldn't figure out what.

Peeking around the chimney, she looked across to the other building but there was no sign of the sniper. She crawled toward the front of the building and looked down at the parlor across the street. She immediately realized that the sedan was missing and wondered what had happened. Did this happen before or after she moved towards the building? Did the other sniper radio his accomplices so they could escape or were the two left behind as a trap?

Pressing the transmit button she asked, "Did you see the vehicle leave?"

"No, I'm sorry. I was too busy searching for the other sniper."

"Understood. Watch my back, I'm heading in."

"I can't," said the young girl and Laura was sure she heard a tremor in her voice. "I destroyed the drone. It... it won't respond to commands."

Understanding hit Laura like a punch in the gut. She realized that the girl had done the only thing she could do to protect Laura, and that was to use quad-chopper as a weapon. She reached over and rolled the corpse off the rifle, another Russian "Vychlop", and put it to her shoulder. It only took seconds for the high-powered scope to find the body of the other sniper, lying in a heap among the other discarded debris. With all his attention on Laura, it would have been easy to catch him unawares with an attack from above. A little push with the drone and gravity would have done the rest. No wonder the girl sounded so lost. She had killed the man, and that was never an easy thing to deal with; let alone for a teen that had been already traumatized.

Laura had to struggle with the maternal instinct to return and hold Gabrielle. It would have to wait. She had Rachelle counting on her. She almost slid down the same conduit and circled the building. There was no movement on the street and although she saw no one watching, she instinctively knew there was a multitude of eyes watching the afternoon's events unfold. She figured she didn't have to worry about someone calling the police; it might happen if there was nothing to salvage from the leftovers.

She dashed across the street, half waiting for the impact of a bullet from a third, unseen attacker, but it never materialized. With her pistol extended at the ready, she surveyed the front of the tattoo shop through the glass doors. Seeing no threat, she entered the storefront tracking for any movement. After checking behind the counter, she moved to the rear of the unit where the only door leading deeper into the building stood closed. Crouched low to one side of the door, she twisted the doorknob and pushed the door open, expecting a barrage of bullets to follow, but was met with silence. Allowing her pistol to lead the way she saw Rachelle tied to some kind of chair that looked like it belong in the estate of the Marquis de Sade, but focused on clearing the room. Once satisfied, she moved towards her ally, only then noticing the pool of blood surrounding the chair.

She suddenly felt the weight of the world fall on her shoulders. She had been too late and failed her newfound friend.

Rounding the chair, she saw the shocked and painful expression frozen on the police officer's beautiful face. The agony was carved in every graceful curve of her skin which had glassed over with that sick gray-yellow sheen of a corpse. Protruding from between her breasts was the object of her pain; the black neoprene handle with a silver knob at the hilt.

On a table to one side, she saw a hypodermic needle and a small glass vial. Picking the vial, she sniffed it, recognizing it as the psychoactive drug or one of the many derivatives. She knew the effects of the drug and wondered what they pulled from the woman.

Laura crouched down in front of the corpse, a drop of falling blood periodically disturbed the crimson pool below. It had been the first time she had ever teamed up with anyone and she had failed them. Biting her lip, she closed her eyes and tried to hold back the pain of loss that threatened to overwhelm her. With an effort, she swallowed her grief and felt her stomach churn as it converted to something dark and cruel. She let it grow.

When she next looked up at what was left of Rachelle, all emotion had dried up, she studied her friend with a cold clinical eye. Feet and hands bound to the chair, her entire chest cavity seemed to push outward as if she had been dead for a while and the body's internal gasses sought an escape. That the blood was still dripping and that Coutu's men had just left, she knew her friend had been killed only moments ago. Probably while she was dealing with the sentries. To be that close and still fail stung even more. She centered on the murder weapon and tried to understand why a knife would need a button. Bracing herself, she stood and reached for the knife. When she pulled the blade from the woman's body, a rush of air escape startled her causing her to let go of the hilt. Taking a deep breath, she took hold of the handle and pushed it to one side allowing the built up gas to escape. Rachelle's chest seemed to deflate like a slowly leaking balloon to its normal proportions and the corpse relaxed in the chair. Pulling the knife completely out, Laura examined the blade, but it was covered with a sheen of blood. Pressing the button at the top of the hilt caused a spray of fine blood particles to caress her cheek. She froze at its touch in horror as the thought of her friend's blood on her face sank in. With a shudder, she continued the inspection of the knife and unscrewed the base of the hilt to find a small CO_2 cylinder, which explained the knife's real purpose.

Whoever used a weapon like this, killed for the enjoyment.

The ball of anger that had been growing became even denser. This would not go unanswered.

Wiping the blade with a cloth that sat on a tray with several tattooing pens, she took one final look at the police officer who had sacrificed so much for Laura and the children, then turned and left the building. She had one thing to do before she could unleash the stone-cold killer that was growing inside her and it was something she dreaded.

Chapter Nineteen

"No!" Gabrielle shook her head in defiance, making her beads swing back and forth. "We had a deal. I've held up my end of the bargain so you need to honor yours."

Laura knew she would have a fight on her hand, but was surprise at the passion that her young ward was displaying. This wasn't the typical teenager tantrum with sulking and name calling, not that she expected that kind of behavior. That would have been easier to deal with; especially if accompanied with the silent treatment. But Gabrielle had not been exposed to the regular high school dramatics and attacked with logic and sound arguments. Laura had to keep reminding herself the girl was only fifteen.

"This is not a game," Laura said. "And these people are playing for keeps."

"I understand that. I have an intimate knowledge of these animals."

Laura closed her eyes and drew in a steady breath. "You didn't see what they did to Rachelle." Reaching for the girl's hands, she looked her in the eyes and said, "The fact they have no fear of killing a police officer speaks volumes about what they would do to you."

"I'm nothing. It's you they really want."

Laura nodded. "That's just it." She cupped the other's cheek. "They would use you to get to me. And I wouldn't hesitate... and then we'd both be dead." She felt the unwanted tears slide down her face. She could not get over how hard or fast she had fallen for this young girl. Why after all this time, did this maternal instinct rear its head and I have the urge to raise and protect this perfect stranger?

Is it because her decision to fight the good fight had taken away any chance of ever having a normal life? Or, she thought cynically, is Gabrielle just a replacement for her best friend Janice, who she had to leave behind for this crusade.

Both women leaned forward, foreheads touching as tears fell with no shame.

"I need to know you are safe and out of harm's way so I can concentrate everything on taking these people down and finding any of the other children. I can't do that if I'm always looking over my shoulder to see if you're safe. It's only a matter of time before I make a mistake because of it."

"But who'll have your back?" Gabrielle swiped at her eyes and a mischievous smile cracked worry lines. "You'd still be stuck on that roof if I hadn't been there."

Laura gave her a slap on the shoulder. "I won't miss that smart mouth of yours, that's for sure," she said with a laugh.

"Yes, you will." The light had fled from her eyes, leaving shadows of uncertainty and fear. "What will happen to me?"

"I will drop you off at the Canadian Embassy. You'll be completely safe there. Arrangements are being made to fly you to Canada where you'll be able to start a new life away from these people." She gave her an excited smile. "Just think. You'll be able to go to school, make friends and be whatever you want to be without ever having to look over your shoulder. It'll be a fresh start and you'll be in the driver's seat."

"But you won't be there with me." Tears filled those dark eyes and slid down her cheeks. Laura reached out and caught them before they could drop further.

"I'll be here," said Laura placing her palm on the girl's chest. "I'll always be here."

"How are you doing this? I thought you were a fugitive there."

"I still have some friends in high positions that are willing to do me a favor." She was speaking about Darren Forbes, the head Canadian Security Intelligence Service or CSIS, who had helped her friend Janice, avoid some nasty political fallout over Laura's escape from Canada. He had offered to help her out if he could. It had taken only a couple hours for him to arrange things from his end. Laura was not blind to the thought she would one day have to return the favor, but ensuring Gabrielle was safe and able to live a normal life would be worth it.

"So, I'm to live in Canada's version of SOS Villages d'Enfants?" Gabrielle said in a scared voice. She was referring to a foster system used in France and other parts of the world.

"God, no!" Laura said stopping in her tracks. She pulled the girl into her embrace and said, "I would never do that to you." She felt some tension leave the girl's shoulders.

"Then, what will happen to me? Where will I live?"

Laura steered her into an open-air patio and under the shelter of an umbrella. After ordering them each a coffee, she took the other's hand and gave her a soft smile.

"This is happening fast, I know," she said. "And for that I apologize. I have so many details in my head I haven't fully explained everything." She paused as the waiter brought their coffees. "My best friend, Janice is a police officer in Canada—in Ottawa in fact. She is the only person in the world I would trust to help you. Like you, she was abused when she was young, but like you, she had the strength and determination to rise above it."

"So why would she agree to take care of me? She doesn't know me."

Laura felt the squeeze of the girl's hands on her own and imagined the fear and anxiety she must be feeling. "You and Janice are more alike than you know. I think you both will be good friends. Unlike a social worker with too many case files, Janice needs you as

much as you need her. Since I had to leave her and my country behind, she has been hurting." She would never divulge the numerous emails Janice had sent through their joint account. Most were
painful and more than a couple were hateful messages as she cried
out her loneliness and helplessness since Laura fled. Her crusade had
left a major gap in Janice's life and she was struggling to find her own
place without her friend. All she had was her job as the Director of
the Child Exploitation Center for the RCMP. She needed human
intimacy and companionship, something her past made difficult, especially with trust. Gabrielle should fit that bill perfectly and vice
versa.

"So, we're both damaged goods."

"It depends on how you look at it," Laura said leaning back and
assessing the girl. "We all have to decide how we respond to different
experiences that life throws at us. Either we let it destroy us or make
us stronger." She raised her hand to ward out the retort she saw jump
into Gabrielle's eyes. "I'm not making light of what you have gone
through; neither you or Janice. But you have to decide if your scars
are ugly or beautiful. Are they a sign of weakness or strength? If you
and Janice can help each other move forward, then you both win. I
think... rather I know you are both more than capable to doing just
that."

"But what about you?"

"I have my own path to follow. I made this decision; right or
wrong, and I have to see it through." She reached over and cupped
the other's cheek. "I need to stop Coutu and people like him from
hurting children and other innocent people. They need to know I
can't be bought or bargained with. Nor will I be scared off. Because if
I allowed myself to walk away, people like Rachelle would have died
for nothing. And that is unacceptable."

THE RECENTLY RENOVATED Canadian Embassy for France was an imposing building that jutted out and over Rue du Faubourg Saint Honore. Gone was the original Haussmann architecture with its wrought-iron balcony railings that made the building standout from its neighbors. Prefab cement panels and barred windows reflected the security realities of the new era. They designed even the entrance with enough reinforcement to hold back a platoon of dedicated terrorists.

What had not changed Laura concluded was the brilliant red and white Maple Leaf flag that signified peace and goodwill the world over.

Knowing that as a fugitive, Laura could not enter the consulate without being arrested, Forbes had arranged for one of his people to meet them out front of the Embassy. While she and Gabrielle walked towards the entrance, she studied the lone man with a USA Today newspaper under his arm which had been an arranged sign to show it was safe to approach. She was under no pretense that the man wasn't an agent of CSIS nor that there weren't others watching the meet. He was lean and average height and could blend in with any crowd which was a good thing considering his trade.

As they approached, Laura said casually, "Celine spends so much time in Vegas, she might as well be American."

"Maybe Rush would be more to your liking," the man said not even looking her way. "Three good Toronto boys."

Laura nodded at the man having heard the simple code that Forbes had texted her. She turned to Gabrielle, ignoring the puffy red eyes and pulled her into a huge hug. In her ear, she said, "Never forget that I love you, so no regrets. I will watch from afar. Give my love to Janice." She felt the girl's arms clutch at her as her body trembled in sobs. Laura broke the embrace and nodded at the agent who had the decency to give them their moment. With long strides, she put distance between her and a life she never realized was there for her. She never looked back because it would have been her undoing, but in the cafe window across the street she saw the man half guide - half carry Gabrielle into the safety of the Embassy. Her own eyes stung, and she used the memory of Rachelle's broken body to burn the tears away.

This crusade of hers was costing too much.

THEY KEPT THE LIGHTS in the room dim to help those monitoring the multiple high definition screens concentrate on the traffic cameras that littered the streets of Paris. Like most countries, France kept regular passive surveillance on the consulates that peppered the city. It was a regular counter-intelligence strategy that all sides played in this international dance of diplomacy. Law enforcement also used the system as a monitoring device using facial recognition software to locate individuals of concern.

Agathe was one of those technicians who monitored the traffic cams. She still could not believe the man she had met three months ago and the scattered nights they had together. He was so handsome and gentle. This was so new to her. Shy and reserved, she rarely met, let alone went out with men. They had met on the train on the way into work and after sharing a bench for two trips he had asked her out for dinner. One thing led to another, and she returned to work without having gone home. He was a hero of France who worked to hunt down terrorists. When she had told him of the work she did for a living, he showed so much admiration and interest she soon offered to help him in the hunt for extremists.

Last week, he took her up on her offer and had sent her two names and photos that his team was actively hunting.

"You understand, my love," he said as his fingers traced the curve of her hips, "that you must keep my team's involvement to yourself. It could be a death sentence if anyone of my team was identified publicly considering our undercover work."

She nodded seeing real fear in his eyes. "I would not tell a soul. I would do nothing to endanger you."

She blushed at the memory of how he had thanked her.

When the camera near the Canadian Embassy beeped a specific tone that identified a known criminal or Person of Interest, she immediately hit the record button on the video feed. The system created and stored digital copies of the entire network but her system allowed her to create a separate file of the specific encounter that could be emailed to the originating police officer that had sent in identifying information to the system. In a city that multiple terrorist attacks had rocked, investigators were always searching for known radicals or criminals that might be the lead they need to avert the next attack. Although there were thousands Persons of Interest in the system, her computer brought up two names.

Laura Amour - terrorist at large

Gabrielle Pichet - missing child

What an alleged terrorist was doing with a missing child was anyone's guess, but Agathe worried for the girl's safety.

The software sent another audible alarm when the suspect was no longer in the camera's view. At this point Agathe typed in another command which stopped the recording, logged the start and end time of the record as well as the camera location and date. She brought up another window on a separate computer and entered the file number into the database. Attaching the recorded file, she pressed enter, and it sent the file to the original investigator for his consideration.

This should have been the end of her duty, but before leaving the system, using a patch cord to her phone, she downloaded the video file. She sent a quick text to her supervisor explaining that she had to attend the bathroom. Once confirmed, she logged out of the system and left her station. Taking the elevator, she rode to the ground floor and left the building. Crossing the street, she entered a restaurant and ordered a green tea. While she waited for her order, she hit a speed dial.

"Oui?" answered a male's deep voice.

"Rollan, it is Agathe. We had a hit on the Canadian and the black child."

"Where and when?" he said, his tone not gentle like the night he had slept with her and promised he would love her forever.

"Ah... outside the Canadian Embassy. The child went inside and the Amour woman left the area. I have the video file and am uploading it as you requested."

"Excellent." His voice changed with the news and she dismissed the concern that had reared its head.

"And the child did not come out of the consulate?"

"No. She was escorted into the building by a man."

"Interesting."

"When will I see you again, Rollan?" Don't beg she scolded herself.

"Soon, my love. This woman is causing a lot of grief for France and I've been very busy. You'll let me know if she reappears?"

"Oh yes. To help you put that horrible woman away before she can hurt France, I will do anything."

"I'll wait for your call, my love."

Chapter Twenty

Laura stood over the kitchen table of her latest safe house reflecting that if she gave up this way of life, she could at least put down some roots. This continued shuffling of properties was getting old fast even though it was a safe alternative. With luck, she might call this home for more than one night. On the table was an assortment of tools and weapons which she was inspecting and cleaning. It had been ridiculously easy to attain the array of weapons she needed. It was no wonder that Europe was having trouble with terrorist attacks.

She was planning on shaking Coutu's tree to see what would fall out. A frontal assault on his home might make the criminal mastermind react in a panic and could lead her to the next target. There were also possibly other victims in his human trafficking organization, both the sexual and the organ harvesting sides. They were her priority if she could find where they might be hidden. Once she could confirm there were no more innocents at risk, would she cut the head off the snake.

She wiped a thin coating of oil over the receiver of the FN SCAR-L/Mk. 16 rifle before giving the 40 mm grenade launcher mounted under the front stock a wiggle to ensure it was secure. The long noise suppression barrel caused it to be front-heavy, but she couldn't afford to have the police react too quickly. This Austrian beauty was the go-to assault rifle for many Special Forces around the world and she had to contain her excitement in front of the dealer or it might have cost her a lot more. She laid it on the table beside the familiar Remington 700 with the PGW silencer. This older rifle had been in use since the Vietnam War and was still an effective long-range rifle.

Her Browning waited in its holster, already attached to the Osprey combat harness which she would don later. She had packed the pouches to the brim with ammunition for the different weapons, plus she had a bandolier for the 40 mm grenades. It might seem extreme, but with Coutu's private army, she needed to be ready for anything.

Regardless of how busy she kept herself, she kept glancing at her watch. Janice should arrive in Paris in a few hours to pick up Gabrielle for the return trip to Canada. The sooner the girl was safe, the sooner she could get her head in the game, because she was having a lot of trouble planning her next move. Shaking her head as if that would clear it, she sighed and rewound their parting conversation. She'd known the feisty youth for such a short time and yet leaving her behind, even though Janice would be the one who cared for had hurt her more than she thought possible. When she had left Janice last year, they had both felt the emptiness and loss of each other, but this seemed deeper and more personal.

For the first time since she started this fight, she seriously questioned the cost of her choice. Janice had been the first thing she had lost. Not that her friend didn't still care and love her, but Laura was still on the Most Wanted List which made regular visits between the two next to impossible. If she was arrested here in France, after serving a long prison term here, Canada would look to extradite her to answer for those crimes she committed in her home country.

And that was the second cost. Her country. She could no longer hope to live there, except in the confines of a jail cell. Even with Canada's liberal view on incarceration, she would ever taste freedom again if she had given herself up to the authorities. She had backed the government into a corner and forced its hand to bring tougher penalties against child abusers. Even though it might have been the right thing to do, that would be viewed as unforgivable by the upper echelon that ran the country. Hell, they had even tried to have her killed, rather than captured.

There was no going back.

Finally, there was Gabrielle. She knew it was the right thing to do. This was no life for a teen. Hell, it wasn't much of a life for her and she had freely chosen it. At least the child would be out of harm's way. With Janice, the girl would have a good chance at a normal life, safe from this underbelly of the world. Laura knew that with Janice's love and support Gabrielle would have no excuse not to move forward. Not that it wouldn't be difficult, but at least in Canada, she would have a fresh start where no one would know what she had been through.

Of course, that was part of the issue. Although she knew Janice could reach the girl at a fundamental level, Laura knew she wanted to be the one that Gabrielle leaned on. Whether that was a latent maternal instinct or a leftover from her counseling days, she didn't know nor cared at this point. She wanted to be the one.

She swiped at her eyes which betrayed her yet again.

Bending, she snatched a large duffel bag off the floor and loaded the weapons and equipment. Anything to clear her mind. She zipped the bag closed and her phone chimed indicating an email. Glancing at the time, she frowned, knowing it was too early for Janice's plane to have arrived. Checking the message, it surprised her to find that it was from Yusuf Rahal, Rachelle's Muslim friend who had taken the children. Opening the message, she saw that he had left a phone number.

Always concerned about security, she packed up her equipment and left the safe house. If it was a trap, she wouldn't allow them to trace the call back to the last refuge she still had in place.

Thirty minutes later, she walked into the Bristo Vicienne which was part of the famous Galerie Vivienne, a covered shopping mall, just down from the Louve. The area was teaming with tourists and offered multiple escape routes in the event she needed to run. She was armed with three throw away cell phones.

"Hello," said the familiar voice.

"Yusuf, it is Laura. You asked me to call?"

"Yes. Yes. Laura. I have some information you might find interesting. I could not contact Rachelle-"

"Yusuf, she's dead. I cannot get into the details now, but you must tell me what you have found." She heard the sudden gasp on the other end and felt sorry to break the news so bluntly. "I may have to hang up in case your phone is being traced."

"Do you think—" The surprise seemed genuine, but she could not take any chances.

"Hurry, Yusuf."

"Of course. Ah... After we found out about the children, my people made some subtle inquires with those still in the camps. People, children and adults are still going missing from the camps."

Glancing at her watch which she had in stop watch mode, "Is that any indication when this is happening or by whom?"

"It seems a few each night and — "

"I'll call you back," Laura said and dropped the phone in a trash can next to where she stood. She didn't bother ending the call as she was hoping to see if the call was being traced. She retreated to the exterior and crossed the street to the Royal Gardens. The mist from one fountain competed with the afternoon's heat as she waited on a bench that gave her a good view of the Bristo. That no team of anti-terrorist soldiers or any of Coutu's men rushed the place didn't tell her anything either way. There might have been a technological glitz, or they were not in the area to arrive soon enough, or the phone wasn't compromised. Paranoid maybe, but she'd be dead the minute she took things for granted.

Keeping among a group of tourists, she walked a short distance towards the Louvre. She left the group and descended the stairs into the Carousel, an underground shopping mall where some of the most famous sculptures in the world surrounded stood vigil. She marveled at the grace and the beauty of the European display of masterpieces in a subway. Like Moscow, there was no graffiti on the walls or trash to step over. The society harbored a deep love of art and culture. Perhaps it came from seeing your cities and countries torn apart during the last world war.

Checking to ensure she had coverage, Laura redialed the number that Yusuf had supplied.

"Is everything all right?" that man asked once she identified herself.

"I'm just being cautious. Please continue. You were saying people are still going missing."

"Yes. Many moved north and have set up a camp in the forest outside Grand-Synthe waiting in hope of a passage to England. The camp is overflowing so it is hard to keep track of people, but some are noticed. My sources tell me that a group of three former smugglers are involved but they are not taking them to the UK but rather to somewhere within France. They do not follow the regular trails to the coast."

"That doesn't sound good for your people," Laura said while she turned the matter over in her head. "I'm going to move again. While I'm gone, figure out who I can meet at this camp who might act as a guide. Someone who speaks English or French." With that, she once again discarded the burner, this time under a pile of overpriced sweaters in a woman's clothing shop that she had been strolling through as she talked with Yusuf.

The third time she called, the man gave her a name and a general description of a woman who volunteered at the camp and would meet her at the eastern end of the facility. She thanked him and made for her car.

Possibly, it was a trap. But it might offer a lead to where the refugees were being taken. Either way, she would be prepared.

Chapter Twenty-One

Laura allowed the car to coast to a stop just off the roadway, outside of Grand-Synthe. The town was just south of Dunkirk where Canadian and British soldiers were slaughtered by the German forces as they tried to retreat across the English Channel. Now there was another group trying desperately to cross the same barrier. Through the trees, she could see the flickering glow of several bonfires. She knew from a quick online search that they had recently moved the migrant camp to a drier location. Doctors Without Borders had stepped up when the government of France refused to, and built over three hundred huts to house the refugees.

She stepped from the vehicle and allowed her eyes to adjust to the darkness. In the camp's direction, there was a murmur of voices. She loosened the pistol in the shoulder harness and patted her jacket for her extra magazines. Locking the vehicle, she listened to the night, waiting for the contact that Yusuf had arranged. This could still be a trap, but she was as prepared as she could be. Moving off the road, she positioned herself so she could spot anyone approaching the car, but in cover so they could not surprise her.

The wait wasn't long before she heard someone approaching through the brush, the scrape of a branch against fabric. It was obvious that the person was not comfortable moving in the dark as they stumbled and cursed softly as they moved. A slide of gravel announced that the person was climbing the shoulder of the road. The individual moved towards the vehicle and leaned over to look in through the window. The shadow stood uncertainly looking into the darkness.

"Laura?" called a nervous whisper. "Are you there?"

Having not heard anyone else moving in the area, Laura moved closer, careful of where she stepped. "Here, Banaz," she whispered the name that Yusuf had given her.

The figure jumped, showing just how scared she was. The woman held her arms around her chest as Laura approached.

"We must go. It is not safe for a woman to be alone at night. There are too many single men in the camp and some are known to take advantage." Without waiting for a reply, she turned on her heel and moved towards the light of the camp.

"Wait," Laura hissed causing the woman to turn in fright. Taking the woman's arm, Laura led her to a large cluster of brush and pulled her into a crouch. "Before we enter," she explained in a whisper, "I need you to explain where you are taking me and what's been happening."

"The smugglers always do their work at night, but there is one group that even the others will not associate with. Those who attempt to help the migrants cross the channel tell us that this group is not to be trusted. That they offer no escape, but rather work for criminals within France. None they have taken has been heard from again. This group is at the rear of the camp. They have set up a tent which I will point out to you when we are closer."

"Okay, take the lead and I'll follow. I don't want to enter the clearing, so try to circle around and stay in the woods. Keep low and slow."

As the woman moved out, Laura pulled the pistol out of its holster and screwed on the silencer. Ensuring the safety was engaged, she followed leaving enough room so she did not get slapped by any branch that the other had bent forward. They entered the stand of pine trees, their progress silent on a bed of needles. She kept her eyes moving, searching for threats. Off to their left, loud laughter erupted by one fire showing that even under the harsh living conditions, people found something to find positive. Beyond the fires, they set line after line of sheds up. She knew this new camp, named La Liniere after a former flax cooperative, in the area was a far cry better than the last camp, Basroch. The former was a cluster of tents on a floodplain that had been overrun by migrants when the Calais Jungle was shuttled. Mud, garbage and wide-scale sexual assaults were the norm. Much had changed, but tensions were still high as the refugees awaited results from immigration applications.

Finally, the young woman pulled up at the edge of the tree line and crouched beside a cluster of bramble. Laura knelt down beside her. The woman pointed to a lone tent in between a group of trees. Someone tied nylon tarps to the surrounding trees to allow water to run away from the enclosure. Four or five people sat cross-legged in front of a small fire, several children among them. While she studied them in the low light, Laura realized that they were tied each to the other by the neck. There was no need to tie the children as they clung to the adults, which she presumed to be their parents.

Out of the tent, two men emerged and stretched. They kicked at the people on the ground to stand. With difficulty, they struggled to their feet and Laura realized that the captive's hands were also tied behind their backs. Banaz's suspicions been right. This was no regular human smuggling group.

She reached a hand on the woman's shoulder and pulled her close so she could whisper in her ear. "Is there a road near this end of the camp?" The woman nodded in the dark, her expression unreadable and pointed off to their right. "Let's go."

Without hesitation, Banaz set out with Laura trailing. Unimpeded with a chain of captives, they reached the road well ahead of the other group. A Renault closed box truck sat idling alongside a weed-filled ditch.

Laura indicated that Banaz should stay low before crawling, crab-like towards the vehicle. A lone male was pacing back and forth on the roadway trailing cigarette smoke. Seems nervous. Scared of the dark or the police? Moving slowly through the ditch, she pushed the tall plants aside to avoid making noise. She eased up onto the asphalt behind the truck, listening to the man's footsteps to gauge his location. She tensed as he came towards her. When the glow of the cigarette came in sight, she threw a throat punch inches below the ember. The driver gave a ragged cough that had nothing to do with smoking and collapsed to the ground, too withered to draw a breath. She didn't give him a chance, clubbing him on the side of the head with the butt of her pistol.

She jammed the firearm back into its holster and dragged the man into the tall grass on the far side of the road. Once safely concealed, she called to Banza in a hushed voice to join her.

"Get down in the ditch and wait for my call," Laura said, pointing to a spot away from the unconscious thug. She didn't wait for the girl, but turned her attention to the forest for any signs of the smugglers. The night still hid them but could not disguise the tramp of feet on uneven ground. She used the chance to jump off the roadway, run down the trail which was a lighter shade of dark and crouch down in the overgrowth.

A few minutes later, the group of linked migrants shuffled past her hiding spot. One smuggler led the train with a length of rope attached to the bound wrists of the first weeping child. Laura had to bite her tongue when the man yanked on the rope causing the first two children to trip and fall to the ground in a heap. The entire string of souls would have tumbled like dominoes except one of the adult males behind the kids braced himself and took their weight. The guard's evil laughter turned to rage as he cursed them to rise and continue towards the road. Laura spied another guard walking along the string of captives while a third followed behind. When this last one past her, she rose from the cover like a phantom and silently clubbed the man in the back of the head. He collapsed without a sound.

Crouched low, she hurried forward on the balls of her feet. She placed a hand on the last captive in line. His eyes went round as he perceived her small shadow. She pressed her throwing knife into his hands, figuring he would know what to do with it and moved forward. She slipped past the next couple detainees, hearing the sudden intake of breath, but no one cried out. She needed to disable the guard before he could alarm the leader. She was five feet from her goal, when a small boy, surprised by her sudden appearance, cried out and pulled as far as his tether would allow him. His frightful scream was cut short as the rope around his throat took his weight, but it had caused the guard to turn around in exasperation. He rushed towards the child and Laura raised her pistol towards his head. Before she could shoot, the large man behind the boy, perhaps his father, stepped forward, looped the rope around the sentry's neck and yanked on the cord, like an improvised garrote. Even in the dark, Laura could see the white of the man's eyes as he frantically tried to pull the rope away from his neck. She stepped forward and clubbed him with the pistol butt and he went limp, hanging from the rope.

"Keep moving," Laura hissed.

Up ahead, the leader of the column stood on the road looking back in the darkness to see what the holdup was. With gentle urging, Laura got the father, as she thought of him, moving towards the road so the entire train could continue. Stepping over the unconscious smuggler, she ducked behind the big man and assumed a position in the line. They trudged up the embankment and milled around the roadway, unsure what would happen next.

Not seeing his comrades in the group, the leader pulled out a long knife that look more like a machete and stared off down the trail while calling for his men in a harsh whisper. Laura used the distraction to move behind the man. She wrapped an arm around the man's neck and rammed the pistol's silenced barrel into the base of the man's skull.

"Drop the knife or die," she said in a growl.

The clatter of the steel rattling on the pavement broke the quiet of the night. One of the former captives moved and retrieved the knife and untied the others as Laura pushed the man against the grill of the truck. It gratified her to see the man's hands tremble in the glow of the truck's headlights. It would make things easier if he thought he would die. She had no issue mainly because he was willing to sell his own people.

"You only get one chance and then I'm turning you over to these people to deal with you. Do you understand?"

The man's Adam's apple bobbed as he gave her a nervous nod. He was just a soldier that was following orders she knew but that didn't excuse him from his crimes.

"Where were you to take these people?"

"They'll kill me if I help you."

"What do you think," she whispered into his ear, "that father over there will do to you when I tell him you were planning on selling his son into sexual bondage?"

Wide-eyed, the smuggler brow became sweat covered as he contemplated the retaliation he might face.

"There... there is a warehouse in Paris where we bring all the new candidates," he said in a rush.

"And you can take me there?"

He was silent for a minute and Laura figured that he was trying to figure how he could turn the tables on her. She sighed and tuned to the father who stood with his son, watching her exchange with the leader as did all the others. What happened here affected them all. With a tip of her head, she motioned the father to her. He spoke quiet words to his son and moved towards the truck. It had the effect she was looking for, because the smuggler began to shy away from the man, even though she had said nothing else.

"Yes, I can take you there or to any other of the other locations you want. Just keep him away from me."

To the father, she said, "Please tie him up and help him into the passenger side of the cab."

Without hesitation the man did as asked. The smuggler cringed as someone grabbed him. The man she had given her knife to, moved forward with a length of rope and together, secured the smuggler. A few minutes later, the man was hoisted none too gently to the front of the truck.

"There are two more of them along the trail. Can I get some of you to tie them together? In the morning, report what they have done to those administering the camp." A woman and man broke from the group with handfuls of rope and disappeared down the trail without a word.

"Ji bojiyana min û keça min spas dikim!" one of the woman said bowing, one hand holding tightly to a young girl.

"She thanks you for her life and her daughter's, Lady," the man at her side said, his hand holding her knife, hilt first. "She is Kurdish."

She nodded, taking the weapon back and returned it to its sheath on her hip. "Tell her I was happy to help, but she must be more careful."

She called out to Banza that it was safe and the girl came at a run. Many of the migrants recognized her even in the low light and bowed to her as she too helped free them. The girl spoke excitedly mostly to the women and children of the group in a rapid fire dialect that Laura assumed was Kurdish. Once finished, she stood waiting for Laura's next request.

"Jump into the back of the truck and I'll drop you at my car. I need my bag. You'll take my car and head over to Yusuf's. Your volunteering days are over until this is dealt with. Understand?"

The girl nodded slowly as she realized the danger might still exist.

The group started back down the trail towards the camp. Only the Kurdish man stayed behind watching the others fade into the night.

She turned to him and he said, "I can help." Before she could protest, the image of Rachelle flashing across her mind, he continued. "I've been fighting most of my life. First against the Iraqis and Turks, and then against ISIS. When the Russians shelled our camps, my wife, children, and I joined a group out of the war zone."

"Then you need to stay with them," Laura said with an earnest tone.

Fierce eyes fixed on her, "I lost both to these vultures during our travels. My heart cries for vengeance!"

Chapter Twenty-Two

Laura felt the truck come to a stop and winced at the grinding of gears as the Kurd, Mazar backed the truck to a warehouse loading dock. They had gained the yard when the smuggler who sat in the passenger's seat with a knife pressed into his groin, was recognized by the lone guard in the security hut leading to the rear of the property. Through the dirty windows of the rear doors, she could make out several large loading doors, but the one behind the truck was rising to the back alarm of the truck. Three armed guards appeared in the opening. Only one of them carried his rifle loosely by the stock while the other two carried them by the strap with a bored expression. Two of the men even lit cigarettes. The scene told her they had never had an issue in the past, other than to shepherd scared, confused people to their next destination. No real threat.

Until today.

Mazar engaged the parking brake and shut down the truck. He opened the driver's door and stepped out as one guard approached the rear doors and pulled on the latch. The moment that Laura heard him grab the handle, she lifted her foot and tensed her body. The door opened, and she drove her foot into the door panel so it barreled into the guard, knocking him senseless and he fell to the concrete dock in a heap.

With the Browning leading the way, she dropped the one guard who was half more alert than his companions. He was just raising his rifle when a pair of 9mm slugs slammed into his forehead with the sound of a couple of hand claps. The third guard stood dumbfound with his mouth wide open, the cigarette hanging from his bottom lip. Seeing his friend die in front of him and the bulbous silenced barrel tracking him, took all the fight out of him. His hands rose above him as if in a benediction to God.

Mazar grabbed the stunned guard at the rear of the truck and disarmed him as he pulled him to his feet. He shoved the man forward before passing Laura's FN SCAR-L/Mk. 16 rifle to her. He guided both guards forward under the threat of their own weapons, with Laura guarding their back.

Once inside, she hit the button to close the loading door and crossed to a small office that stood in the corner. On the desk, a bank of monitors showed different views of the property, including the guard shack they had just been waved through. There was a control box that allowed the operator to cycle through the different cameras and a toggle that controlled each unit. While Mazar secured the two guards, rags already stuffed in their mouths, Laura played with the security setup and after trying a few switches, found cameras that monitored the inside of the building. Ignoring the loading dock and Mazar's efforts, she concentrated on the cavernous warehouse. A tall chain-linked fence separated half of the large area, topped with rolls of razor wire. They also divided this into two distinct areas by a curtain of white fabric. A closer inspection, showed men on one side and women and children on the other.

On the far side of the chain enclosure, another curtain of fabric blocked off the area from the prisoners, however from Laura's bird's-eye view, she could see that it held several separate enclosures, each with an observation table like you would find in any doctor's office and a few chairs. The rooms seemed to have a variety of medical equipment on mobile medical trays. Each of the examination rooms held an individual, either waiting without hope or tied to the table. A doctor and a nurse moved from one room to the next with practiced efficiency.

Laura had seen enough to know they were on the right track. She took the time to count the guards and note their positions. The only thing she was unsure of was what their protocol was in the event of an intrusion. Would they cut and run or kill off the witnesses? From the amount of effort, resources, and risk Coutu had taken to get the children back, she didn't think he would destroy the merchandise unless there was no other choice.

Normally the number of guards would have been too many to even contemplate making an assault, but the warehouse having been subdivided worked in her favor. And she had Mazar to back her up. She explained what she planned and he nodded.

"Silence is key, but keep an eye on the back doors. If we have unexpected guests, I need to know you have my back. Noise won't be an issue if that happens."

"Why not call the authorities? They could bring enough men to secure the property and the prisoners. They would also capture those criminals," he said indicating the monitors.

"I need to know where the victims are taken from here. They have to be stored elsewhere, like the children I found. Once the police are involved, there'll be a ton of lawyers more interested in the criminal's rights rather than those being held hostage and we'll never find out." She pointed to two different monitors. "I'm guessing either the doctor here or this guard who seems to run the security might have the information we need."

"I'll keep your back covered," he said raising the rifle he had liberated. "But I can't promise it will be quiet if things get crazy."

She tapped him on the shoulder in acknowledgment and left the small office. In what was becoming a habit, she checked her weapons a last time. She added a few shells to the pistol's magazine and checked that the rifle had a round in the chamber. She threw the rifle so it hung down across her back, but could easily swing around quickly if she needed it. Because of the enclosed environment, she kept the grenade launcher empty. Making sure nothing rattled that might give her away, she crouched before the interior door that led deeper into the warehouse. Before turning the knob, she looked back towards the office where Mazar stood watching her. He turned back to the monitor and then gave her the thumbs up that the way was clear.

Slipping through the doorway, she eased it closed and scurried to one of the fabric walls. Overhead, long rows of florescent lights ran the length of the warehouse. They were high up, so she didn't think she would cast a shadow on the wall which felt like a light canvas, but she would have to keep it in mind as she moved around. From her study of the floor plan, she moved along the synthetic wall that moved gracefully with the airflow in the building. At the end, she knew the lead guard had a desk that acted as an entry point to the interior labyrinth. He watched a few video feeds on a bank of monitors that were more than likely the same as in the office she had just left. That no alarm sounded told her that there was no feed from the entrance to this guard station.

She had been lucky.

From her pants pocket, she pulled out the telescopic mirror and edged it past the curtain. Stretching inward from her corner, the drape moved to create one wall of an examination room. The man's desk was pushed against the exterior wall of the warehouse across from the opening in the curtain. From his position, the central area of the examination area was completely visible. She couldn't just walk up to him with her gun drawn because anyone in the middle section that happened to be looking his way would see her and sound the alarm. She would have to draw him towards her, but in a way that would not sound an alarm.

As silly as it sounded, she decided on a child's game called Penny Toss. Back in elementary school, she and her school friends would toss pennies towards a wall. The closest toss won the other pennies.

The game she remembered only lasted a short while until the next time Mom had change.

Before she began, she dropped to the floor and peered under the sheet to see if anyone was in the first examination room on the other side of the canvas wall. No one. She pushed herself slowly into the fabric so that to see her, someone would have to come around the corner. The drape pulled taunt on its curtain rod which hung from the rafters by a steel cable. Readying herself, she checked once more with the mirror that the man was alone before securing it in her pocket.

From the front pocket of her pants, she pulled out a few Euro coins she kept on hand for parking. With a flick of her wrist, she tossed the coin high in the air so it came down and hit the concrete floor with a clink and spun in place before rattling to a stop. The sound was not loud, but the open area seemed to cause a minor echo. Not hearing any movement from the guard, she tossed another coin. This one bounced a couple times creating a soft jingle with each hop. It rolled and died against the wall.

"Ce que le...," said a man's voice. The sound of a chair's legs being pushed against the hard floor made her tense.

Tossing the last coin in the air, Laura drew the Browning and tensed. The timing worked as the coin hit the floor just before the man turned the corner. His attention was focused on the sound and not at the arm which grabbed him around the throat. Reacting instinctively or from training, he slammed his elbow back into Laura's ribcage rather than grab for her arm. The blow would have knocked the wind out of her had it not been absorbed by the ceramic plate within the flak jacket she wore under the tactic harness. She jammed the barrel of the pistol viciously into his lower back, aiming for his kidneys. His back arced at the excruciating pain and Laura used the distraction to pull him off his feet and over her shoulder. She followed with her shoulder, landing on his chest, driving the air from his lungs. Rolling off him, she slammed the back of his head against the concrete and he went limp.

Ensuring he was unconscious, she scurried back to the corner and had to use two hands to quiet the shaking of the telescopic mirror caused by the rush of adrenaline. There was no movement or outcry that signaled an alarm. Returning to the man, she heaved him into a sitting position and crisscrossed his arms. She noticed the familiar tattoo on his right hand and knew why he was in charge. She reached around his chest and under his armpits before locking one hand over the other wrist. Lifting with her knees, she leaned back and duck-walked backwards towards the door she had entered the warehouse from the loading dock. Twice she had to stop and slow her breathing. She could feel the sweat rolling down her back and knew her skin was flushed. She was thankful for all the exercise she did, but made a mental note to increase heavy lifting to her workout. It was tough work as the dead weight was more than she could boast or would want to. Fortunately, Mazar having seen her efforts via the security camera had the door opened and took the load from her.

With the warehouse door closed, she could finally draw in deep breaths without fear of being heard. It took a couple of minutes before she stood. She walked over to where Mazar had tied the unconscious guard to a chair that they had tied one of the other sentries to. That unlucky fellow lay on his side on the cold floor, but the fear in his expression told her he wouldn't be logging a complaint.

She turned back to see Mazar holding the flame from a lighter to the blade of a knife.

"What are you doing?" she asked concerned.

"We need information and this is the fastest way of extracting it," he said without looking up. The flame was leaving a trail of sooty carbon on the blade as he waved it up and down its length.

"Let's see if he'll talk without having to go that far."

"You do what you wish, but if you are unsuccessful, we'll do it my way." He looked at her with eyes as hard and sharp as flint. "I don't think he and his friends gave my family a choice."

Unsettled at the Kurd's viciousness, she stepped in front of the man tied to the chair. She slapped his face hard enough so his head rocked to one side. After the second blow, he came around, his eyes unfocused and glazed. Drawing a ragged breath, he looked up and seemed confused as he took in his surroundings, including the fact they had bound him to the chair. He pulled at his bindings and tried to speak over the rag stuffed in his mouth. When he realized his predicament, he looked around the room frantically as if for some miracle that would rescue him. When he found the two bound guards lying on the floor next to a corpse with no face, he fought his bindings with maniacal strength to no avail. Exhaustion and resignation slowed his struggle.

During the entire episode, Laura had stood quietly staring at the man. When his eyes finally met hers, she moved aside so he could see Mazar with the flame to the knife. This time, a whine escaped the improvised muzzle, and he began the struggle with renewed vigor. She waited until he finally ceased fighting before putting her finger to her lips to show he should be quiet.

She leaned forward and said, "I have some questions. If you can't help me, you get to talk with him," indicating Mazar. "Just to let you know, your people took his eight-year-old daughter and wife. He's not very forgiving." She watched the blood drained from the man's complexion, leaving him pale and shaking. Beads of sweat blotched his forehead as if he had been sick with a high fever. Not once had he looked away from Mazar and his knife.

Moving around the man so he had an unobstructed view of the big Kurd, Laura put both hands on the guard's shoulders and put her lips next to his ear. "Are you ready to answer my questions?" Laura whispered.

He jumped at her voice so close to him but nodded anxiously.

"I need to know where they are taking these people after they complete the medical tests. Do you understand?"

It was like he hadn't heard her. She looked over his head and saw Mazar was playing the sadist part to a tee. He had an evil grin that almost cracked his face and his eyes seem to bore into the captive man's very soul. Okay then, good cop, bad cop. Reaching around the man's head, she tugged at his gag until it dropped to the floor. His expression did not change, his mouth wide open as if the rag was still stuffed behind his teeth.

Mazar took a slow step forward and in a menacing voice that threatened violence said, "Answer the fucking question."

The thug looked like a stranded carp, his mouth opening and closing as he sought water and Laura would have laughed if the situation hadn't been real. She took hold of the man's jaw and twisted his head towards her. When his attention was on her, she said, "Are you ready to answer my questions?"

His head bobbed frantically, trying to please her.

She moved her body so it blocked Mazar from the guard's the line of sight. "When the good doctor is finished with the patients, where are they taken?"

"Ju... Juvincourt," he said, his voice raspy.

"Where in Juvincourt?" It was a small town an hour and half north-east of Paris.

"The old aerodrome. When the government sold it, Coutu picked it up for a song."

"How many people are being held there?"

"Three to four hundred. It chang—"

"What?" Laura cut him off in shock

The man cringed as if she had struck him. He looked everywhere but at Laura.

"What are they doing with that many?"

"They hold them there until... until they have buyers for all the parts-"

She grabbed him by the throat. "Say it!"

She could feel him try to swallow under her gloved hand, his eyes bulging out in terror more than pain. She felt Mazar step in close so he looked over her shoulder, glaring at the man.

"Or-organs," he stammered.

Mazar reached for the helpless ex-soldier, but she shrugged her shoulder to hold him off.

"Do they keep a list of these people they process?"

Tears fell from the guard as he nodded; maybe realizing for the first time how sick an endeavor he had involved himself in. Or maybe it was just fear. She didn't care. "The... the doc... the doctor keeps everything on his tablet," he said, moving his head to indicate the warehouse.

She turned to the hovering Kurd, "That tablet that the doctor uses might give us some clue as to what happened to your family and the others. I need to get it."

He nodded his face a mask before casually drawing the blade of his knife across the prisoner's throat. A stream of blood shot across the concrete floor like a geyser, in rhythmic streams that shorten with each pulse.

"Why?" Laura asked in surprise. "He told us what he knew."

"And for that, he saved himself from being skinned alive."

Chapter Twenty-Three

Still shaken at the unnecessary and callous killing of the guard, Laura leaned over the security monitors showing the warehouse's interior. Although she had killed many, most either deserved it because of their crimes or it was for self-defense. To kill someone just because he might have played a part in the man's family's disappearance seemed more brutal than she was willing to allow herself to contemplate. The fact the man had told them what they required and was tied to the chair added to the moral gravity of the situation. Being skinned alive was too horrible to contemplate. The Kurd must have seen or been part of some horrible experiences. It might be better if she didn't know.

She watched the doctor make his never ending rounds of the makeshift examination rooms. From what she observed, the examination comprising an orderly who asked a number of questions and entered all answers into a tablet. He would then take several blood samples and handed out plastic jars for a urine sample. Afterwards the doctor would perform a regular physical examination on the individual. If the subject refused, it took seconds before a handful of soldiers forced the issue. She expected that for the majority who were Muslim, this was a major infringement on their customs and beliefs.

After each examination, one guard would escort the patient back to the holding pen and bring back another. The entire process took about forty minutes. After each physical, both the orderly and the doctor transferred the information to a laptop that sat on a workstation in the central area of the examination area.

That laptop was her target.

To get to it, she would definitely have to expose herself. That issue wasn't what worried her. In any assault, there was a good chance of getting hit or worse, but there were victims to think about. She didn't think the guards would hesitate to attack regardless if there were non-combatants in the way. The patients were worth a lot of money alive, but an attack on the facility put everything at risk and if the price of saving the entire operation was a few dead bodies, she didn't think they would hesitate.

Pointing to the screen she looked at Mazar who was also studying the monitor. "Here's the laptop. From what I can tell from these views," she said, pointing a two other angled views, "I'll be exposed long before I can reach it. When the shit hits the fan, I need—"

"Shit?"

"Sorry, it's a western expression. When the bad guys see me, they'll either yell or shoot at me. I need you to cause a distraction. But there are innocent people, like your family in there, so we can't just start shooting the place up."

"What do you suggest?"

After a moment's thought, she said, "Start yelling, 'Police'. That might make them hesitate enough that I can get behind cover."

The big man nodded and pulled his rifle off his shoulder.

Laura grabbed one of the ball caps that each of the guards wore and rammed it over her shortened hair. She had to push down the memory of Gabrielle's first time attempt in haircutting and the laughter they had shared. She needed to keep focused. The two checked their weapons and the placement of equipment. There would be no time during a firefight. Everything would have to be instantly attainable with little to no scrambling trying to find the right pocket.

Ready as she would ever be, Laura crossed one last time to the security office to ensure it was clear of personnel by the entrance of the warehouse. She saw one guard escorting a woman who was holding an infant to her chest to one of the examination rooms directly behind the entrance. The camera showed that all the makeshift rooms held patients waiting to be examined.

"I will try getting these people out first," she said to her partner. "It will get them out of the line of fire at least."

"Better make it fast," he said pointing at another monitor. It showed the one guard who had escorted and deposited the woman and child into the room, make his room to the supervisor's table. After some hesitation, he walked over and looked towards the entrance door as if wondering what had become of his superior. With a shrug, he turned and retreated into the curtained off area. "They have noticed his absence."

Laura nodded. "Then let's hurry."

The two moved to the door, and she quietly opened it while Mazar held his rifle ready, a finger across the trigger guard. Risking a quick look to ensure the way was clear, she tiptoed towards the hanging curtain and crouched down. Listening for the doctor or nurse, she lifted the drape and looked around. On the examination table, looking pathetic a boy who looked around thirteen years of age, sat rocking in nervous anticipation. Seeing her, his head tilted like he could not understand what he was seeing. Putting her finger to her lips, she waved him towards her. Tentatively, he stepped off the bed, his head swiveling towards the room's fabric entrance. He crouched down and crawled under the sheet that Laura held for him. The boy rose but froze when he saw Mazar in the doorway with a rifle at his shoulder, barrel pointed downward. Laura lent him a hand to stand and repeating the signal to stay quiet, pointed towards the formidable-looking Kurd. With a nod, Mazar indicated the boy should escape through the door.

Laura did not wait to see the boy disappear into the loading dock area, but moved further down the flimsy wall and checked out the next room. That one lay empty, so she continued on. The third room held an adult male and with quick hand signals that would have been universal, coached him towards her and towards Mazar.

Using the silenced pistol to lift the canvas on the last room, the woman inside let out a loud gasp. Laura's finger slapped hard against her lips but she could already hear the footsteps moving towards the curtained room. Dropping the sheet, she waited with both hands wrapped around the butt of the firearm, ready to return fire but keeping in mind where the mother and her child stood. When the sound of the boots came closer, they were drowned out by the brawl of a baby. She heard the fabric slide back and could imagine the guard looking in. The curtain closed with a whipping sound of canvas sliding on a steel line.

Laura let out a ragged breath as the patter of boots moved away. She raised the curtain again and saw the woman guiding the child back to her breast. The harsh cries of the child settled to a satisfying mewing as it latched on and continued feeding. The woman gave her an apologetic smile and with her child tight to her chest, followed Laura's gesture to scamper under the cloth.

Once the woman and child were ushered through the door by Mazar, she gestured him to contact the police. Knowing they were outnumbered and stood no chance to free all the victims, they had agreed to contact the police and inform them of this facility just as she was making her run for the information on the next site. They were better suited to deal with a hostage situation.

Laura rolled under the canvas and in a crouch stepped to the door. Pulling back the sheet, she put an eye to the opening to see the doctor and nurse at the workstation. They exchanged a word before moving to separate examination rooms on the far side of the enclosure. The laptop sat on the table. From her vantage spot, she watched as a guard wearing a similar ball cap as hers came out of a room further down, his hand clamped around the arm of an older woman. He headed towards the prisoner's enclosure with the woman. With no one else in sight, this would probably be her best chance.

Steeling herself and holstering the pistol, she pulled back the curtain and walked towards the table with a purpose. She allowed her eyes to scan the area, but avoided looking around like a tourist. She hoped to suggest to anyone who saw her that she was supposed to be there. Even if it made them pause, it could mean the difference of success or failure. But her luck didn't last.

A cry went up, and she dropped all pretenses and ran for the computer. Snapping her head towards the prison area, three guards at the gate were pulling at their firearms. She saw movement at the far side of the enclosure and slid the remaining distance to the table like a baseball player in a run for home plate. The report of a large caliber rifle crashed and echoed in the closed quarters only to be drowned by the scared cries of the prisoners.

Grabbing the laptop under her arm, she flipped the table and squatted behind the flimsy cover. The table shook and slammed into her side as several holes appeared in the particle board table top. She might as well be in the open for all the good this was doing to protect her. Giving up, she bolted towards the exit when Mazar's deep voice cut across the warehouse space.

"Police! Put your weapons down!"

Laura didn't wait to see if any of the security did as the command had ordered but ran as hard as she could towards the break in the fabric wall. She could see the canvass dance in front of her like a haunted freestyle ballet as bullets hit the loose material. She passed the entrance guard's position and the door of one of the examination rooms opened to expose Mazar, his rifle extended from the hip. She skidded to a halt behind the white wall as he opened up on the three closest approaching thugs. By the time she looked back, all three lay on the ground in a heap of arms and legs. Another rifle report had both her and her partner ducking behind the insubstantial shelter.

"Mazar," she yelled. "Pull back."

Running for the door, she almost tripped as the Kurd rolled under the linen wall. She reached down to help him up, but he waved her off and together they tumbled through the exit door that led to the loading dock.

"There's no way to lock the door."

"Don't worry. The cops will be here in seconds. We have to make ourselves scarce."

Pulling the pistol from its holster, her arms securely around the laptop, she used her butt to open the door that led to the truck. With the pistol leading the way, she scanned the dark lot from beneath the bright halogen flood lights. An army could have waited and she would not have seen it. Over her shoulder she said, "You drive."

Mazar didn't argue and ran for his side of the vehicle. He started the heavy-duty diesel as she lay her rifle across the dash and rammed the gearshift forward. The truck lurched, throwing Laura back, so she bounced off the secured smuggler with a grunt before settling in the seat. When the Kurd turned the truck towards the gate, its glare caught three figures like a deer in the headlights. Laura recognized them as the people they had just help escape.

Dropping the laptop in between her seat and the truck's center console, she told the Kurd to stop.

"We will be caught between the police and that group back there," he said throwing his thumb over his shoulder.

"So will they. We have to help them."

The big man rolled his eyes, yet engaged the reverse gear and backed the vehicle in a violent motion towards the refugees. The truck skidded to a halt beside the scared displaced group. Laura jumped out and shepherd them into the back compartment with frantic hand gestures. Handing the woman and child off to the others, she slammed the rear door and ran back to the cab. Across the yard, the door of the loading dock burst open and a number of the guards came running out, weapons at the ready. It was obvious that they were as blind as she had been when she first left the building, but that wouldn't last.

Mazar had the truck moving before she slammed the door closed. Reaching for her rifle, she pulled it towards her as she hit the window button. Pushing the barrel out the window, she switched the fire selector button to auto and sent a burst of rounds towards the on-coming guards. She didn't think she had hit anyone with the speeding truck bouncing on the uneven ground, but they scattered like so much chaff in the wind.

Ahead of them, the door of the security hut opened, and the guard exited the building. He had his hand on a pistol which was holstered to his hip as he squinted into the darkness. With the truck barreling towards him, Laura threw a few rounds his way which sent him diving for cover as the truck roared out of the backyard. They didn't slow as the wooden gate exploded with a smash, sending splinters of yellow and black flying.

Mazar put the truck in a hard skid as they met the road, the g-force knocking the wind out of the frightened smuggler when Laura slammed into him. When the truck settled, he hit the gas leaving a trail of smoke and rubber across the pavement.

In the distance, Laura could see the approach of red and blue lights and knew they would encounter the police within minutes. "Slow it down, and turn north at the first chance you get."

He didn't answer, but she felt the vehicle's speed slacken off to a more reasonable pace. Seconds later the truck pulled into the next cross street and continued towards the lights of the city. Leaning forward to check the side mirror, she could see multiple cruisers scream past the intersection, heading towards the warehouse.

She hoped they could rescue the remaining prisoners with no casualties on their part. Hopefully, she could provide them with evidence of the other holding area at the World War II airport in Juvincourt with its ties to Coutu. Tonight's one-two punch should shake Coutu's confidence and help her get to him. He still had an army of those ex-soldiers but she hoped that some of them might bail from his sinking ship. The more that cut their losses and faded away into the night, the less she would have to go up against.

Minutes later when they were assured that they were not being pursued by the police, they dropped the smuggler and his former captives on the steps of the same newspaper where Gabrielle had told her story. The only difference was that they handcuffed the man to a bike-sharing stand outside the building. A phone call told the astonished receptionist the role the smuggler had played and the ongoing hostage situation at the warehouse. Laura was grateful to see a handful of journalists sprint from the front doors to greet their new guests while another group raced for vehicles.

Looking across the cab at Mazar's hard face, she pushed the laptop towards him.

As his eyebrow rose, she said, "The information you need to find your family is in there. It lists both as being at the airport."

His mouth dropped open, and he stared at her while the statement sunk in. "They're alive."

"According to the information on here," lifting her chin to show the computer.

"Then let's go. There is no time to waste," he said reaching for the ignition.

"No, Mazar. The police are better suited to handle this part."

His face darkened, "But—."

"Listen," she said reaching over and grabbing his arm. "Any mistake on our part might get them killed. They train the police for this type of situation and they have the resources to make sure none of them get away." His features eased as her assurances hit home. "Trust me. It's the best chance to see them again."

"But to sit here helpless..."

"You're not helpless. What you have on the laptop will force the police to act immediately. You can even tell them I plan on contacting the press. They are very familiar to my methods," she said her face cracking into a mischievous smile.

He nodded and asked, "And you?"

"I'm going after Coutu. This ends tonight."

"Then I will help you. I know my way around a fight."

Laura shook her head. "No, you have a wife and kid to look after. The last thing I need is to tell them is that you will not be around. I started this and I will damn well end this. After tonight, Coutu will never hurt another—" She was going to say child, but this had grown so much bigger, "—soul."

Chapter Twenty-Four

Michel Coutu sat staring at the family Coat of Arms that dominated the wall. The gold Fleur de Lie on either side of an ancient key was centered over a white cross that was mounted on the white shield had been a design of his father's. The key was the tool used by his family in their rise to respectability and represented taking what you wanted to claim, as your own. There had been no one of noble heritage within his ancestry that might have earned such a distinction. He snorted at the idea. It was all window dressing for the part they played. It made for a great talking piece when influential guests were being entertained. The most comical aspect was that even those with authentic backgrounds didn't question it. They took it for granted that no one would ever dare infiltrate their ranks.

His gaze took in the other props around the room and he shook his head at the waste. Like his father, they seemed essential at the time, but now as his entire organization was falling around him, he realized that it had all been for nothing. It was all a facade. A mirage. Compared to the money involved in the organ transplant part of his business, this room—no this home was a pittance. But now that the foundation had been exposed to the light, no amount of shoring up would ever stabilize him or his organization.

All gone. In less than a month. By one woman.

He drained his glass; the alcohol no longer burned as it slid down his throat. His senses had grown numb. Not that it mattered. He wasn't going anywhere. Pulling back the heavy drapes, it took a moment for his blurry vision to focus on the police car on the street beside the front entrance. He was under house arrest he supposed. Obviously he was a flight risk to someone within the government.

It was to be expected as that Canadian bitch exposed one part of his organization after another. God Damn her to hell! She wouldn't sit still for a second but dashed from one spot to the next. It's like she had a map across his entire network and knew just when and where to hit.

He felt his anger growing at the thought of someone within the organization helping her. She had to have an inside connection. No one in the police or government suspected a thing about his involvement or his second, hidden life before she showed up. His beloved wife had not known. She might have suspected, but they never spoken it about. Whether for her peace of mind or for the sake of their marriage he would never know.

The door to his den opened, and he made out the silhouette of Antoine entering the room. The end must be near if the man would enter unannounced or invited. A sudden coldness seized him from the pit of his stomach to his groin. Was this the final betrayal? Did the man plan to kill him? He took a step back as the man moved towards him like a lion stalking his prey.

Antoine stopped a few feet away, studying him like an insect tacked to a spreading board. Coutu squirmed under the man's scrutiny.

"You're drunk," said the younger man, his nose flaring the only sign that he was upset.

"Who are you to judge?"

"Have you given up so easily? All these years I thought you were solid as a rock, but at the first real challenge you have ever encountered, you fold."

Indignation fought against the rage within him at the insolence in the man's tone. He let the anger build like a heated pot of espresso until it exploded in righteous glory. His vision cleared as the rage burnt the alcohol haze away and his lip curled in hate. He would crush this man, this insect for his disrespect. His hand reached for the hidden knife within his jacket, anticipating the feel of the blade as it bit deep.

Antoine gave him a sinister smirk, "Now, there is the man I chose to follow. Welcome back."

Coutu blinked at the change in the man's demeanor. He had risked death to save his employer from himself. Leaving the knife in the built-in sheath, he pulled at the jacket as if straightening it, returned to his chair and waved Antoine to sit beside him.

When both were settled, he said, "What do we know?"

"The Amour woman attacked the warehouse we used for the initial medicals. Seconds after she left, the police showed up en mass and captured the facility. Most of our hired guards fled at the first signs of the police. They have caught a few and they are in custody. Our legal people will meet them after they have been processed. We'll try to contain what we can."

"What difference does it make? The building is owned by one of our sister companies."

"True, but buildings are leased by third parties and that is exactly what our documents will show once the authorities get around to inquiring. It'll all be speculation like all the other allegations. If anything, our legal team will offer the seed that some third party was out to set you up in the event it exposed them. While everyone is looking at you, a beloved patriot and seasoned statesman, the real culprit slips away with the help of this Amour woman."

The rational helped dispel any further doubt Coutu harbored. He had panicked with the continuous attacks. He would just continue in the role he was born to play and everything would clear up in the long run.

"Anything else?"

"The police are at the airfield."

He closed his eyes and took a deep breath to center himself. "So, it compromises the entire operation."

The ex-soldier nodded and Coutu felt the man studying him. *He fears this news will send me reeling again,* but there was no way he would give the younger man the satisfaction. Although they had grown close over the years, he knew his place in this relationship and so did Antoine.

"That's almost a half a billion lost in one night."

"We'll re-build," said Antoine with the confidence of youth. "This might have raised the suspicions of the police but there's nothing they'll be able to prove categorically. When we move forward, we'll put safeguards in place so the authorities remain blind to our dealings."

He was right. His other enterprises were totally separate from the human trafficking and organ harvests. He already had a substantial base from which to grow again. Bigger and better. He looked at his longtime right-hand man affectionately. He had proved that he was loyal to Coutu especially at this time of great upheaval. Maybe it was time to trust him with more responsibility. Allow him to take charge of the rebuilding of the lost operation. He and his ex-soldiers were more than a match for the Eastern Europeans who must already plan on swooping in to tear his organization apart. It would not be as if he was handing the reigns of his family empire over to the man. At least not anytime soon. He still had plenty he wanted to accomplish, but he wasn't getting any younger. He would see.

He nodded. "We will rebuild," he said aloud to his lieutenant. "And I will put you in charge of the entire resurrection of that arm that has so easily been destroyed."

He savored the look of incredibility on the man's face. Antoine sat up straighter as the immense boon he was being offered sunk in. His eyes sparkled and Coutu knew the man was already starting to visualize the new and improved branch and the ways he would put his personal stamp on it.

Power was the world's most incredible and addictive drug and he could see the young man yearning for a taste.

"Before we get ahead of ourselves," he said bringing his new protégé back to earth. "All things come at a price."

"Name it," Antoine said without hesitation.

Coutu leaned forward in his chair and gave the man a tight grin. "I want Laura Amour dead, but I want her to suffer for what she has done to us. Make it as public as you can because we are sending a message to anyone else who would challenge us."

The young man smiled and Coutu realized he had never seen the man smile before. It was a good smile. A handsome smile. Something he should do more often. "What is it you find so amusing?"

"I had already promised her head to you before you extended this incredible offer."

He smiled back and said, "Now you have more motivation."

Chapter Twenty-Five

A canopy of trees shielded the area around Coutu's mansion which did not lend itself to a long-range assault, yet she still carried the Remington. It was still the tool she used to reach out and touch someone across open spaces. While she approached the property from behind, it amazed her how hidden the wide open spaces were from the satellite imagery she found on the internet. It could see only the massive roof top and the driveway in the foliage's cover.

In reality, there were massive gardens that looked immaculately groomed with banks of prize-winning roses fronting a walkway that lead to a massive modern-day swimming pool with covered sitting areas. The heady aroma of the roses carried to where Laura lay under a manicured hedge. Steam rose from the heated water which was lit up in the evening's dusk and gave off a false sense of safety and serenity. But she wasn't fooled.

She had found three sentries already; the first by sheer luck. When she had started towards the property, the neighbor's cat found her irresistible until it sensed something in the dark more interesting. Due to the cat's curiosity and its rigid body language, she had crouched down to watch. Ten long minutes later, she was rewarded by a rustle off to her right and the hiss of a threatened feline. Circling the area, she crept towards the area to find the near invisible guard trying to discourage the cat's interest by throwing twigs into the night. Poor discipline. Two rounds to the back of his head ensured he never made the same mistake again. Whether it was the quiet cough of the pistol or the smell of blood, the cat gave up the game and scampered back the way it came.

To ensure her escape route was free and clear, she invested over an hour finding and dispatching two others who were watching the rear of the property. Neither one heard her as she crawled on her belly inches at a time. Like with the others, she performed a quick search of the corpse and confirmed the weapons were all fitted with sound suppression. Like her, they didn't want the police to respond with anti-terrorist troops. And with the police cruiser parked at the end of the properties entrance, she knew the response would be quick. That no alarm was raised told her that no one was doing radio checks or they knew someone was out there but were waiting for her to commit before closing the trap behind her.

Hunkered down under a rosebush, the ceramic plates in her body armor fending off most of the thorns, she kept her eyes roaming the rear of the house. It was a three-story monstrosity that could house twelve or thirteen families by North American standards. Windows walked across the entire back of the building in uniformed rows which stemmed from the building style which had the framing studs running from the base straight through to the roof. Wood was cheap back in the 1800s. A massive brick chimney hugged the back wall and rose fifteen feet over the roof-line. The roof itself peaked to either side, meeting a mansard-styled roof in the building's center.

Her Intel had mentioned that Coutu lived alone since the death of his wife. The property boasted two guest cottages; one of which was the home of Coutu's security officer, a man named Antoine Boivin. Records showed that he was wanted for abandoning his post at a Legionnaire post in central Africa. How ironic the Minister of Foreign Affairs employed a fugitive, and he also lived on the man's property.

The entire building was lit up both inside and out. Occasionally a shadow would pass in front of a lace-covered window; not enough of an outline to confirm who it might be but enough to tempt an anxious hunter. She did not fall for the bait. There were no shadows close to the house, except in one small corner next to what she assumed was a changing room for the pool. Like everything she'd seen on the property, it was oversized and shouted money. She could not pierce the darkness partially because of the glare from the patio lights. From a pocket she extracted a small night vision monocular with painstaking patience. Movement or a noise might give her away if there was a guard in that patch of blackness.

The vision in one eye turned a sickly shade of green as she powered up the unit. She kept the other open so she would at least have one conditioned to the night. Experience told her that the enhanced eye, due to the brighter light, would suffer a purple haze until her vision reconditioned itself. Centering on the area in question, the sentry stood out in sharp detail. He sat in a lawn chair, his rifle across his lap, totally invisible to the naked eye.

There was no way of getting closer and taking him out like she was able to with the others. She would stand out on the open lawn like a jack-lighted coon. She pulled the SKAR from her back and looked down its sights, but could not see any sign of the man. Remembering seeing a setup on-line, she pushed the monocular forward, so it sat in front of the weapons scope. Looking through the scope, she could pick up the reticle from the scope with a little difficulty because of the green on green. Satisfied with the experiment, she dug into another pocket and pulled out a roll of black electrical tape. Three slow turns around the monocular and the front stock of the rifle had it secure enough she no longer had to use her hands to hold it steady. Not fancy, but it did the job.

When she was ready, she centered the cross-hairs on the man's chest and squeezed off a round. The impact knocked the man backwards, and the chair folded into itself. Both lay still in a dark mass. The sound of the shot seemed loud in the night air and she froze, extending her senses in all directions. Using the improvised night scope, she scanned the areas to either side of the building but nothing was moving. She knew a thermal unit would have shown any warm body no matter how well hidden they were, but it was all the weapons dealer offered on short notice. Rising in a crouch, the thorns pulling at her jacket; she raised the rifle to the roof, and the results were much different. A ghillie suit might have helped the sniper if he had been scoping from the cover of a bush or tree, but on a rooftop, it did little to help him blend in with the hard angles and flat surfaces.

She tracked what she could see of the building's rooftop, but saw no other sentry, knowing that meant nothing. You could hide a platoon on a roof that size. Returning her aim to the familiar outline of a green sasquatch, she drew in a breath and slowly exhaled. When her lungs were half filled, she held the breath and in between heartbeats, squeezed the trigger. The rifle jumped in her arms with a cough and it threw the man back from his perch beside a masonry chimney and slid him out of sight behind the parapet. Once again, she held her position to see if there was any reaction.

After a full ten minutes, she moved towards the house, using what cover she could and avoided the light as much as possible. In the deep pool of shadow where the dead guard lay tangled in the lawn chair, she risked a small penlight and examined his hands. There was no tattoo on either hand. So this wasn't one of the specialists, just another goon. She wished she had checked the other men on the parameter. She had been fortunate so far, but the lack of movement was unsettling. There were no roaming guards, just the stationary positions. She had expected more from ex-military personnel and her gut was telling her she might be walking into a trap. It had all been too easy. With Coutu's money, she expected that the security might have used electronic counter-insurgency tools, like sensor pads or motion detectors. If she had planned it, the sentries would at least have been equipped with some type of night vision.

The last twenty feet was in a fast sprint, bent low. Her back against the wall, she pulled the rifle to her shoulder and checked her back trail with the infrared scope. Seeing nothing, she rose to one side of the corner window and peered inside. Though covered by a light sheer material, she could see the room, a formal dining room, was empty. She went along the rear wall, checking each window to find that each was locked and there seemed to be no one in the house. She dismissed the thought as she recalled the shadows passing across the windows.

She considered whether Coutu was even home, but the fact that a police vehicle was in place, she figured that he was under house arrest. Not that he couldn't leave the property in a similar way as she had entered. She also knew part of the property had water access, so he could have fled that way. It didn't matter, she decided. She had to check. Even if he had left, there might be evidence of his whereabouts. If he fled, she would follow. He wasn't getting away with hurting all those people.

There would be an accounting.

AT THE END OF THE BUILDING, Laura once again did a scan with the SCAR and its make-shift IR scope, but found no movement in the area. If there were sentries on all the perimeters, they would be too far from her current position to pickup unless they were in the open. Rounding the corner, she continued to check each window for life. All were locked until she came to a small basement window that was half hidden by flowers. This swung upward and after exploring the area by feel, she found a bent nail turned to hold the half rotten window frame open. After searching the room with the scope, she lowered herself and backed her way through the opening feet first. When her feet touched, and she found that the room was low enough she could reach out and grab the two longer rifles from the ground, but then left the Remington hidden in the vegetation. There was no need of it within the close quarters of the interior.

She lowered the window back in place so that from the outside it did not look disturbed, but ensured that it wasn't wedged in place. She might need a fast exit.

With the SCAR at the ready, she used the scope in the near complete darkness to navigate through what she now realized was a crawl space. The floor was hard-packed earth and smelled like a root cellar with a damp musk. The main joists were rough hewed logs mounted on masonry cribs showing how old the structure was. Shuffling forward, she made her way across an open area that held the heavy brick base of the fireplace system and took up a huge area. Metal hinges held a large steel door snug into the masonry was obviously a clean-out for the ashes. No servant of the original home would have had to brave the winter weather to perform this daily chore. An old furnace and a boiler sat in the corner beside the older heating system. They had mounted a newer electrical panel, phone and internet to a sheet of plywood. She considered cutting the electricity to the building but decided against it. Not only would it alert her quarry, but moving through a dark, unfamiliar house would take away any advantage she might have. Using the rifle and night scope in a compartmentalized building would be cumbersome and the field of vision too narrow. Better to see what she was shooting at.

Along the rear wall, a narrow, wooden set of stairs rose towards the main floor. With exaggerated care, she climbed the steps, keeping to the wall side to help muffle any creaks. She put her eye to the key-hole, thanking the gods that the original doors that used a skeleton key were still in place. The room was a large kitchen. She could see a bank of modern looking stainless steel fridges from her angle, but little else.

With a squeeze of the locking button, she compressed the shoulder butt of the rifle to shorten it. It would make it easier to swing around if required. She also took the time to undo the monocular to reduce the weight. Turning the doorknob in tiny increments, she found that it was unlocked. Straining to hear if anyone was nearby, she pulled the door inward and with the rifle held ready. She snapped a look in both directions but saw nothing to alarm her. She could not hear any movement either.

Keeping low so they would not see her from the exterior of the building, she moved through the kitchen to the dining room, clearing every corner as the numerous SWAT teams she had worked with while a counselor for PTSD had taught her. They thought it was hoot that a civilian, let alone a woman, would want to run their courses. Of course, had they known she was learning these skills for her crusade against child abusers, there was no way they would have helped. They probably would have locked her up at that point.

Shaking her head of those memories, she scolded herself for not focusing on the task at hand. She pivoted on her heel and retraced her steps back through the kitchen to the other rooms in the home. A broad staircase that Scarlett O'Hara would have envied was a centerpiece of the home. The dark wood shone with the polish of a hundred applications of wax, each spindle in the railing hand turned on a craftsman's lathe. The center of the stairs was covered with a rich green carpet that pulled the eye. It rose to the second floor, circled round and continued to the third.

Before she could ascend, she had to clear the main floor. Crossing the entrance of the huge room, she moved through a parlor designed for entertaining with high ceilings and a massive mantel over a stone fireplace that originally been used for cooking. Either Coutu or a previous owner had renewed the hearth as the original spit and cooking racks stood waiting for an ambitious chef, but no fire had marred the brick for years. Rich tapestries covered the walls with scenes of blooming gardens and graceful waterways.

Beyond was a library that any archivist would have died for and finally a fully windowed solarium facing the south. Plants of all types were spread throughout the room which offered a relaxing atmosphere. She didn't enter the room, because with the room lit up, she would be fully visible from the outside.

Returning to the entrance, she slowly walked backwards up the stairs with the rifle held ready to fire. She kept her eyes moving, watching for any sign of a threat, her thumb on the fire selector switch, finger stretched taut across the trigger guard. When she reached the second floor, she checked both ends of the hallway, but still saw no one. The stillness was spooking her. The building felt like a tomb. She heard no movement or voices yet she had seen that shadow, hadn't she?

Moving down one hallway, constantly looking back to see if someone is following, she found nothing but bedrooms, most sharing a bathroom. One by one she cleared the rooms. It felt like she was in a hotel rather than a home and she constantly had to force herself to keep up her guard. The massive hotel featured in The Shining, jumped into her mind and she shuddered. The farther hallway took as much time to clear, but yet again, there was no one around. Glancing at her watch, it surprised her to find that it had been almost two hours since she first started her infiltration and still there was no alarm going off to announce the dead bodies she left in her wake.

Her nerves were stretched as tight as a drum and she could feel the pounding throb of blood in her temples.

She forced herself to stop in one bathroom and quickly chewed an energy bar, washed down with a handful of water. It helped settle her down. Although she was eager to finish this, to rush was to throw caution aside. With a deep breath, she pulled the SCAR into the ready position and moved to the staircase.

Repeating the same technique she made her way to the third floor, moving to the right as they had taught her. She entered a dark room that was only lit by a solitary table lamp. Even in the room's gloom she saw a large coat of arms was the centerpiece of the room. There were portraits of stern looking men for years gone by glaring at her from the shadows. Two leather high-backed chairs faced the fireplace, and she circled around to ensure they were empty. A solid wood table set between the two chairs, a short stemmed, round bottom brandy sniffer sat half full of a golden liquid beside a bottle of cognac. The rifle barrel swung with her eyes as she re-checked the room. Nothing. Why would someone leave an unfinished glass of expensive liqueur? It was as if its owner had to leave in a hurry. Could he be in another room?

Feeling confident she was close, Laura turned to continue her search when the door to the room slammed with a bang. A loud metallic grinding sounded within the door and she felt sure a heavy duty locking system had been engaged. The finality of it sounded like a prison door sliding into place. Swiveling, she scanned the room for obvious threats, but she was alone. To be sure, she crossed the room and tried the door. They'd locked it.

Her head snapped at the harsh jangle of an old hand held phone. Knowing it was for her, she walked over and picked it up.

"Welcome to my humble abode, Ms. Amour," said a male's voice.

"Afraid to answer for your sins, Coutu?"

A thin chuckle came through the line. "What you would call sins, I would consider business deals."

"Your deals destroy lives."

"Maybe so, but if I didn't do it, there would be others. Business is supply and demand. I wouldn't make any money if there wasn't a desire for my product. And if you look around you, there is a lot of demand."

"You won't be able to run far enough Coutu. I'll hunt you down."

"I have to admit, your escapades have cost me dearly. I must leave France for a while until my lawyers sort everything out. My man, Antoine will see to you as my pilot is having my jet prepared and I must go." He followed the aristocratic dismissal with a whisper, "Adieu."

Chapter Twenty-Six

Laura looked around the room for a means to escape. She wasn't planning to wait for this Antoine character and his men to come for her. For the first time, she realized there were no windows. That threw her off, because from the exterior, windows were spread across the entire building in a uniform design. From the layout of the room, there should be at least two windows.

She approached what should be the exterior wall and rapped the butt of her rifle against the paneled wood. The sound it made told her it was solid, but common sense said otherwise. Unless the windows she had seen upon her approach were just a facade, there had to be an opening behind the paneling. She moved down the wall, sounding with her rifle, but there was no difference in the tone.

The other walls seemed as solid. She paused to consider. Building frames from a hundred or more years ago had changed little. The studs were usually sixteen inches to two feet apart. So she should hear a difference when banging in between the studs. There might be a major renovation over the years and this wall might have been build right over the previous one or the wall had been sheath in wood. She remembered back to some stories her fire fighter friends had told her about the crazy stuff people put in the walls for insulation. Everything from newspaper to wood chips. Some even hid their wealth in between the walls, not trusting the banks.

She didn't know how long before her reception party arrived, but she had to move. A beautiful roll-away desk was positioned along one of the shorter walls. She made her way towards it, flipping on a lamp beside the unit and looked through the drawers for anything that might help her. Rolling up the top, she found three monitors and a tower computer on the floor. Firing up the computer, she kept checking the room while it booted up.

Running her hand across the wood paneling, she barely felt the seam because of the superior craftsmanship. With true regret, she sent a silent apology to the tradesman as she wiggled the tip of her knife into the wood. It took a few seconds before she could gain traction. Throwing her rifle over her shoulder by the strap, she used both arms to heave on the knife. The wood gave a little. Sliding down the plank, she wedged the knife in and took another bite. Little by little she was able to pry the panel away from the wall.

Concrete?

Moving to another wall, she fought with the wood until she tore another piece loose. She found the same hard gray cement behind the wood coating.

Realization struck her like a hammer. This was Coutu's safe room. A room built for those who lived in places in the world where kidnapping was a risk, the rich, criminals, and the paranoid. The issue was why Coutu didn't just lock himself in here. There would have been nothing Laura could have done to get at him. It would have been the ultimate stalemate. He could have even contacted the police to storm the building to apprehend her.

Unless he wanted to capture her. Seeing Rachelle's lifeless body in her mind's eye, she made a promise to the universe that it would cost them dearly if they thought she would just roll over and give up.

Seeing the computer had finished booting up, she walked over and hit the space button. The center monitor came to life, and she saw a rugged, handsome face staring back.

"Ah, Ms. Amour." The cultured voice was gentle which surprised Laura, knowing this man was probably another ex-Legionnaire. "I had hoped you would try the computer. I am Antoine."

She nodded. "So, what do you have planned? Another interrogation before killing me with my hands tied behind my back like a coward?"

The man's expression turned to regret and hurt. "I am sorry for your friend's ending, but there was no way we could allow her to live. My colleague, Hans, is a rather nasty individual, but I gave him only a limited time to do the deed to save the good Capitaine a great deal of pain." He spread his hands as if it absolved him. "It was the best I could do for her, at the time, but of course she ended besting us in the end, didn't she? She and you must have had some agreed to code word or phrase to indicate I had compromised her."

Laura waited, not giving him the satisfaction of answering.

Antoine gave a heavy sigh, "As for you, my orders are to ensure that you do not leave the building. If you haven't figured it out yet, you are in a secured, fortified room with no chance of escape. I do not plan to waste any more of my soldiers on this endeavor. My employer will start anew, so no longer requires this property. I have decided to make it your tomb."

The screen changed to show an individual dumping a fuel can full of liquid across the broad central staircase. He descended the steps. He moved off camera towards the area that housed the library. After a moment, the man returned and backed himself into the doorway of the kitchen area. He pulled out an object that Laura recognized at once. Unwrapping the top, he pulled the short piece from the whole and struck the two together to ignite the flare. From the shelter of the doorway he threw the glowing shooting star towards the staircase. White, blinding light consumed the camera, and it snapped off to a black screen.

Antoine's image replaced the dead display. "If by some miracle, you found your way out of that room, my men will be waiting below. The only hope I can offer is that you will succumb to the smoke long before the flames reach you."

With her heart racing, she ignored his look of remorse.

"Goodbye Ms. Amour."

The screen went black a final time.

Turning back to the room, she let her eyes scan the room from right to left, forcing herself to take the time needed to catalog each feature. Panicking would not serve her. She had to stay calm and think her way out.

The first thought she had was to use the grenade launcher mounted to the underside of the SCAR on the door, but decided to wait until she had exhausted all other means. They meant the reinforcement within the door to hold up against dedicated efforts to break in. All she might do is breach the door to allow smoke and flame to enter.

She located the vents within the floors. This was one path the smoke would take as it rose that came directly into the room. She used her knife with vicious efficiency on the leather chairs and used the severed fabric to stop up the vents. It would buy her time, but unless she found a way out of the room, it would only take that much longer for her to die.

Her gaze slid over the fireplace, but returned to the huge, soot-stained centerpiece. She thought back to the position of the chimney on the back wall, the massive base in the basement and the other fireplace in the room off the entrance. All were part of the same system. Because of the size of the system, might they be navigable? An image came to her of a chimney sweep; soot covered tall thin men or children with chimney brooms over one shoulder. Would this chimney be large enough for someone her size?

As she strode towards the brick emplacement, she pulled a coffee table with her. There was a metal plate on the floor and lifting it she saw that it descended straight down. All the way to the basement clean out, she figured. Below the firebox, the ash dump looked big enough to take her thin form, but what about further down? There had been only one clean out at the chimney base in the basement so it made sense that the clean outs from both fireplaces joined somewhere. It was that connection she worried about. If there was any tightening of the tunnel or extreme angle, she could end up stuck in place. If that happened, she would either roast slowly as the building was consumed or suffocate as the smoke traveled through the tunnel. Neither was appealing.

Setting her rifle aside, she ducked into the enclosure and carefully allowed herself to stand. Reaching above her she followed the opening and found the damper which in this case was along a thin piece of metal of plate steel. It was rusted in the open position. With her flashlight, she could see the inside of the chimney for several feet before it disappeared in Stygian darkness. What she could make out was that the rough mortar and brick were covered with fine soot that fell and covered her face having been disturbed. The cavern seemed to narrow to approximately twenty-eight inches before disappearing.

From her position on the third floor, it would not take her long to climb to the top, however with Antoine's promise of men waiting for her, she would be a sitting duck and she would still be in the fire's path. There was also the matter of a three-story drop to the ground.

It was a coin toss.

After considering the risks, she decided on the ash clean out. The only issue was she needed to enlarge the opening to the vertical tunnel. With no sledgehammer on hand, the only thing she had that might break apart the brick floor of the firebox was a grenade. She only hoped that it didn't bring the whole building down on her.

She ran to the furthest corner, wedging herself between the room's entrance and a large bookcase built into the wall. Loading the grenade into the breach of the grenade launcher, she aimed the rifle at the fireplace floor. The weapon jerked in her hands as the round flew across the distance and erupted in a flash that lit the room.

Shrapnel and brick clattered and thudded across the wooden interior of the room, one chunk narrowly missing Laura.

She opened her mouth in an exaggerated yawn hoping to pop the assault on her ears, but the ringing didn't dissipate very much. If she didn't escape, her hearing would be the least of her worries.

She moved towards the hearth but had to wait for the smoke, dust and soot to settle. The explosion had done its work only too well. Not only was the entrance to the ash pit opened, but so was the second flue from the main floor cookery. Smoke from the main floor pushing its way up the chimney entered the room and rose to the ceiling. It wouldn't take long before the smoke filled her room.

From a pants pocket, she pulled out a length of tightly weaved rope. Taking off her combat harness and body armor, she tied one end of the rope around metal loops on the vest and garments to the front strap of her rifle. She quickly lowered the heavy load down the shaft of the clean-out until the rope became slack. She unwound the rest of the rope and tossed it across the room. There was no way to know if the bundle had descended all the way to the basement or if it was hung up partway down. She might have to extend it further down and need the extra length.

Before lowering herself into the shaft, she tied a piece of fabric over her nose and mouth to act like a filter from the ash and dust. Dropping her legs into the hole, she wedged her back against one side of the shaft and her knees against the other. With only scant inches of space to move, the walls closed in on her. With an effort, she pushed the mounting terror back. Moving in small increments to avoid falling uncontrollably, her back pressed pushing on the rough brick. Eyes tightly closed, not that they were any good to her here, but she didn't need to see the light from above slowly dwindle. That in itself was reason to panic.

Within minutes, it felt like there was no more skin left intact on her knees and across her shoulders. The uneven surface, pushed in and her own weight tore as she lowered herself.

Knowing most building floors were ten feet in height and she started on the third floor, she determined that it was a thirty foot descent, give or take. Try as she might and moving by inches there was no way for her to figure out her progress. No choice but to keep descending until she reached the basement or some kind of blockage. No! Stay positive! There will be no blockages. To ensure all the ash, embers and un-burnt wood made their way to the basement for extraction, there could be nothing hindering the fall.

Her legs and arms shook and quiver from the strain and she stopped in place to rest. By wedging her knees almost to her chin, her entire body plugged the hole taking the strain off her extremities. She tried to swallow, but even with the mask, the fine soot had covered the inside of her mouth and it felt like she had not drunk anything in days. To get her mind off her thirst and the trickle of blood sliding down the small of her back, she brought Gabrielle's face to the forefront of her mind. Smiling at the remembrance of that special soul and felt the tension lessen.

After a few moments, knowing she raced the fire somewhere around her, she pressed on with her snail pace. While she dropped further, the shaft seemed to heat up, but she was unsure if it was due to her exertions or that she was nearing the area involved in the inferno. Feeling the panic rise again, she slid downward and before she could stop herself; she had dropped a couple of feet. Only by pressing herself against the tunnel was she able to stop her plunge, but rough surface dug deep into her flesh and she groaned aloud. The pain rocked her body, and she wasn't sure she could continue, but the heat coming through the wall burnt her knees and she forced herself to keep moving.

Over the scraping noises and her own grunts, she heard a roar through the brick surface. It sounded like a hurricane caught within a tunnel. She pictured the billows of a blacksmith's forge charging the coals to a white hot heat that could create as well as destroy. There was another sound in the shaft and after a minute, she realized that the scared whine came from her as she coped with the terror of burning to death or being buried alive.

She came too close to letting herself fall, if anything to escape the flames, but some inner stubbornness kept her moving downward in a controlled descent.

Her hands trailed to each side, taking the weight as she shifted each knee. Suddenly, she felt an emptiness to her side, and she almost lost her balance. She stopped and explored the opening and she realized she had found the clean-out for the lower fireplace where it angled slightly to meet the shaft she was in.

She must be only feet from the base.

Heartened, she continued downward, inch by inch, until something jabbed her buttock. Wedging her body so she wouldn't slip, she reached down to explore what she had come up against. It took her scraped and bleeding fingers seconds to realize it was the barrel of her rifle. Lifting it, she dropped it and it stopped with a thud. She sounded the area beneath her in different spots. The last thing she wanted to do was to step down thinking it was the base to find it was just a shelf and fall uncontrollably, but the rifle moved some fabric which she figured might be her armor.

Tentatively, she lowered one foot until it touched the hard base of the clean-out. And then she was standing freely, her knees aching as they straightened up. Moving the equipment to the side, she crouched down and reached out with her hand to find the steel door to the cleanout. Giving it a shove, she had to fight the rising panic when it didn't move. She thought back to when she saw the door and remembered that it had a simple bar welded to one side that sat in a cradle on the frame. To open the door, she had to lift the door so it could swing free. With her hands, she tried to manipulate the action, but her hands kept sliding on the metal because of the dust. In a burst of impatience, she dug through her equipment until she found her knife. Guiding the tip under the lip of the door, she pushed downward knowing she would ruin the blade, but at this point not caring.

With a clang and a rush of fresh air, the door swung open.

Feet first, she crawled out of the mason box, sucking in the clean air. This caused a bout of coughing as she expelled the carbon dust from her throat and lungs. Dragging her equipment to her, she pulled at the hose on her outfit that extended to a bladder of water sewn into the suit. It took two full mouthfuls of water to rinse the worst of the dust out, before she could swallow the liquid into her parched throat.

Above her, one of the ceiling joists groaned to remind her that the fire was right overhead. Grabbing her equipment and rifle, she staggered across the crawlspace to the window she used to enter the building. It took longer than usual for her to put on her kit because of the damage to her knees and back. The blood made the fabric stick, and she had to tug to pull it over the raw skin. It would be a bitch to take it off later once it dried.

She could hear sirens in the distance and see the light from the flames dancing across the lawn. The only good thing was that if Antoine's men were still in place, they wouldn't be able to use night vision equipment. The light of the fire would defeat the technology. She on the other hand was in a perfect position to use it. Within seconds, she found two watchers in the trees. Both were about fifty feet back and almost blended in with the vegetation. She had spotted them because they couldn't sit still.

Once again, she wrapped the monocular to the SCAR's front stock. Two shots later, her way cleared, she struggled to climb out of the basement window, biting her lip so she would not scream out her pain as her body wiggled through the opening. Limping, she made for a spot in between the two dead sentries and allowed the night to swallow her whole.

Chapter Twenty-Seven

Laura lay up to her neck in the tub, the hot water numbing the pain of her injuries. The water had been tinted a blushed pink from the blood that still leached from her knees, back and hands. But it was not the alarming red from the first of three baths since arriving at her safe house as the night sky surrendered to the day. When the water cooled off, she crawled out of the tub and patted herself dry.

From her first aid supplies, she coated the raw skin in an antiseptic cream that would help fend off infection and hopefully keep the skin moist enough that it shouldn't tear as she moved. Sucking back another bottle of water, she eased herself under the bed's linen sheets and fell into a dreamless sleep of fatigue.

Much later she awoke to a noise she could not identify. Her hand found the pistol under the sheets and she was content she had not abandoned all security thoughts before collapsing into the warm nothingness of unconsciousness. Laying still her eyes cracked open, she waited for the noise to come again, but it did not repeat. Throwing back the sheet, she winced as the cloth which had dried to the newly healed skin of her leg, pulled and reopened the wound. Carefully she rose and moved to the doorway, not bothering to dress. If there was an intruder, they would be shocked to find a naked armed woman ready to battle. She had to bite her lip at the thought and realized that she was still exhausted.

After confirming that there was no threat, she picked up her phone and found a message from Janice and another from the CSIS Director, Darren Forbes. One or the other would have raised no concerns, but seeing messages from both, she experienced a sudden premonition of disaster. She got up from the kitchen table and padded barefoot towards her bag in the living room, before stopping to stand, still naked in uncertainty. The trepidation that was consuming her threaten to overwhelm her, and she took a series of deep breaths to calm herself.

Once centered, she moved to the bedroom and pulled on some clothes. It was a regular task that allowed her to gain some emotional traction. Moving to her gear, she pulled out another burner phone and sent a text first to her computer nerds to track down Coutu's flight plan and any reservations he might have made. It would give her a place to start.

She forced herself to put a pot of coffee on in an exercise to calm herself. Depending on the news her two Canadian friends had for her, she would need to think logically. Part of her could guess what they were calling about, but she refused to entertain the thought. Finally, with a cup of coffee in front of her, she texted the phone number of the new phone to Janice. She hadn't finished her first cup before the phone rang.

Taking a deep breath, she answered, "What's happened?"

"They have Gabrielle," said Janice's familiar voice, the certainty driving a spear through her heart. No way Janice would mislead her on something this important.

"How?"

"When I arrived, they told me she left with someone who was posing as me."

"As you?" Laura gasped. The implication was immediate. Someone within the Canadian Embassy had betrayed her. Her first thought was Forbes, but she dismissed it immediately. He had her in his sights last year, but refused to follow the kill order by his superiors in the government. Although a patriot who would do almost anything to protect his country, the man had principles. She would let the man answer for himself when she contacted him next.

"A dark-haired woman came to the Embassy and showed them a Canadian passport identifying herself as me and told them she was there to pick up Gabrielle for the trip to Canada. Because of the circumstances, they didn't question it."

"They must have her on video. Have they identified her yet?"

"Forbes is on it personally. He's already identified the individual who leaked the information and to who. He's waiting for your call."

"Okay. I'll call him right away."

"Laura," said her best friend. "I'm here in Paris. You don't have to do this alone."

She closed her eyes and clenched her fists, as close to losing it as she ever had, knowing what Janice was offering. But to accept would drag her friend into the dark life she had made for herself. She had chosen this while Janice had chosen the law. If she allowed her friend to help her, there would be no going back, and it was something that Laura could never take away from the closest person she could call family. Janice needed to stay true to herself and Laura would never allow her to do otherwise.

"Thank you. You taking Gabrielle is the greatest thing you can do for me. Someday I'll be able to tell you how much it means. But I need to deal with this myself. I made her a promise. I intend to keep it."

"I understand."

Laura heard the relief in the other's voice and knew Janice was ready to give up for her friendship.

"Stay close to your phone. I'll let you know what I find out."

Hanging up, she texted Forbes and poured another cup. Once again the wait was short.

After an earnest apology, Forbes wasted no time. "The leak came from one of our rising stars. Obviously, he was rising too quickly and got in over his head with a woman that was looking for an opportunity to exploit. From what we have uncovered, he somehow got access to my private email. We're investigating this breach, so hold off using it until you hear from me," he sighed and Laura could hear the frustration and stress. "He was attempting to use you to take out Coutu who was blackmailing him. When they threatened to expose him, he gave up Gabrielle. I have him locked away in a secure location outside Paris. He's yours if you want him."

"I'm tempted. I'm sure Canada knows what to do with traitors. What have you learned from him?

"Not much I'm afraid. The name was an obvious alias. He said he had met her at a body art display at one of the modern museums. We're checking into it but she sounds like a pro and I'm not hopeful."

"Body Art?" she said in a hush. "Do you mean like in tattoos and piercings?"

"Yes. Does it mean something to you?"

"It might. Thanks Darren. For this and for setting things up for Gabrielle. It means more than you know."

"Well, I feel that I failed in that regard." The regret in his voice was authentic and Laura felt guilty for ever doubting this man; even for a moment.

"No. You jumped at the chance to help her. The fault doesn't lie with you. Keep the offer open. I'm going after her."

"I'll be waiting for your call."

At least she had a starting spot. The woman's interest for tattoos was too much of a coincidence considering the Legionnaire tattoos and the location of Rachelle's interrogation and murder. Last time she had stalked that building, Gabrielle had saved her life and took on the burden of an adult's life. She could only hope she was as successful.

Ignoring the torn skin, she pulled on her dark clothing, even as she felt fresh blood soak her garments. She took the time to clean and service her weapons. The last thing she needed was to have a malfunction at the moment she needed it the most. She should have done it before she had bathed, but her exhaustion and injuries took precedence. When the last magazine was loaded and shoved snug into her battle vest, she changed the batteries on the night vision goggles and loaded the gear into her duffel bag. It wouldn't do to have some truck driver looking down into her open vehicle and see a cache of weapons on the back seat. Before leaving the house, she grabbed a bottle of over-the-counter painkillers and threw a few down with some water. She had stronger medicine, but needed a clear head. There was no room for error.

Ninety minutes later, she tucked her car into a back alley three streets from the tattoo parlor. She backed the vehicle until her bumper nudged the cement retaining wall. This would hold back a dedicated thief, but should keep her gear safe during her reconnaissance of the surrounding neighborhood. In case there were shooters in wait, she approached from another direction.

Armed only with her pistol and the night vision gear, she made her way to a more modern high rise. Broken glass in the mezzanine and graffiti artwork on the brick was signs of the type of tenancy the building held. She didn't want trouble, but she needed the vantage point for its height. Anyone that got in her way would quickly find out just how little patience she had tonight. Taking the elevator to the top floor, she took only minutes to find the roof access. She chuckled when she saw the chain with the padlock, still engaged lying on the floor; a couple of cut links kicked to the side. She pulled out the pistol before she opened the door and stepped out onto the roof. After checking behind the heating and cooling equipment that littered the area to ensure she was alone, she moved to the side that overlooked the grid of streets that included the parlor. Lowering herself to the roof, she laid on her stomach to help steady the goggles and scanned the night. Street lights and storefronts glowed a bright green-white while cooler surfaces were darker shades. Taking her time, she allowed her gaze to glide over the rooftops looking for the shape or movement of a man with a rifle. She gave herself a good half hour to study the area, not only for sentries but also to plan her approach.

She heard them coming from the roof access, trying to sneak up on her but the excitement was making them jittery. She sighed and rolled over as three young punks spread out around her. Poverty made them desperate, their numbers made them tough. They took what they wanted and didn't give a damn about the destruction they left behind. They were no different from their counterparts in any large city around the world. She read their intentions and knew better than to plead for compassion.

"It was nice of you to join us tonight, woman," the punk in the center said, his hands clutching his pants like it was the only thing holding them up.

"So, let me guess," she said. "Each of you plan on riding me whether or not I'm willing?"

"Ah, ya," he said, her lack of fear making him pause. After eyeing his two henchmen he said, "We're gonna fuck you silly."

"Well, come on big man," she said with a growl. "Show me what you've got."

The three of them were bouncing from foot to foot, eying each other. Their prey rarely reacted like this and it was unnerving them.

The tough in front of her, threw out his scrawny chest, trying to assert himself. Groping for the zipper on his pants, he took two fast strides towards her and dropped himself towards her. She let him come until he was close enough. Like a striking cobra, her leg came up, and she caught his descending body on the base of her foot. Without trying to stop him, she reached out and pulled him towards her while pushing her foot upward like a piston. She watched his eyes and saw the instant he realized what she was doing. His mouth formed a large "O" that matched his eyes, before he flew over her head and into space. He must have fallen three stories before he re-membered to scream. It followed him down and ended abruptly.

Without waiting, she rose with the pistol suddenly in her hand. The two thugs had not moved and stood in total shock at what had just gone from a night of hardcore sex with this strange bitch to see-ing their friend do a swan dive for eighteen floors. Reality snapped for both, when she said, "Who's next?"

Hands raised to ward off a bullet, one tough began to break-down, his face contorting as tears fell freely. The other didn't wait, but ran for the roof access and she hurried him along with a round in the meaty section of his ass. The cry baby used the distraction to bolt for the door as well and Laura let him go. She had no time for this nonsense. Maybe next time, they would think twice before attacking a woman.

She had to wait for the elevator, but listened to the two of them thumping down the stairwell. They were still going when she stepped into the cage and dropped back to the street. Seconds after leaving the building, she was just another shadow.

After gathering her armor and rifle from the trunk of her car, she followed the route she had planned from the rooftop observation. She took her time, ensuring she kept to the shadows and so was not observed. While she was anxious to get to Gabrielle, she knew the girl was just bait. She was the big game they were hunting. The plan to grab the girl from the embassy had originated before she attacked Coutu's home and after the risk they took, they probably wouldn't hurt Gabrielle until she outlived her usefulness. Either way, if they intercepted if her before she even reached the building, she be doing the girl no favor. Patience was essential.

Chapter Twenty-Eight

The back of the tattoo parlor was covered in poor imitations of Andre and Azyle graffiti street art, partially hidden in shadows. The shop was part of a small strip mall with several businesses all lined together, sharing central support walls. Most had rear exits that opened to a small parking lot for employees fed by a tight lane. A quick scan with her goggles ensured she was alone, and she ran bent over for the back wall. Without slowing, she leaped up and grabbed at the natural gas pipeline that ran up the building. Hand over hand, she walked up the cinderblock wall and threw a leg over the roof's edge to pull herself onto the tar and gravel surface.

Careful to move quietly, she glided towards a large roof access trap door, three businesses over from the parlor. From her perch on the high-rise, she had spied this access and was sure it entered a service area for the heating and cooling systems for the entire block.

The square lid was secured with a padlock which she examined with a quick flash of her penlight. From a pocket on her vest, she pulled out a small aerosol can and a leather pouch that contained several lock picks. She used the can of lubricant spray on the hinges for the lid. The time it took to open the lock, would allow it to penetrate and hopefully quiet any rusty screech it might produce when operated. Propping the lock with her knee was difficult because of the raw skin, so she ended up using her tip of her foot. She inserted the tension wrench and turned it slightly in the direction the key would turn. This added pressure to the pin chamber, so it was locked in place. Next she pulled out a Triple Crown pick and inserted it into the keyhole until it hit the back chamber. Applying a little upward pressure, she began 'raking' the pick across the row of pins until they all lifted up to their designated spots. Adding a little more pressure to the tension wrench turned the ensemble, and the padlock snapped open.

The entire process took her less than a minute and she shook her head remembering the weeks of frustrating practice it took to master the skill. What she once had considered impossible to master, she now did with little thought.

After putting her tools away, she grabbed the lid by both corners and pulled up in a steady, even motion. There was a slight groan from the hinge, but she was sure it wouldn't carry. She secured the trapdoor with the attached hinge lock and with her rifle hanging across her back; she lowered herself into the opening. At the bottom of the ladder, she quietly stepped on a plank walkway that stretched both ways through the common ceiling for the building. The catwalk was surrounded by a sea of insulation and allowed service personnel to reach the heating equipment for each storefront. Silver, foil-covered conduit tubing ran back and forth to heating and cold air return vents. Smaller access ways branched off at different sections. She knew the parlor was the last unit, so slowly made her way to the end, careful of her foot placement.

Knowing her IR monocular would be next to useless in this almost complete darkness, she used her pen light with care. Being late, the businesses would be closed and quiet. Any noise she made would transmit through, warning the occupants of her position. She walked like she was crossing a field of egg shells, carefully placing each foot before gradually easing her weight down.

At the end of the main catwalk, it branched left and right. Visualizing the inside layout of the tattoo shop and the back room from her last heartbreaking visit, she figured the left branch might end up over the display room while the right would put her over the back room. If Gabrielle was being held here, she would definitely be in the building's rear. She had to push away the image of Rachelle's distorted body and the chair they bound her to, but she had to steel herself in case she found the young teen tied to the same chair.

The people that had taken her had better not... She stopped, breathing hard, knowing she had to get herself under control. She needed a clear head to save the girl. If — if the worse scenario played out, then she might trade some of the Kurd's methods for dealing with their enemies.

With difficulty, she calmed herself using breathing exercises and clearing her mind. She had a job to do, and she swallowed her fear.

Following the right branch, she stopped and knelt beside one of the flexible conduits and carefully pushed the insulation away from the tube. Once the area around the ten inch hose was clear, she reached in to her vest again and pulled out a screwdriver kit and selected a standard driver and slowly undid the adjustable metal clamp that held the tubing to the ceiling vent. Holding onto the clamps so it wouldn't drop onto the vent cover, she wiggled the tubing up and off the vent. She moved it well out of her way and peered down into the room.

It took a minute for her vision to adjust to the bright light within the room. From her position, she could see the entrance to the back room but little else. Gathering her tools, she moved further down the walkway and repeated exposing the vent.

Squinting through the vent openings, she had to move her head to see different parts of the room. Almost directly below her, she saw the target of her fears. Gabrielle lay tied to the same chair where Rachelle had been. The difference was that Gabrielle was very much alive and giving someone one out of view an ear-full. Her barrage was cut short when a woman with florescent green hair walked into view and slapped the teen across the face. Her head rocked from the blow and only her bindings kept her in the chair. From somewhere else in the room the roar of a man's laughter reached Laura but she couldn't determine where he stood because of the distortion of the sound. The woman said something, but it was muffled. She walked out of sight.

Using her light, she saw that there was one more vent further back. She needed to know exactly where these people were if she hoped to catch them unaware. The last thing she needed was to drop down and have someone behind her. She had wanted to use her telescopic endoscope, but worried the small camera would not fit through the vent's openings. To force it would make a noise that might give her away.

Twenty minutes later, she was bent over the last vent and could see the woman and a muscle-bound man leaning against the back wall, talking in low tones. Beside the man, she spied a wicked looking Israeli IWI X95 assault carbine with a sound suppressor. From the size of the magazine, she knew it carried the heavier 5.56 mm round. This guy obviously knew his weapons, and it was one clue he was a well trained, season operator. Not someone she should underestimate.

The woman, her arms crossed across her chest, didn't seem to be armed, but Laura had to expect the unexpected.

Watching the pair, they looked occasionally towards where Gabrielle sat, but nowhere else. If she had to hazard a guess, there were no others in the room other than the three. That made her job easier.

Extending herself over the vent, she checked the area beyond the man and found that it was clear for at least eight feet. She wanted to drop behind the pair, but needed to ensure she wouldn't come down on something that might hinder her from attacking. The drop was around ten or twelve feet.

She pulled on a pair of safety goggles which would keep her eyes protected from the falling insulation and dust and dragged up the neck piece on her suit so it covered her lower face. It would double as a simple air filter from the same particulates.

Using all the caution she could muster, she followed the wooden ceiling joist away from the catwalk for about five feet. She cleared the insulation from one of the ceiling tiles that hung from metal strapping, pushing it behind her so it was out of the way. In the closed in area, it didn't take long before she was sweating freely, mentally cursing the "non-fog goggles."

Adjusting the strap on her rifle so it sat ready to use, she pulled out what her buddies on the SWAT teams had dubbed, the 'party cracker'; a stung grenade. The thin grenade fit easily in Laura's hand. She pulled the safety pin and released the secondary pin at the same time she pulled on the ceiling tile. She dropped the armed flash-bang through the gap and shoved her fingers into her ears. Even then, the noise was tremendous.

The concussion knocked down several ceiling tiles, and she was able to drop through the ceiling, landing and rolling to her left, her rifle already tracking one kidnapper. The man had his eyes tightly squeezed and blood ran from his ears, but he was operating by instinct. Already he had the carbine in his meaty hands and let a stream of bullets fly behind him where Laura had originally landed. How he knew while being blinded and deafened by the concussion, she would never know. Not second guessing the fates, she flicked the fire indicator to automatic and squeezed off a burst that stitched the man's huge torso. He was flung back against the wall and collapsed in a mass of muscle, his jacket smoking from the rounds.

The woman staggered in circles, her hands covering her head as she tried to gain her balance. Laura sent a single shot that centered her forever, before swinging her rifle across the room, looking for other targets.

"Clear," she said aloud from a forced habit.

Gabrielle was struggling to sit up but the effects of the grenade on her senses caused her to flop against her bindings like a fish hauled into a boat. Laura ran to her and with a quick slash of her knife, helped the girl stand. Laura had to almost carry the girl's full weight with one arm as she aimed the rifle with the other towards the front door, in case there were others stationed there.

"You... came," Gabrielle slurred, spittle streaming from loose lips.

"You know it, kiddo," she said with relief. "Let's get you somewhere safe."

It would take a few minutes for the worse of the effects to wear off, but they had to get back to her vehicle before any police showed up. The blast from the grenade might have them responding at this very minute.

She guided her young ward towards the rear of the room and used her weight to push the panic bar on the rear door. With the rifle leading the way, she was helping Gabrielle through the door when the muffled tatter of an automatic firearm opened up behind her. It walked the wall beside her before closing and catching her below the shoulder. The force spun both of them in a macabre pirouette before they tumbled across the pavement of the rear parking lot.

Burning pain engulfed the top of her arm and she dropped the rifle from dead fingers. Blood saturated both sides of her armor and she knew instinctively that they hit her bad. She needed to stop the bleeding and fast or she'd bleed out.

"Laura," the girl groaned under her. "What happened? You're crushing me."

She propped herself up with her good arm; her gloves giving her some purchase on the rough pavement. She drew her pistol with her left hand, feeling the unfamiliar awkwardness of it.

"I'm all wet," Gabrielle said, still confused about her surroundings. "Oh my God, is that blood?" She moved her hands over her body looking for a wound.

Laura ignored her, raising the pistol aimed at the steel door they had fallen through. The front sight of the pistol wavered but her right arm would not respond.

Oh shit! It's you," the young girl cried. "What can I do?"

"My pant leg. Med kit. Pack it."

She wasn't sure if the girl had all her faculties, but she didn't lack in enthusiasm, tearing at the zippered pockets.

The door burst open and the monster she had killed stumbled out, his weapon erupting as he spewed a torrent of bullets in a huge arc, meant to have anyone waiting, ducking for cover. With the two of them lying on the ground, the rounds screamed over their heads towards the neighborhood buildings beyond.

Not waiting to understand why the man was still alive, she fired as he staggered away from them, unable to keep his balance, but trying to swing the carbine around as he sensed her return fire. The Browning sounded like an automatic as she squeezed off round after round. Unable to keep the weapon steady with her ineffective left hand, she missed all her shots except one. The last bullet caught the behemoth in the leg just as he put his weight on it. The leg collapsed, and he went sprawling in a tumble with a grunt.

She fumbled with the pistol to drop the clip to load a fresh load when she felt Gabrielle's frantic hands grab the edge of her vest and ram in the dressing to help stop the bleeding. The minute the dressing hit the entry wound, her head exploded in bright sparks as the most excruciating pain over whelmed her world and everything went black,

WHEN SHE CAME TO, SHE was lying on her side; her gaze turned at a right angle. Her shoulder throbbed, and a groan escaped her throat as she tried to rise.

Across the pavement, not twenty feet, the wounded man pulled himself towards her with his arms, his leg being dragged uselessly behind him. His teeth were drawn back like a rabid dog with only her death in his eyes as he stalked her. Seeing she was conscious, he redoubled his efforts.

From her right, there was a blur of motion. She focused, seeing it was Gabrielle, and she tried to cry out for her to get away. She was no match for this killer. Of course, neither was she in her state. She struggled to rise again, ignoring the waves of pain and nausea that threatened to push her back down.

She watched in horror as the girl tried to kick the man in the head. He easily caught her foot and laughing hatefully he yanked her off her feet so she lay on the ground beside him. Raising one of his hammer-like fists, he brought it down on the side of her head and she went still. So he was sure she wouldn't cause him any more issues, he raised his fist a second time.

Laura screamed her anguish and malice at him stopping him with his arm raised.

"Come on you fucking animal," she spat. "It's me you want, not her."

The man gave her an evil grin, his eyes slivers in the low light. "But her pain hurts you more, ya?" he said in a heavy Germanic accent, but he relaxed his fist. "I will kill you and then I will take my time with the girl."

"Well, come and try soldier boy. You'll find, I'm not the helpless victim you're used to dealing with."

A sudden look of doubt showed briefly across his dark features, but the grin came back with a vengeance. "Oh, this will be so much more fun than the time I had with your cop friend."

As the words sunk in, Laura's mind pulled up the image of her short-term friend and the damage this sick bastard and his knife had caused. "So you're Hans. Good." She went numb and felt the primal rage deep within her grow and spread through her. This was the ultimate source of vengeance she always kept wrapped up, buried deep in the depths of her soul, because to release it was to lose all control and thought of herself.

Ignoring her body's protest, she lurched up onto her knees. She held there swaying; her damaged arm dangling like a corpse hanging from a noose. With her good hand, she reached behind her back to the sheath built into the rear of her vest and readied herself. She would only get one chance. If he overpowered her, she, then Gabrielle would be killed by this psychopath. Coutu and his headman, Antoine would set up shop elsewhere and the horrors would continue and they would have all died for nothing. The ball of anger and spite kept growing and she let it build until there was nothing left.

He stopped just out of her reach. Measuring her. She saw his eyes take in the blood that had slowed to a trickle oozing out from under her vest and the position of her arm. Like a striking cobra, he lunged across the distance reaching for her throat and shoulder. He meant to crush her with his bulk while attacking her wound.

She dipped down so that the hand reaching for her shoulder missed completely, but allowed him to engulf her with his gargantuan form. There was no way she could match him in strength, so she didn't fight his advance but welcomed it. When his weight hit her and pushed her back, she pulled the knife out of the back sheath and pushed it between them. His bulk, falling across her in what might have been an intimate hug, did the rest. The blade slid effortlessly into the lower stomach, just beneath his own vest, which explained how he survived being shot in the chest. He let out a large breath and rolled off her, his hand around the knife's hilt. He raised his head from the pavement to examine the wound.

Before he could extract the blade, Laura reached over placing her hands over his. Looking up into his surprised eyes, she asked, "What does this button do?"

She waited until she saw the recognition of her words reflect in his gaze before she mashed the button with her palm. The reaction was immediate and his body arched as his vest expanded like a water-activated life preserver. The zipper could not contain the pressure and tore from the fabric. Blood gushed from his throat as his entire body shook at the assault it had been subjected to.

Leaving him, she crawled slowly, cradling her arm, to Gabrielle. The girl was breathing but already the side of her face was swollen from the brutal hit Hans had dealt her. She lifted the girl's head onto her leg and reached for her phone. Under her breath, she said, "Regis, I'd like to call a friend."

Chapter Twenty-Nine

Laura lay under the harsh Brazilian sun, a floppy hat and large sunglasses protecting her eyes, a book across her knees. Her skin was becoming dark, and the locals were becoming familiar with seeing her by the pool every morning. The puckered scar on her shoulder was still pink but her mobility was almost back to normal thanks to the quick and quiet surgery that Forbes had arranged by a patriotic Canadian doctor living in Europe. She had kept up the prescribed physiotherapy, and it helped bring her back from the devastating gunshot.

That had been three months ago and the pain at having to send Gabrielle off with Janice was still more devastating than all the therapy she had endured. She missed the girl immensely and in her lowest moments, contemplated giving up this insane crusade. It would be nice to have a normal life with someone who relied on you. But it was for Gabrielle and all the other children were still in danger every day she would not quit. At least not while she could still stand up to the animals of the world.

She looked across the pool area to see a distinguishing gentleman open the enclosures gate and take up the same spot near the bar he'd been coming to for the past two weeks. Ducking under the dry palm leaves that covered the large shade hut, he lowered himself into one armchair. A tall, broad-shouldered man who scanned the occupants around the pool with an intense scrutiny accompanied him. She felt his gaze flicker then return to her, but she didn't look up from her book as she turned the page. A melody of chimes announced an incoming call and interrupted his scrutiny as he answered the device.

After a moment, he ended the call and approached the bar to place the same order he requested each day; a glass of Sauvignon Blanc from the Bordeaux region which had been special ordered on behalf of the older guest. The man brought the glass to the shaded area his patron preferred and handed him the wine. He spoke to the older man and with the tip of his head, left the pool area.

Laura could guess where the ex-Legionnaire was headed.

It had not taken long for Laura to discover where Coutu and his lapdog, Antoine had disappeared to. While Coutu's mansion burnt to the ground, he had flown first to Morocco and then after news of the international warrant for his arrest became public, thanks to a hefty file delivered to both the French Press and the Police on all his illicit activities and contraband, to Brazil. Her computer friends had captured his flight plans even before his jet had touched down.

Once Laura had been cleared by her 'private' doctor with strict orders to continue her exercises but to avoid more dangerous pursuits, she followed the pair discreetly. It hadn't taken her long to find that they were reestablishing their lucrative organ harvest organization, but with one subtle twist. Instead of using the Syrian and Kurdish refugees, they now preyed on the slums of Brazil, the Favela. With over 11 million of moradores da favela jammed into these hillside ghettos, it was easy to exploit the desperately poor.

Although she expected to find fear among those affected, she also found anger and a thirst for retribution. Having been pawns between drug lords and government forces for years, the tolerance of these people was close to boiling over. She found several groups of families who had lost three and four children to the sex slave organizations and begged her to be part of a tangible solution. The chance to strike back was strong in these downtrodden people.

Today, they would get their chance.

An hour pasted with people refreshing themselves in the pool. Like most days, the pool area cleared out with the lunch hour. The sun was at its hottest and many of the inhabitants of the condo resort jumped at the chance to savor the Spanish custom of siesta; of course in an air-conditioned room.

She rose from her chair, gathered her tablet, book and towel before walking the length of the pool towards the exit. When she came even with Coutu, he raised his glass to her.

"Good day, Mr. Coutu," she said, her smile brilliant against her darkened skin.

"Mrs. Davis, would you care to join me for a glass of wine?" he asked, using the name she had given the first time they encountered each other a week ago. The story she told was that of a widow from South Carolina who had traveled south to try an experimental treatment for her terminal ovarian cancer after doctors in the States had offered her no hope.

She tilted her head as if considering the offer before nodding. "A glass of wine would be refreshing; however the doctors have suggested I drink sparingly while in between treatments." She ducked under the awning, lowering her possessions onto one of the empty chairs before accepting the chair he held for her.

He waved at the bartender for a second glass of wine as she pulled off the sun hat and wiped her bald head of perspiration. Shaving her head was not only part of her story but also ended being the perfect disguise. Even her eyebrows were naked. She had sat across from both Coutu and Antoine and was not recognized as the person who had taken down one of Europe's largest criminal organizations.

Once the glass was in front of her, he raised his and said, "Never more have I meant the words, 'To Your Health.'"

Nodding her thanks, she sipped the dry, crisp fluid. "That is delightful."

"I hope you do not find me too forward if I inquire how you are feeling?"

"Not at all. The weakness lasts for a couple days, but the sun rejuvenates me. The doctors seem to feel they should be able to determine if the treatment is working."

His eyebrows rose. "That is good news indeed."

"Have you given any thought to the donation?" she asked tentatively.

"Yes. I have read all their material and I feel that this new treatment holds some ground breaking results." He gave her a dazzling smile. "I would be happy to donate, let's say $25,000 as an initial sum and possibly more once they tabulate the preliminary trials and their results."

She put her hand to her mouth in surprise, "My God," she said, the accent a sight heavier than normal. "That's most generous, Mr. Coutu."

"Please, my friends call me Michel. You can have the institute send me whatever papers they require me to sign at their convenience."

"Oh, there's no need," she said in delight. She reached onto the seat beside her and picked up her tablet. "Modern technology. The institute has downloaded their donation form onto my notepad and you can sign it right here."

She pretended not to notice the slight annoyed expression that flashed across his face when she dropped it in front of him. With her finger, she deftly moved through several files until a form opened on the page. She handed him the stylus with another ecstatic smile.

With a force grin, he scanned the form, filling in his information and then signed the line indicated.

Taking the tablet back from him, she hit a couple more buttons and then replaced it with her book and towel. Grasping the glass again, she said to him, "You have no idea just how many people you will help save, Michel."

"Happy to help."

The bartender moved towards their table and Coutu didn't notice. He was so used to being waited on that he felt nothing out of place before the man's arm wrapped around his throat and a hand covered his mouth. Suddenly, he noticed the man.

His eyes bulged in surprise and when he realized he could not shake the man's grip, the shock turned to fear.

"Michel," Laura said in French, "Thank you for your hospitality, but I must confess that I have deceived you." She took off the hat and glasses and placed them on the table. "You see, my real name is Laura. Laura Amour."

His eyes widened even further, and he struggled frantically but the man behind him kept him secured.

"Did you actually think I would just give up after you fled France like a coward? Too many people have suffered because of you and your organization and now it's time for you to pay the toll. Before we part, I have something you should see." Retrieving the tablet, she opened a live link thanks to the resorts WIFI and placed it before him. "The poor of this country have little they can call their own. What they have and what they cherish the most is their children. When I offered to help them avenge their lost children, they were very accommodating."

His eyes fell on the screen and froze at the scene playing out.

It centered the camera on the hard features of Coutu's aide-de-camp, Antoine. His hair was out of place and blood ran from his forehead, down one cheek.

"Hello Antoine, this is Laura Amour," she said leaning over the tablet. She smiled as his nostrils flared however the gag that pushed between his teeth prevented him from answering. "I figured you would appreciate the irony of the situation because the last time we talked, you had tried to burn me alive. Today, my associates, who are the parents of some children you kidnapped, have decided to send you to hell already burnt."

The camera pulled back, and it showed a masked man stepping forward and dosing the contents of a red, plastic gasoline container over the ex-soldier. He struggled wildly, swinging on a rope that hung overhead. Without warning, the tablet screen flared up as the man's body was engulfed in flames. A loud, inhuman wail erupted from the device's speakers.

Coutu threw himself backwards as if the flames would jump from the screen and ignite his own clothing. The bartender had to struggle to hold the man in place, his face turning red with exertion. Tears crept down Coutu's darkened face.

Laura reached over and pressed the screen with her fingertip, which closed the horrible sight and Coutu sagged with relief. While he fought to control his breathing, she stood up and walked to the back of the bar. A small printer lay on the counter, just out of sight. She collected the forms that lay in the tray and returned to the table. Coutu's eyes had followed her the entire time.

"Personally, I don't think you deserve any less Michel, but I think if there is a hell, you'll burn for a long, long time. Considering the harm you have caused so many however, I think this is more appropriate. Sorry for the ruse concerning the institute. You are making a donation today, but it's not monetary."

She slid the form in front of him and his gaze found the form's title:

The Gift of Life

Organ Donation Pledge Form

All the boxes denoting the individual organs was checked off. His eyes dropped to the bottom of the sheet where his signature sat beside today's date.

Laura stood up, gathering her possessions as the bartender's strong hands wrapped around Coutu's throat and squeezed. She watched as the man fought his fate. The struggle slowed after a moment, one foot hammering a tattoo on the ground, before ceasing all together.

She passed through the pool entrance and nodded at the two ambulance attendants who would ensure that Coutu's body was kept viable until it reached the hospital. The tearful story of a rich European who wanted to die with dignity surrounded by his loved ones rather than in a hospital had guaranteed they be waiting. Of course, the $25 thousand would go a long way to purchase much needed medical equipment.

Epilogue

The breeze off the Ottawa River brought the first hint of fall and Gabrielle hugged her bare knees to her chest. The uniform outfit for her new school did not consider warmth a big argument to neatness or uniformity. Not that she could complain much. She had made friends since arriving in her new country and Janice when she saw her was fantastic. They had given her a bus pass and a tour map and set her loose on the Capital city. It wasn't Paris, but it was more personable and the people so friendly and open. Having never experienced winter by Canadian standards, she couldn't wait to skate on the canal and Janice had promised to take her skiing in Quebec.

It had been months since that horrible night. Janice and she had stayed long enough to ensure that Laura would make a full recovery, but in the end, it was Laura who pushed the two of them to move on. She still planned to continue her fight and there was no room for friends and family. It had hurt her to her core to hear those words, but she now knew those cruel words were more for Laura than for she and Janice.

She was still wary of strangers, especially men, but Janice assured her it was to be expected and there was nothing wrong with it. Janice was very forthcoming and told Gabrielle her story. The shared trauma helped them bond and their friendship had grown quickly. Janice, having never had children, treated her like an adult which after her experiences felt right, but was there for a hug when needed. Laura had been right, they belonged together.

For the first month or two, she feared even leaving the condo, but thanks to her new friends and excursions to different events, she was becoming more comfortable every day. But regardless how perfect her new life was, there was always that missing piece. Sometimes she missed Laura with such intensity she ached. She had only known her for a few weeks, but it was like they were attached at the hip during that time. She owed her life to Laura and although Janice would protect and love her without hesitation; it was Laura she needed and longed for.

She got up, brushing her skirt of any dead grass and climbed back up to the street. Flashing her bus pass to the driver, she leaned her head against the cool glass, her eyes taking in the sights while her mind wandered. This mystery man, Forbes, which they had warned her not to speak about, had arranged a Canadian Passport in the name Gabrielle Williams. She liked the name because it made her part of Janice's family. She belonged somewhere for the first time in her life. It felt good.

An hour later, she stepped off her bus. At the entrance to her building, she stopped and checked for mail and found a brown envelope addressed to her in clean, crisp lettering. Other than her health card, it was the first letter she had ever received. Excited, she rode the elevator to their floor and entered the condo she now called home. Janice would be home from work in an hour or two, enough time to put together some food.

She tossed her coat aside and flopped down on the couch, her fingers excitedly tearing at the opening of the letter. She opened it and saw a number of items. Shaking the contents out on the cushion beside her, a news cutting coming up on top. It was a story of a wealthy European that had died while vacationing but whose organs had saved over eight people. When she saw the name, she began to shake and rung her hands together. A second news story told of a tourist who had wandered into a bad section of Rio, one famous for drug dealers, and was found burnt alive.

She put that story aside and snatched up a flashy postcard showing white beaches with scantily dressed bathers. Come to Brazil was scripted across the top. She frowned because she had never been there and knew no one that ever had.

Turning the card over, she read, "Stop looking over your shoulder! Live for both of us! L."

I HOPE THAT YOU ENJOYED my story. Reviews are essential to an author. If you could spare a moment, please consider leaving a review wherever you purchased the book or at https://www.goodreads.com/author/dashboard

Thank you so much for your support.

Author's Note

Although the story you have just read is fictional, the growing increase in organ harvesting is becoming an International issue. Usually it is those desperate souls in third-world countries that are the subject to this horrible and selfish crime. In the U.S. alone, over 98,000 people are waiting for a kidney and more than 50% will die before a donor is found. Because there is such a demand, organized crime is filling the orders throughout the world including the UK and North America.

The best way to battle this type of crime is to sign a Donors Card. One person can save up eight others. If we all gave this gift upon our own deaths, we would stop the market overnight. It is important to sign that card but also talk with your family to ensure they know and understand your wishes.

Be a Donor. You too can be a hero and save a life.

About the Author

Photo by Chris Kemp

DAVE WICKENDEN HAS spent time in the Canadian Armed Forces before the Fire Service, so is as comfortable with a rocket launcher as a fire hose. He has brought six people back from the dead using CPR and a defibrillator and has help rescue people in crisis. He has learned to lead men and women in extreme environments. He loves to cook, read and draw. Dave ran his own home based custom art business creating highly detailed wood and paper burnings called pyrography. One of his pictures of former Prime Minister Jean Chretien graces the walls of Rideau Hall in Ottawa.

At home in Sudbury, Dave and his wife Gina are parents to three boys and three grandsons. His two youngest boys are busy with minor hockey and fishing, so you can guess where you'll find Dave when he's not writing.

After 31 years in the Fire Service and attaining the rank of Deputy Fire Chief, Dave retired to write thriller novels full time. He has been a member of the Sudbury Writer's Guild since 2014 and the Canadian Union of Writers. His first novel, IN DEFENSE OF INNOCENCE was released April 2018 and his second, HOME-GROWN released June 2018. He also has a couple short stories published. He is currently working on his sixth novel; a political thriller.

Don't miss out!

Visit the website below and you can sign up to receive emails whenever David Wickenden publishes a new book. There's no charge and no obligation.

https://books2read.com/r/B-A-NTFJ-SUNCB

BOOKS 2 READ

Connecting independent readers to independent writers.

www.ingramcontent.com/pod-product-compliance
Lightning Source LLC
Chambersburg PA
CBHW032228050726
47591CB00001B/308